
SCORING FAST (RIVALS)

CATHRYN FOX

COPYRIGHT

Scoring Fast

Copyright 2023 by Cathryn Fox
Published by Cathryn Fox

This is a work of fiction. Names, characters, places, brands, media, and incidents are either the product of the author's imagination or are used fictitiously. The author acknowledges the trademarked status and trademark owners of various products referenced in this work of fiction, which have been used without permission. The publication/use of these trade-

Discover other titles by Cathryn Fox at www.cathrynfox.com. Please sign up for Cathryn's Newsletter for freebies, ebooks, news and contests: https://app.mailerlite.com/webforms/landing/c1f8n1
ISBN ebook : 978-1-998943-25-8
ISBN Print: 978-1-998943-40-1

JEMMA

How did I get here again?

I continue to ask myself that one question as I sit on the edge of the pool outside our sorority house at Scotia Academy, watching the hockey players shove each other into the water as the warm September sun beats down on us.

How did this introvert—me—find herself living in an extroverted setting? Honestly, who would have thought that I, Jemma Maloney, book nerd extraordinaire—a nobody from rural Nova Scotia—would currently be hanging with the popular students, drinking fruity cocktails, and sliding into the DMs of the in-crowd? So, how exactly did I get here again?

Simply put, you orchestrated it, Jemma.

Right, right. That's exactly what I did. Yeah, I'm here getting light-headed on fancy cocktails because I'm pretending to be everything I'm not. Nothing about *this* me is real. From my blonde hair right down to the tiny bikini showcasing far more skin than I've ever dared to show before. I casually adjust the top to cover a nipple that is determined to break free, then finish my drink, needing all the liquid courage I can handle for this poolside party. I'm pretty sure no one from back home would even recognize this version of me, and I guess that's the whole point.

I was always orbiting the popular girls back in high school, always looking in from the outside. Sure, the book nerd they loved to call Maloney Baloney was good enough when it came to helping them with their homework, but forget about friendship or being invited to any of the parties. Last fall, after I received my acceptance letter from Scotia Academy, I devised a plan to transform myself by emulating the girls in my sorority, especially my roommate Brynn. Her brother Kace is a senior and one of the best players on the hockey team, and Brynn is the epitome of popular. Not just because of him, but because she's gorgeous, confident and isn't afraid to put herself out there.

Alison, my best friend from high school, is here at the academy too. She never cared about being popular, and in the three weeks that I've been here, we've already drifted apart. My stomach tightens. I really miss her, but she doesn't want to have any part of sorority life, and she's not a fan of hockey. I wasn't either, until I realized fitting in with the popular crowd meant showing my support—in very slinky clothing. Ugh.

What is it that I'm called now? Oh yeah, a puck bunny. I don't particularly like the term—correction, the old Jemma doesn't particularly like it—but this new version of Jemma, she's just fine with it. At least she thinks she is. It's what makes her popular, after all.

But is popularity all it's cracked up to be, Jemma? Everything you've ever dreamed of?

Give it time, it's only been three weeks, I quickly remind myself. A group of loud hockey players at the other end of the pool catch my attention as they line up on the edge of the pool and jump, clasping their knees so they can cannonball and splash my sorority sisters. Shrieks saturate the air as the guys drench the girls and they scramble from their lounge chairs, pretending to be angry. It's easy to tell they secretly love the attention.

They laugh and tug on their tops, and the beginnings of a wet T-shirt contest flashes before my eyes. I tighten my arms around my body. I'm not all that comfortable with the idea of exposing myself, and while I sit here and pretend otherwise, I resist the urge to slink back to my room and crawl under the covers with a good book.

"Jemma, come on," Brynn says, taking my empty drink cup from me and pulling me to my feet. "It's been three weeks and you haven't even officially met Kace yet. I just know you two are going to hit it off." She gives me a little wink.

I groan inwardly. She talks highly of her brother, as do all the other bunnies, and she likes to joke that maybe someday I could be her sister-in-law. The thing is though, there's something in the way Kace looks at me. I truly don't think he likes me. I mean, we haven't officially met, like Brynn said, but I don't get the sense he wants to meet me either. Forget about love at first sight. I think for Kace Andrews it was hate at first sight. Maybe I'm just being paranoid, the old insecure Jemma seeping through the cracks.

Seriously though, from what I've seen in my short time here on campus, the man loves the puck bunnies. Just not *this* puck bunny. Brynn drags me along and I lift my head to see Kace, who is easy to spot in the crowd, and not just because he's tall. He's sideways to me, talking to Sierra. I like Sierra. We bonded quickly after I moved into the house. Probably because I'm Brynn's roommate and she clearly likes Brynn's brother. Sierra is a senior and is the most popular girl in the house and it feels good to be liked by her. I'm sure she never would have given the old Jemma the time of day, though.

I turn my focus to Kace and study his tall frame. My gaze follows a bead of water as it slides down his chest, disappearing into the band of his swim shorts. Warm sensations rocket through me, and I'm pretty sure it has nothing to do with the late day sun. I work to control my racing heart, not wanting to appear breathless when I reach him.

As if feeling my eyes on him, he angles his head, and his gaze meets mine. The second our eyes lock, his lips tighten, and he stands up a bit straighter, like he's preparing for battle—with an ogre. Yeah, I'm pretty sure the man hates me. What I don't know is, what is it about me that offends him so much?

"Kace," Brynn calls out, grabbing my arm to drag me forward when my feet slow.

Kace nods, turning away from Sierra, and eyes his sister. "Hey. What's up, sis?"

Sierra stands there for a second, her gaze going between the three of us. With his attention no longer on her, Sierra touches his arm and his gaze cuts her way.

"Catch up with you later?" she asks.

"Yeah," he agrees and Sierra gives me a smile before walking away. Oh, I get it. She's hooking up with Kace tonight and wants me to know it. Like I could actually compete with a beautiful, outgoing girl like her anyway. I wouldn't even know where to begin which makes me wonder why Brynn thinks Kace and I would be a good fit.

"Kace," Brynn begins, and his head slowly turns back toward us. "This is Jemma." Brynn shoves me until I'm standing directly in front of him, and I fight the old urge to shrink into myself. "My roommate. Jemma, say hello to Kace, or as he's known on the team, Dragon."

"Why...would they call him Dragon?" I ask, glancing at Brynn over my shoulder.

She grins. "You'll have to ask him."

I turn back to Kace, who looks less than impressed. Yeah, no, I'm not going to ask him why they call him Dragon. My imagination can figure it out. Kace stares at Brynn over my head, his eyes narrowed. Brynn must take his disinterest for confusion, because she says, "What's the matter with you? I told you all about Jemma. Remember..."

What the heck did she tell him?

"Yeah, Jemma. Your roommate. I remember." He finally looks at me. "Hi Jemma."

"Hi," I reply for lack of anything else, and fold my arms across my chest, unintentionally plumping them up. "Nice to meet you." That's when his eyes drop to my cleavage. But it's not lust or want I see there. He tears his gaze away, but not before I glimpse the...disappointment? What the hell is wrong with this guy? I don't know and I really shouldn't care if he likes me or not. Heck, I don't like him. I'd never tell Brynn that, though. She adores him. I guess with him being her brother, she sees something I don't. Although he did call her sis, and that's kind of adorable.

"Yeah, nice to meet you too," he finally replies and runs his thumb over his jaw. "I'm going to get a drink," he grumbles, about to step away. That's when he notices the empty glass in Brynn's hand. "You guys want anything?" he asks, staring at his sister again, like the sight of me makes his skin crawl. What a jerk.

"Of course, we do," Brynn answers and while I'm sure I've had enough, I nod in agreement. Truthfully, I'm a lightweight and those drinks I've had are already messing with me, and we all know overdrinking at a poolside sorority party can only lead to good decisions—said no book worm ever.

From the corner of my eye, I catch a couple more hockey players coming around the corner with more coolers, and Brynn waves. Sebastian Turner, who I met earlier, and who is Kace's roommate, grins at me.

"Drink, baby?" he asks me. "I'll make it a stiff one."

Kace shakes his head, disgust on his face. What's his freaking problem with me? I shrug, playing it cool, like I'm not already halfway to drowning in the pool from alcohol poisoning. "Yeah, sure."

"Heard you like stiff ones, but no worries, baby, you've never had a stiff one like mine before."

"Jesus," Kace mutters and rubs the back of his shoulder, like he's trying to work out a strain.

"It's Saturday," Brynn bursts out. "You guys won against the Islanders last night. We need to celebrate in a big way. Stiff ones all around." She weaves her arm through mine and while I truly don't know her all that well yet, I worry she might be a bit self-destructive. But hey, who am I to judge? "Right, Jemma?"

"Right," I agree and plaster on a bright smile. I lift my head and find Kace studying me, the darkest eyes I've ever seen narrow in on my face as a scowl mars his handsome features. My entire body freezes, everything inside me telling me he can see right through me, see that I'm just an unlovable, boring book nerd—Maloney Baloney—that no one wants to be around, and probably shouldn't be here. God, I really do need another drink. Or ten. Although when Sebastian talked about a stiff one, I'm not so certain he's referring to alcohol.

We follow Kace to the coolers, and the chill radiating from him as he pours a little bit of this and a little bit of that into a glass, knowing exactly what we're drinking, freezes my blood. He finishes and hands me a cup. When my skin touches his, warmth ripples through me. My God, what is wrong with me? The man hates me—I hate him—and I shouldn't be thinking about what it would be like to have his hands on other parts of my body.

I'm a virgin, for God's sake. Virgins—who have no idea what it's like to be touched—don't suddenly begin to fantasize about guys' hands all over them, do they? It's not like I haven't touched myself over the years, however. Although it's been happening more often these last three weeks after watching Kace play hockey. He's known to be a fast scorer, and I'm guessing the bunnies aren't just talking about his on-ice skills.

Just then, Sebastian comes up and throws his arm over my shoulder, like he's laying claim to me. He's not my type, but I don't want to offend him. He glances at the cup in my hand. "What are you drinking, baby?"

"Oh, it's ah..." Okay, I saw what Kace put in it, Aperol, prosecco and soda but I have no idea what it's called.

Brynn laughs. "It's a prosecco cocktail."

"But I made you a drink, baby," Sebastian pouts, and I can't help but steal a glance at Kace as he folds his arms across his broad chest and stares at me. What is he waiting for?

"What's in it?" I glance at the concoction in the red cup.

He grins. "All the good stuff." He sips it, as if to prove it's safe, and holds it out again. Kace reaches out and takes it before I can try it.

"She already has a drink," he says. "I'll take this one."

"What the fuck, Drag," Sebastian yells, shortening Kace's nickname as Kace takes a big swallow from the cup. He winces and wipes his lips with the back of his hand.

"Gin." A hard quiver goes through Kace as his lips pucker. "That's fucking strong."

"Like I said..." Sebastian pauses to wink at me. "A stiff one. It's my own special drink."

"Gin is panty remover," Brynn pipes in with a laugh. She glances at what's left in the cup and pokes her brother. "You might not want to finish that."

"If I wore panties, maybe I'd be worried." His gaze strays to me, a possible warning in his eyes as he puts the cup to his lips and finishes it.

Sebastian tightens his arm around my shoulder, pulling me against him. "Come on, baby, I'll make you another one." I walk away with Sebastian, my stomach tight as he makes me a drink and I keep a close eye on what he's doing. I know all about drugs getting slipped into drinks. My older sister, Krista, who is in her third year at Montreal College, warned me all about college life. She didn't come home after her second year, something about working on a research project, and I miss her like crazy. I make a mental note to call her again, even though she hasn't been answering me.

But I'll think about that tomorrow, because right now Sebastian is tipping a cup to my lips. For the next hour or so, I drink gin, party, swim and...I'm not sure what else, because my brain turned fuzzy and the world around me went black. The next thing I know, I'm waking up in my bed, my tongue stuck to the roof of my mouth. What the hell happened last night? I groan and that's when someone moves beside me.

There's someone in my bed? Oh my God there's someone in my bed! What the ever-loving hell did I do?

I try to control my breathing as I slowly turn my head, not wanting to move the mattress, but there's nothing I can do to quiet the moan of regret crawling out of my throat when I see who's beside me.

Kace peels his eye open and winces at the sun creeping in through the open curtains. His gaze lands on mine, and he quickly sobers. "What the fuck?"

"Kace," I say, as I too try to wrap my brain around the events of last night. How did Kace end up in my bed—dressed in his bathing suit from last night? Panicked, I quickly glance down and find myself in a T-shirt—one I've seen Kace in before—and my bathing suit bottoms. I scramble to pull the blankets up.

He shakes his head and pinches the bridge of his nose. "What the fuck did Sebastian put in that drink?" he asks.

"Gin," I answer quietly.

"Yeah, I'm sure there was more than gin in it."

"A lot of gin."

He moans and presses his palms to his eyes. "I'm going to kill that fucker." He groans some more. "Did he make you one?"

"Yes." I close my eyes, and sort through the foggy memories from last night. Drinking. Partying. Swimming. Dancing. Wait, did I lose my bathing suit top? Is that why I'm in Kace's shirt? I gasp for breath, pretty damn sure I've gone ghostly white.

"What?" he asks, his brow furrowed as worry narrows his eyes.

"I was drinking.... partying..." I look down. "You were there..." I point to the mattress as memories take form. "You...you took me back here. I remember laughing, and then you dragging me away."

He runs his hand through his hair, his head down. "Did we..."

I glance at the bed and find the sheets clean. I'm a virgin, so I'd expect a trace of blood or something. When I don't immediately answer, he jumps up.

"Jesus Christ," he swears, and starts pacing. "This was a mistake. This never should have happened. Fuck me."

I swallow against a tight throat, and tears threaten. As far as I know he's been with numerous puck bunnies. Why would I be such a mistake? I'm not sure, but heck, maybe I should let him think he slept with me. Maybe he doesn't deserve the truth after telling me I was a mistake.

"I have to go. I have to run home before I head to the rink... practice." He walks to the door, puts his hand on the knob and stops. He takes a big breath, turns back around and zeroes in on me. There's genuine concern on his face when he asks, "Are you okay?"

"I'm okay," I manage to get out without a tremble in my voice as I lift my chin high.

He gives a tight nod and walks out the door. I throw myself on my bed as memories of what I'd done last night come back to haunt me. Although I can't remember when or how my bathing suit top came off.

God, is this really who you want to be, Jemma?

I stare at the ceiling for a long time, my blood pounding like thunder through my veins as the minutes tick by. A long while later a knock comes on my door, and I sit up. "Who is it?"

"It's Kace. Can I come in?"

My heart jumps into my throat and I try to sound casual. "Sure." I hug my blankets to my body as his big frame walks through the door and overwhelms my senses.

His face is hard, his jaw clenched so tightly I'm sure he's going to crack his teeth. He has something in his hand as he takes two steps, stops at the small dinette table, and slaps his palm down. "Found this in the locker room." He glares at me, hard disdain in his eyes and my heart stops beating. "Thought you might want it back."

Unable to speak, I nod, and stand on wobbly legs. I keep the sheet wrapped around my body as I take a tentative step closer. His big body towers over mine, every muscle tight as I lean forward and see the picture he just slapped down.

The world around me spins, and tears pool in my eyes. I put my hand on the table, bracing myself before I fall—before I lose all contents in my stomach. Who would do this? Better yet, why did I ever take my top off, which I can't even remember doing? I don't know what is going on, but what I do know is that this...this mistake...could have followed me around forever, ruined me. Thank God Kace got to it before anyone saw it. Wait, did he really find it?

"Did you..." I lift my eyes to his and find anger brewing.

"Jesus Christ, Jemma." He grips his hair, the look he's aiming my way full of anger. "Of course, I didn't take it."

"Who did?" Whoever took it must still have a copy on their phone. What if it resurfaces. I'd die of embarrassment.

"I don't know. I saw it, ripped it down and brought it here before anyone could see it. At least I think I got to it before the other guys saw it."

I open my mouth and try to speak as I work to sound nonchalant, like this is no big deal. That's what the new Jemma would do, right? I mean, it's just my breasts, right? Half the population has them. God, if only I really felt that way. I try not to take deep gulping breaths in front of Kace. I look back at the picture, and my throat squeezes so tight it hurts. I am such a fool. Is it too late to run back to Shelburne, crawl in my bed and stay there for the next ten years?

"Jemma," he whispers, his voice so soft, so tender and so full of concern, it does the strangest things to my insides. Is this the side of him his sister knows? I tear my gaze from the picture, and take in dark eyes that are waiting for an explanation. But how can I tell him who I really am—a book nerd that no one here would be friends with—and avoid humiliation? Dammit, I'm in too deep now, and what would he think of me if I suddenly told him I'd fabricated a new life just to feel accepted. I can't do that. I can't turn back now. Right? Heck, I've already let him believe we slept together.

How could I have done that?

"Oh that," I say, my voice filled with laughter, even though my insides are in turmoil and I'm seconds from racing to the toilet to vomit. I wave my hand. "Fun and games." How could I have been so stupid? I force my lips to part in a smile, and grip the table harder to keep my hands from shaking as my stomach churns.

"Fun and games, huh?"

"Yeah," I answer, a lightness in my voice that doesn't reflect anything going on inside me. Maybe I should be taking acting classes instead of English literature, because I'm not too sure I'm pulling this off.

"Right." He turns his back on me and walks out the door, clicking it tightly shut behind him. I crinkle the picture in my hand as I run to the bathroom before I lose everything in my stomach. As I grip the porcelain, I groan out loud, because I'm beginning to believe that being popular isn't all it's cracked up to be, and that I've gotten myself in too deep to turn back now.

2

KACE

I stand outside Jemma's sorority room, my back against the wall and take a couple of deep, fueling breaths. Last night is still a bit of a blur to me, and while I want to kill Sebastian—he must have put something in her drink—the fact of the matter is, I didn't have to drink it.

I only downed it because Jemma already had a drink in her hand and maybe there's a part of me that just doesn't trust my roommate. Then again, it's not like Sebastian needs to liquor up a girl to get her in his bed. Not only is he a hockey player, a jock, his father is a well-known political figure here in Nova Scotia. Talk about money and power. The ultimate aphrodisiac, right? The girls here fall all over Sebastian and Jemma is no exception, which fucking pisses me off.

Why?

Oh, believe me, it's not because I want her—it's because I don't like her. Which, when it comes right down to it, means I shouldn't give a shit what she does or who she does it with. But she's Brynn's good friend and roommate, so by proxy, I guess, I do care about her well-being—hell, I care about every woman's well-being—but it doesn't mean I have to like Jemma.

The more my brain fills in the gaps from last night, the more I'm sure I didn't sleep with the girl I woke up beside. Why does she want me to think I did? Probably because she's pretending to be something she's not. Yeah, I can see it. Every time I look at her. When she has no idea she has an audience of one, I can tell how uncomfortable she is with this whole party scene, the whole sorority puck bunny persona, and I hate her for pretending otherwise.

I hate liars. Thanks to my old man and the double life he led, of course. Yeah, I know. A man with two families sounds surreal, the stuff of fiction, right? But it fucking happened, and because of it, I hate liars with every fiber of my being. Imagine, pretending to love and care for your family when you secretly have another. How can I ever again trust a person who lies about who they really are? I know Jemma and Brynn have grown close in the last month, but that doesn't mean I have to be friends with her too.

Just then a noise sounds on the long set of stairs leading to the main level, and I push myself up to my full height. I catch Sierra's eyes and she angles her head. Curiosity, and maybe even a hint of anger, passes over her gaze when she spots me outside this particular room. I think she was looking to hook up last night. Will she think I'm visiting Brynn, or sleeping with her roommate? I don't want her to feel shunned. I'd never do that to anyone on purpose.

"Hey Kace," she murmurs, and runs her hands through her messy hair. She looks like she's just getting home from a wild party. "What happened to you last night?" Her gaze goes from me to my sister's door, and I'm guessing she's putting things together—I slept with the roommate. "You bailed early."

"Yeah, I just uh...had some things to do." I jerk my thumb over my shoulder, toward the door beside me. "My sister," I fib, even though I hate liars and I'm not a very good one. I suppose that's a positive trait to have—until I'm in a situation like this.

She laughs, and it cuts through my brain like a jagged knife, reminding me I drank way too much last night. "Yeah, okay. Sure."

I don't want to continue this conversation, or upset her. I really don't. I just want to go to the rink and practice and lose myself on the ice for a few hours. Before I can leave, she points a finger at me.

"I knew Jemma had a thing for you."

"She likes my roommate," I clarify. "She was hanging with Sebastian."

Her grin widens, and my heart thumps. "If she likes Sebastian, then why were you in her bed last night?"

Maybe because underneath the persona, there's something very vulnerable about her...something you want to protect...and you hate the idea of any guy messing with her.

Whoa. As that thought kicks me in the nuts, blurry visions of her dancing and taking her bathing suit top off rush through my brain. No fucking way was she in her right mind last night, which is why I dragged her away. I vaguely remember giving her my shirt, and sitting down on the side of her bed, just for a moment, to make sure she was okay. Only I woke up this morning, tangled in her sheets beside her.

"It's not what you think." She stands there looking at me like I'm dense and it's exactly what she thinks. I shove my hands in my pockets, digging for my phone. Are there pics of a half-naked Jemma in our group chats? My search for my phone comes up empty. Fuck, I'm always losing the damn thing. Wait, I remember now. I left it at home last night before the party. "She wasn't feeling great last night."

Her gaze drops to my crotch. "I take it you helped her with that?"

I like Sierra, I really do, but I also know she loves to gossip, and before I leave this building rumors of me sleeping with Jemma will spread faster than a brush fire in the dry heat of summer. I know I have a reputation and the girls I sleep with know it and don't care. Does Jemma want that? Does she want others to think we slept together? Fuck, maybe she wanted that naked picture of her breasts in the locker room too.

I shake my head. No that can't be right. She had no idea what she was doing, and someone, I can't quite remember who, screamed something about hazing. Or maybe I dreamt that. Not that I was dreaming of her breasts or anything. I don't think it was Sebastian, though. I'm not sure he'd do something like that. Could it have been one of her sorority sisters? No, that can't be right either. They're a sisterhood and they all protect one another.

I push off the wall, still confused and a bit dizzy. Fuck, honestly, I have no idea what's up or down, left or right. All I know is I'm leaving this situation alone and for the rest of this year, I'm going to avoid Jemma. "Can you drop this?"

Sierra holds her hands up and walks past me. "You got it."

"Thanks, Sierra," I say quietly as she leaves. I listen to her footsteps until they disappear and then I bolt from the sorority house before any other doors open, or anyone comes home. I don't want to explain myself again, and where the hell was my sister last night? Not that it's my business. She's here enjoying her first year like I enjoyed mine. After what we've both been through in our short lifetime, finding out about Dad's secret marriage and trying to keep Mom from falling apart, I need to give her some leeway to let her find herself. As long as she's doing it in a safe and healthy way, it's all good.

Oh, like you are, Kace? Walking around with a heart full of anger— unable to trust or get close to anyone?

Yeah, well, whatever.

My thoughts go back to Brynn. I'm sure after a couple years in this house, she'll want out too. I might not love or trust my roommate—then again, that's sort of a running theme with me—but he pays half the rent, allowing me to live in a house not too far from campus. I refused to take a dime from my father. I'll get my education and get to the NHL on my own. Then I'll show him I never needed him, and that I'm better than him because I made it and he didn't. Yeah, he was never good enough for the NHL.

Will that make you feel better, Kace?

Brynn however, she's not as bitter as me, and I don't know why. Maybe because she's younger, but Dad is paying her way, and she's happy to take it. Maybe that's her way of saying *fuck you, Dad.*

I head back to the rink, and stalk to my locker, glancing around in search of Sebastian. I have no fucking idea if he was behind the picture I found here this morning, or if it had been sent around to everyone.

I turn when I hear a voice, not really expecting to see Sebastian. It's Sunday, and we don't have to be on the ice. I just like to skate to clear my head, and I want to keep my skills up. After getting drafted by the Edmonton Eagles, I want to stay on top of my game. I can't let anything or anyone, not even a ridiculous freshman pretending to be something she's not, get in my way.

"Hey Conner," I call to our goalie as he comes in, ending the call with whoever he was talking to and shoving his phone into his pocket. He was at the party last night, but he looks like he's in much better shape than me. He eyes me for a second. "What?" I ask.

"Dragon," he says. "I'm surprised to see you here." I stiffen. What the hell happened last night?

"Why? I come in every Sunday, don't I?"

"Yeah, but..." He stops and whistles. "You went all fucking caveman last night with Jemma." I sit on the bench and try not to appear panicked.

"She was sick. She's my sister's roommate. I was just helping her out." Okay, stop rambling. It's not making this lie, if it even is a lie, any better.

He grunts out a laugh. "I heard you were doing more than that."

Fuck me sideways.

"Are we practicing or not?" I grouch.

"Practicing." He drops it and heads to his locker. I stand, tugging some gear from my locker as my gaze goes to the spot on the wall where I found Jemma's picture. A hot stab of fire goes through my veins, and I slam my locker shut with more force than necessary. Why the fuck would someone do that to her? Aren't we all better than that? Shit, I can't help but want to tear through Storm House and interrogate every guy on the team until I find the asshole responsible.

"Conner?" I ask as I drop back down onto the bench.

"Yeah?" He turns back to me.

"Do you know if any of the other guys were in here this morning?"

He glances over his shoulder. Other than the two of us, the place is empty. His locker makes a scraping noise as he pulls it open. "No, why?"

I dig into my bag, searching for my phone. Didn't I put it in here earlier when I'd stopped at home before the rink? "No reason."

"You sure you're okay, buddy?"

"Good, just tired." I tug on my skates and lace them, happy that whoever took the picture and printed it out didn't widely distribute it and I managed to pull it down before anyone saw it. Although I'm sure lots of the guys saw Jemma in the flesh last night. Fuck. What was she thinking?

She wasn't dude. Something was wrong.

Then why did she act like there wasn't anything wrong when she saw the picture this morning? Because she's pretending to be something she isn't, and you fucking hate that.

Stop thinking about her.

"Come on, Dragon," Conner says and puts his hand on my shoulder. "Work it out on the ice."

I nod, happy he's not pressing, because what would I say? I follow him onto the ice and we both do a few stretches before he takes up position in the net and I practice my shots. About ten minutes later, a few of the other guys join us and we practice a few plays.

I'm about to call an end to it when I spot Sebastian on the ice. Now that's a surprise. Maybe he's coming in to check on the picture, to see our reaction. Maybe I should have left it up for Coach to see. He would have gotten to the bottom of it. I couldn't bring myself to do it. I saw fucking red and reacted when I walked in and spotted it. Honestly if someone did that to my sister, I'd murder them.

He skates over to me, and I stand there scowling at him. "Hey, you cool, man?" he asks.

"What the fuck did you put in my drink last night?"

He shakes his head. "Gin and more gin. You just drank too much." He bangs his gloved hands together. "I told you it was a stiff one." He nudges me. "Just like what you gave Jemma last night when you dragged her back to her room. She was mine for the night, dude. You fucking owe me."

Owe him? Jesus, what an asshole. I resist the urge to punch him in the face. Wait, does everyone know I dragged Jemma away? Of course, they do, and I know what they're all thinking. Why wouldn't they?

He snorts, taking my non answer as confirmation that I did indeed sleep with Jemma. "It's okay. I don't mind sharing."

I once again see red and before I can help it, I blurt out. "Jemma and I are not a couple. We didn't even...I don't think."

"Oh, then if you want me to share her with you, I don't mind."

"I'm not...there's no sharing. Drop it." Jesus. The next thing I know, I'm blurting out,

"Did you fucking put a nude picture of her up in the locker room?"

His head rears back. "What the fuck, dude? No. I'm not going to risk getting kicked off the team."

I stare at him for a long second, and he stares back, holding his ground. I don't know why, but I believe him. Which is crazy, because I don't know what to believe about anyone anymore. I'm a terrible judge of character, but after my dad's deceit, I've gotten better at spotting liars. Or at least, I thought I had.

I skate backward, putting distance between us. "Fine, I'm out of here."

"Catch up with you later."

I skate off and head to the locker room. I'm still in a foul mood by the time I dress, walk home and head to the kitchen for something to eat. I grab a left over cold-cut sub and take a huge bite. Breakfast of champions right here. I walk around as I eat, searching for my phone. I eventually head up to my bedroom and that's when I spot my phone lighting up on my desk.

I reach for it, and when I see numerous texts and messages from Brynn, the bite of sandwich in my mouth sours as I swallow. I drop what's left and grab my phone. I quickly read the four texts telling me to call her.

What the hell is going on?

My heart thunders in my ears as I call her. She answers on the first ring, and her voice is breathless when she says, "Kace."

I go perfectly still at the panic in her voice. "Sis, what's going on?"

"You need to get over here. Now."

● 3

JEMMA

"What the hell. What the hell. What the hell," I repeat, as I walk around the dorm room, my brain spinning a million miles an hour as I try to quiet the crying baby in my arms. Brynn comes out of the bathroom, her phone in her hand and a stricken look on her face, even though she's trying hard to appear in control, for my sake. When she first burst through our door this morning, she started asking questions about Kace, happy to hear the rumor that he'd spent the night in my bed, but her questioning quickly changed when she saw the bundle on my bed —one I had no idea what to do with.

"I called Kace." She tugs on her T-shirt, sort of pacing back and forth, clearly not knowing what to do.

Everything inside me stiffens. "Why would you do that?"

"He'll know what to do."

"How could he possibly know what to do, Brynn?" My God, what if he calls in child protective services or something? I can't let them take my sister's baby. There was desperation in the note she left, begging me to help her out while she worked to get her life in order. Cripes, I didn't even know she was pregnant, and now...now there's a two-month-old in my care, with a limited supply of diapers and formula. I briefly close my eyes, hoping that when I open them again, I'll be waking from a bad dream.

The baby's screams pierce my brain and my lids fly open. I glance at her red, scrunched face, and bounce her in my arms. Maybe I should call home, let my parents know what's going on, even though Krista asked me not to do that. How the hell does my older sister think I have what it takes to care for a newborn when she can't even do it herself? Why the hell did she keep this a secret? We might have grown up in a strict, religious family, our father's a minister who also runs a big corn farm, but come on. Keeping this a secret, and dropping a little bundle named Emma outside my dorm room with a note is the definition of insanity.

The baby starts to wail, and I put her over my shoulder. "I don't know what to do."

"Kace will be here in a second."

It's great that she has so much faith in her older brother, but I don't know how he can help. What does he know about babies?

Brynn pulls a soother from the bassinet and holds it out to me. "Here, try this?"

I shift Emma in my arms and put the soother in her mouth. She sucks hard, and the tears slow. Her big blue eyes stare up at me, and in that instant, my heart melts. She looks so much like my sister. She sucks hard, and then her face twists and she spits the soother out.

"What do I do?" I'm about two seconds from crying like a baby myself when the door opens and in hurries Kace. It's crazy, because while I don't think he can help, I'm relieved to see him.

"What the fuck," he blurts out, his gaze going from me to the screeching baby in my arms.

"It's her sister's baby," Brynn explains quickly. "She was just... dropped outside our door with a note."

Kace stands there for about two whole seconds—I can almost hear the wheels turning—before he jumps into action. The next thing I know, he's taking three big steps to reach me, snatching a wailing Emma from my arms. He holds her against his chest, his gaze cataloguing the contents in her bassinet. "She's hungry." He touches Emma's bottom. "And she needs to be changed. "Brynn, read the instructions on the can, and get her a bottle. Jemma, throw a blanket down, grab the baby wipes and a diaper."

Now it's my turn to stand there for two whole seconds. "Jemma," he barks out, and it startles me into moving.

I grab one of the blankets from the bassinet and set it on my bed. "Does she have a name?" he asks, as he sets the squirming baby down.

"It's Emma," I tell him.

"So, your sister named her after you." I stare at him, perplexed, and he explains. "Take the J off Jemma and you get Emma."

My heart thumps and tears pierce my eyes. "She named her after me." I lightly touch Emma's red cheek, the bond growing between us. What was that I said earlier about love at first sight? I guess I do believe in it, and it makes me want to protect this innocent child all the more.

"Hi Emma," Kace whispers as he unsnaps Emma's one-piece outfit at the legs to expose her bulging diaper. How does he know all this? Maybe he babysat a lot when he was younger. I did as well, just never with a child as young as Emma. "Pass me a wipe." I do as he asks, and he removes the wet diaper, and washes her clean. "Pass the diaper."

His eyes briefly meet mine as I accidently brush up against him, my legs wobbly, my brain completely overwhelmed with this whole situation. I take in his dark eyes as they move over my face. "Thank you," I murmur quietly, my heart pounding in my ears and he doesn't respond. Instead, he gives a nod and turns his full concentration back to Emma.

In our small kitchenette, the microwave beeps, and I drop onto the bed next to Emma as Kace puts a new diaper on her, hands me the old one to get rid of, and gets her dressed again. Brynn comes over with the bottle, and Kace holds his hand out. "Squirt a bit on my arm."

Brynn shakes the bottle and squeezes a bit onto his wrist. He nods and takes the bottle, remaining calm as Emma continues to scream. I sit on the bed, watching in fascination as he picks Emma up, drops into one of our chairs and puts the bottle into her mouth. She instantly stops shrieking, and gulping sounds can be heard as she drinks.

After a moment, Kace lifts his head. "Okay," he begins, exhaling as his glance zeroes in on me. I sit up a bit straighter under his scrutiny. "Your sister just left her?" I nod. "Brynn said there was a note." I scramble off the bed, grab the note and hold it out so he can read it. I take in his dark, intense eyes as he scans the note. His brow furrows, and he gives a curt nod when he's done. I fold the paper and go back to my spot on the bed. Brynn drops down next to me, and lightly rubs my back.

"First things first," Kace begins. "Put some clothes on."

I stare at him, his words not registering. He already dressed Emma. What the heck is he talking about?

"Jemma," Brynn whispers. "He's talking to you." That's when I realize I'm dressed only in a pair of underwear and a tank top, without a bra.

"Ohmigod." I jump up, and he averts his gaze as I hurry to my closet to grab a pair of frayed shorts and a sweater, which is tight—like all my clothes. I kind of miss sweats and big comfy sweaters. I'd just finished showering when I heard noise outside the door. I opened it to find Emma in the hall. I put the bassinet on the bed, and just stood here panicking when Brynn came home. Chaos ensued, and I'd forgotten to get dressed. I pull my clothes on quickly, hoping humiliation isn't painting my face red as I go back to my perch beside Brynn.

"Have you called your sister?" Kace asks.

"No…I…the baby was crying and, I…" I groan at my stupidity. The first thing I should have done was call Krista. Emma couldn't have been outside my door for any length of time. I'd heard crying and found her. Krista probably isn't too far away. I grab my phone and call my sister, but it goes straight to voicemail. "No answer." Kace's eyes remain on me, and I try not to fumble as I send a text asking Krista to call me, although I doubt she will, after pulling a stunt like this. I put my hand on my stomach, ready to vomit again, from nerves not alcohol this time, and Kace's concerned gaze drops to my stomach. That's when I realize this is the man Brynn knows, this is a side of him he allows only Brynn her to see.

Why is that?

"Child protective services?" he asks.

"No," I rush out quickly. "She asked me not to. She doesn't want Emma taken from her. I..." I rub my aching stomach. "I can keep her until she comes back. She said she was coming back," I say, hope in my eyes as I reach for the note and hold it to my chest. "She's going through something, obviously. I don't want to do anything to cause her trouble."

"Like she's doing to you," he points out.

"Kace," I begin, and go quiet when Brynn's hand lands on my back.

"You can't stay here with her, Jemma. It's against the rules."

My pulse leaps as blood drains to my toes. I shift on the bed, until my back is against the headboard, bracing myself as I grow lightheaded from that realization. "I didn't...think."

Brynn takes my hand in hers as Kace pulls the bottle from Emma's mouth and checks it. He sets it down and puts Emma over his shoulder, lightly patting her on the back. Okay, what the hell is going on with my ovaries right now?

"Maybe you can stay with Kace. You have that third bedroom you guys haven't been able to rent out," Brynn suggests, her eyes big, her lips tight as my gaze flies to hers. I get it, she doesn't think it's a big deal, because she thinks we slept with each other and are destined to be lifelong partners. Good God, I'm the one who wants to be a writer but she clearly lives in a fairy tale world. If this wasn't so insane, I'd think she set this up to get the two of us together, but that's ludicrous of course. This is my sister's baby.

"No," I blurt out.

"You can't stay here, Jemma," she points out softly, but I can hear the exasperation in her tone. She's as stressed as I am. "If she cries and someone hears her, you'll get reported and kicked out. You don't want to get kicked out of this sorority for good for disobeying the rules do you, do you?"

"No. Of course not." She's right about the sorority, though, I realize that, but staying with Kace? "I can't...I mean...No. I'm not going to do that. We'll figure something out."

"You'll stay with me," Kace states, his voice firm, putting an end to my protests. My heart leaps as he settles Emma back in his arms, cuddling her as he puts the bottle back in. Emma's tiny little fingers wrap around his pinkie, like she's thanking him, and my throat tightens. She drinks and stares up at him, and he stares back. Her eyes slowly close, as she takes comfort in his arms, secure against his body.

"Kace," I begin. "I don't know what to say."

"It's temporary." He shrugs. "I'm sure your sister will come to her senses soon. If not, we'll cross that bridge when we get to it." I swallow. How the heck is he so calm about all this and why is he holding Emma to him like it's his duty to protect her? "Right now, Emma needs someone to take care of her." His gaze cuts to mine, and I flinch as the hardness that lives there feels like a slap. "You can't do it here, and you're going to need help."

I grip the blankets and tug as panic bursts inside me. "You have hockey, and work, and school."

"So do you."

I exhale, exasperated. "I don't expect you to help. None of this is your responsibility."

"It's not yours, either."

"Krista is my sister." That totally makes it my responsibility, right?

"You're my sister's friend."

Okay, I get it. He'll do anything for his sister, but this is too much.

"He'll help," Brynn says quietly. "I told you he'd know what to do." I take in her eyes as her gaze meets her brother's, and the love that shines there steals the air from my lungs. The bond they share, the way they trust and take care of one another is incredible, and for the briefest of moments, I'm envious. Although something in my gut tells me they might have gotten to this place together out of necessity, and maybe trauma. "I'll help too. Between the three of us, we'll figure this out."

Tears fill my eyes. "I don't know what to say."

"You don't have to say anything. Get packed up." He puts Emma over his shoulder again, and after she burps in her sleep, he sets her in the bassinet and covers her in blankets.

I push to my feet. "I appreciate this, Kace."

He doesn't look at me. "Yeah."

"I'll do the work. I'll try not to get in the way."

"Uh huh."

"Kace, I'm serious."

"I am too."

Brynn's gaze bobs back and forth between the two of us when I say, "You're saying you're sure I'll get in the way."

He shifts the bassinet from one hand to the other, and looks annoyed when he answers. "Yes, it's exactly what I'm saying. Now, are you ready or not?"

Ready or not?

Hell, I'm not ready. Not ready to take care of my sister's child, and most definitely not ready to cohabitate with a man who is nurturing and caring, and calm under pressure. No, I'm not ready for a man who was upset that he slept with me, and looks at me with disdain, yet removes a half-naked picture of me from the locker room and steps up when needed.

Yeah, so not ready for any of this.

4

KACE

We walk to my car and I stand there for a second, a little pissed off, but anger isn't going to solve anything right now and Emma needs me to be better than that. "This isn't going to work."

"You're right," Jemma agrees, and reaches for the bassinet. "I'll figure something else out."

I hold the bassinet tight as she pulls on it. "We are not playing tug of war with Emma," I point out, and tap her hands to make her let go. "I got her."

"You just said—"

"What I meant was we don't have a car seat. We can't take her in my car." I fish my keys from my pocket. "You drive this to my place." He pulls the keys back. "You drive, right?"

"Of course, I drive. I've been driving tractors for as long as I can remember." I angle my head and stare at her, catching the cracks in her story. Yeah, I'm more and more convinced this whole flirtatious puck bunny thing is just an act and it stirs the anger in my gut.

"You know where I live?" She nods, and I hand her the keys. "I'll walk with Emma."

"I can walk with her. She's my responsibility."

"Haven't we been over this?" She opens her mouth. "She can get heavy carrying her like this. I'm the better choice to do it."

Her nose crinkles, a splattering of late summer freckles bunching together. "That's logical."

"That's me, logical. Okay. I'll meet you there."

"Kace." I pause and take in the uncertainty on her face. "What are you going to tell people?"

I shift the bassinet to my other hand. "That I'm doing a favor for a friend."

A garbled sound catches in her throat. "I just...you don't like...We're not friends."

"No, we're not." Her face tightens. "We might not know each other. But like I said, you're my sister's friend, so..." She nods and I start down the sidewalk, headed toward home. I'm sure I'll run into lots of people I know, and I can already imagine the rumors. Fuck them. They can say whatever they want. No way am I going to let this child feel unloved, or that she's not enough for anyone. There's enough of that going around in the world—in my own life— as it is.

I keep my head down and hurry home, nodding as Jemma drives past us, going slow. How am I going to explain this to Sebastian? Shit, I probably should have run this situation by him before showing up with an infant. He pays half the rent and deserves a say.

Up ahead I spot three sorority girls from Brynn's house coming from the café, and they all start whispering as they walk toward me—a bassinet in my hand.

Here goes nothing.

"Whatcha got there, Kace?" Olivia asks, as I approach.

"Helping a friend out."

"This friend...do we know her?" Kat asks, her eyes narrowed, and I get it. She thinks Emma is mine.

"No, you don't. But my sister does, and so does Jemma. We'll be taking care of Emma..." I hold the bassinet out so they can see the sleeping baby. "Until her mom comes to get her. She needs a caregiver for a little bit. No big deal."

Ally curls her hair around one finger, and juts her chest out, a little pout on her lips. "Does that mean we call you Daddy instead of Dragon now?"

Jesus.

On that note, I start past them, and Olivia says, "If you need any help, you know where to find me, Daddy Dragon."

Fuck me twice.

I hear them saying something about needing a spanking as I continue down the sidewalk. Fuck, I'll be glad to get out of this place and start my life in Edmonton. I reach my house, and my car is in the driveway. Jemma hops out and grabs her bag from the back seat.

Her eyes dart from me to the house and she draws her bottom lip between her teeth. "Sebastian..."

"I'll deal with him." We head to the house and I unlock the door and stand back for Jemma to enter. I follow her in and she stands there, the bag clutched tightly to her, like she's a lamb who just walked into the lion's den. "We're going to need some things," I tell her. "Why don't we check out the online marketplace and see if we can find clothes and essentials?"

Jemma nods. "I have my laptop."

I walk into the living room and set the bassinet on one end of the sofa. Jemma catalogues the room, taking in the big fire-place as I drop down and pat the cushion beside me. "Let's look."

"I saw you run into Olivia, Kat and Ally."

I roll my eyes. "Yeah, they made stupid jokes, asking if they could call me Daddy and then I heard them whispering about spanking." Shock registers in her blue eyes, making them bigger, but she quickly blinks it away and gives a playful smile, like she's remembering her role. Jesus, I don't have time for any of her performances. "Let's look," I say, getting us back on track.

Her demeanor once again changes as she pulls her laptop from her bag and channels her focus. Good Lord, the woman is going to give me whiplash. Her fingers fly over her keys, and she comes across a person selling a bundle of baby clothes, a baby car seat and a crib. "Look."

I lean in close, and her warm sweet scent reaches my nostrils. I breathe her in as I read the ad, and as our legs touch, she clears her throat. "I don't think we'll need a crib," I tell her. "Unless…"

She sighs. "Unless Krista doesn't come back for a long time." Uncertainty dances in her eyes and without thinking, I put my hand on her arm and give it a comforting squeeze. She flinches as her gaze cuts to my fingers, which are lightly caressing her soft skin. I quickly pull my hand back. Jesus, earlier today she wanted me to believe we slept together. Now she's recoiling from an innocent touch. Yeah, no way were my hands on her body last night, and if they were, she clearly didn't like it.

"One day at a time," I remind her as I grip my thighs, my thoughts shifting. One day at a time was how I got through Dad's betrayal. I snort out a laugh that shocks Jemma. Yeah, like I actually got *through* it, found *closure* and came out *stronger*. I take in her questioning eyes as they search my face. "Nothing," I respond and give a fast shake of my head. I don't talk about my past. Neither does Brynn, so there's no way she can know we weren't enough for our own father.

"I wonder if she'll sell the clothes and things without the crib," I ask, and focus back on the ad.

"I'll message her." Her fingers fly over the keyboard, as she shoots off a message, her gaze straying to the bassinet as she types.

"How do you do that?"

"Do what?"

Now she's looking at me. I gesture to her laptop. "Type like that without even looking."

She grins. "I don't know. I guess it's because I spend a lot of time with my fingers on a keyboard."

"Why?"

"I'm a literature student. I write a lot of papers."

"I didn't know." There's a lot I don't know about her, only what my sister had told me, which really wasn't a whole hell of a lot. But there's a lot I do know about her, that I can see with my own two eyes. "A literature student who knows how to drive a tractor. That's interesting."

She smiles, like that might be the nicest thing I've said to her, and it probably was. I don't mean to come off as a dick. I just really dislike fakeness. I wait for her to mention the tractor comment, but she doesn't. I get the feeling she didn't want me to know that.

"Are you and Sebastian..." I begin and she stares at me. "You know...a thing. I guess I'd just like to know, I mean with the baby here." Dark lashes fall and lift rapidly over blue eyes that are suddenly not looking at mine. Really, she's not sure how to answer that? What the fuck? Is she trying to figure out what it is I want to hear, like this morning when we woke up together? "It's a simple yes or no."

"I..."

The front door flings open and in walks none other than Sebastian. "Speak of the devil." I murmur as he slams the door shut, the bang reverberating through the house.

He starts down the hall, his boots coming to a halt at the arc to the living room. He backs up, and stares at the two of us sitting on the sofa. "Hey what's up?" Just then, Emma starts crying, and his body stiffens, his face paling as he holds his hands up, palms out. "Not mine."

"We're babysitting," I tell him.

He takes a tentative step into the room and peeks at Emma, keeping his distance like he might catch something. "How long?" he asks as he looks her over.

"Maybe a week or so." His head turns my way and I arch a brow. "Are you cool if we watch her here? Jemma can't have her in the dorm."

He backs up an inch. "Just keep her away from me."

"We won't bother you," Jemma says.

He grins at her. "I'm saying keep the baby away. You…" He pauses to point to her. "Can come bother me any time you like."

"She'll be staying in the third bedroom," I announce, an edge to my voice that could be taken as anger—or jealousy—even though it's not.

Sebastian wags his eyebrows. "Nice and close to mine."

"Seriously," Jemma begins. "Just go on as normal. Pretend we're not here. Have whoever you want over. Don't let our presence get in the way of your lifestyle." She glances at me. "Same goes for you."

"Nothing about you being here cramps my style, baby," Sebastian says with a laugh. His focus turns to Emma as Jemma gets up and takes the baby from the bassinet. Sebastian makes a face like he'd just eaten something sour. "Yeah, well that might."

"I'll see to it she won't," Jemma assures him just as her computer pings.

"Looks like the person responded." I put my hands over the keys. "Do you mind?"

She places Emma over her shoulder, emulating the way I did it earlier, and starts walking around the room. I watch her for a second, and it's crazy, but that's a good look on her. Better than her dancing around in a bikini at the pool.

Okay, maybe not better...

Fuck.

Sebastian turns. "Yeah, I need food and then I'm going to bounce. I have a list to work through."

"Thanks, Sebastian," I call out. He's a dick in a lot of ways and he could have vetoed this, so he deserves our gratitude. I click on the link and a response comes up that she's willing to sell without the crib.

"A list to work through?" Jemma asks.

I arch a brow. "Do you really want to know?"

"Uh, I think so."

"He's working his way through the alphabet." Now it's her turn to arch a brow. "The girls at the sorority."

Her eyes open wide. "Brynn Andrews."

"Not going to happen," I grind out between clenched teeth. "Your last name is Maloney," I say. "Maybe he's not going in order." I'm still not sure if she slept with him and it's not my business so I drop it and turn my attention back to the computer. "We got it. She took fifty bucks off." I punch the address into my phone. "I'll go get the stuff."

"I can do a bank e-transfer," she says, and I shrug.

"I'll pay and we can figure it out later." I close the tab and that's when I see the word file. I don't mean to invade her privacy but the words on the page catch my eyes. "Are you writing a book?"

She shrugs, almost the same shrug she gave this morning when I brought the picture back to her. I know it embarrassed her, so why play it off, like she's playing this off? Oh right, because she's fake. "Something I'm playing around with."

"You know," I begin. "Brandon Cannon, a former Storm's player, is now a romance novelist. His mom is one too."

"No way," she gasps, her mouth gaping open.

"Have you heard of him?"

She narrows her eyes. "Wait, I think I did overhear chatter about a hockey player turned romance novelist in one of my classes."

"Yeah, maybe he can give you some pointers."

"I'm not writing romance. I'm working on a children's book."

"Still, he might be able to help. I can put you two in contact if you like."

"Thanks, Kace. That would be really nice of you."

"Do you want children?" I ask, suddenly curious, considering she's writing a children's book.

She snorts out a humorless laugh. "Well, maybe someday, but I never thought it would happen like this." She hugs Emma tighter. "Not that I'll be keeping her, but still..."

"Right. Come on, let me show you your room before I go." I walk to the stairs, and take in the uncertainty—the vulnerability—in Jemma's eyes. My heart squeezes tight, and it's in my nature as a big brother—as a man—to protect and care for those that are hurting. If this is who she really is, and I like this girl, why is she pretending to be something else? I'm not sure, and maybe I'm being too hard on her. Maybe she has valid reasons. Or maybe I'm completely wrong about her and she's really a puck bunny who has no problem flashing others.

Hey, don't get me wrong. I have no problem with puck bunnies, not at all. They are exactly who they say they are and we're all on the same page when it comes to what we want. What I do have a problem with is trusting someone pretending to be one when they're really not.

"Do you want me to carry her up?" I ask.

"No, I got her."

I nod, appreciating her courage, and letting her go ahead of me. That way if she slips, I can help from behind. Speaking of behinds, hers is right in my face as she goes up the steps, and maybe I didn't notice what a great behind it was until now. Which is completely inappropriate under the circumstances. Also, maybe I did notice before and just pretended not to, considering all the pretending she was doing.

"This is my room," I tell her, and she slows to peek in. The bed is still made from yesterday, because I didn't sleep in it last night. At that reminder, I touch her arm to set her into motion. "That's Sebastian's." We walk a little further. "You're in here, and the bathroom is right across the hall."

I push open the door, and she steps into the room. "It's small. Maybe too small for a crib if it comes to that." I hang back and put my hands on the doorframe, leaning into the room.

"I'll make it work," she assures me.

"Or I could put the crib in my room." I jerk my thumb over my shoulder. "There's more space."

She gives a fast shake of her head. "No, you need to sleep."

"You do too." Sensing another argument, I say, "One day at a time and if it comes to that, you and I can switch rooms." She hesitates, and I tell her, "I'll be back shortly. Make yourself comfortable. Do you know how to make her a bottle if she needs one?"

"I can read the instructions. Right now, I think we'll just lay down. I'm exhausted."

"Okay." I'm about to leave as she pulls the covers back. "If you need anything, text me, okay?"

"What's your number?"

I reach into my pocket for my phone, to send her my contact information, but my hand comes up empty. "Jesus, what did I do with it now? Hang on." I hurry downstairs, find my phone on the sofa, and rush back up, grabbing a few pillows from my bed along the way. Jemma and Emma are snuggling in, and my throat grows tight in the strangest way when I see how sweet and cozy they look.

How many times did I tuck Brynn in at night because Dad was away 'working' and she missed him? I tried to fill in for him on those long trips. Little did I know he was with his other family. I walk across the room quietly, and pick up her phone.

"I'll put my information in, okay," I say quietly as I put the pillows around Emma to prevent her from moving. Jemma isn't used to sleeping next to a little one, and I want to keep Emma safe.

"Face recognition," she murmurs, and I hold the phone to her face to open it. I put my information in, and set it back on her dresser.

"Get some rest," I whisper, and tip toe out the door. It's really going to take time getting used to a baby in the house. I always stomp around with no regard for anyone but myself. Which is exactly how I like it. Or at least, exactly how I used to like it.

What the fuck am I saying?

5

JEMMA

The house is quiet, peaceful, and I let my eyes drift shut as Emma makes whimpering sounds beside me. At the sorority house, I'm used to shrieks and laughter and doors constantly opening and closing. I snuggle in tight, loving the way Kace put pillows around the little peanut beside me. Thinking of her as a little peanut brings on a soft laugh, which helps me lighten the tension of the day.

As I drift off, I decide worrying can wait until later, but then one thought pops into my head. What was I thinking, telling Kace that I grew up on a farm? I'm trying to run away from the girl I used to be, and I don't want him thinking I'm some hick pretending to be a carefree, hockey loving sorority girl, who parties and doesn't much care about nude photos. I gulp, my stomach tightening. I think I might have died if the guys on the team were all ogling my picture. How did I ever let myself get into a state where I either lost my top or purposely took it off?

The silence of the house surrounds me and the next thing I know, a door opening somewhere in the houses pulls me awake. My lids open, and it takes a second for me to orient myself. My gaze flies to Emma, and I find her staring up at me with her big blue eyes. My heart squeezes tight. I honestly can't believe my sister had a baby and then dropped her off at my door. I certainly wasn't ready for a lot of things today, starting off with finding Kace in my bed.

"Hello there, little one," I whisper quietly, and lightly rub my knuckles over her soft rosy cheeks. "Are you hungry? Need a diaper change?"

She gurgles and I sit up, rubbing the sleep from my eyes. Outside, clouds cover the sun that was shining earlier, and I can smell rain in the air. A shiver goes through me as I slide out from the warm blankets. I hope the baby isn't cold.

The door across the hall opens and I listen to the footsteps. It could either be Kace or Sebastian. My stomach grumbles and I reach for my phone and check the time. I also check to see if my sister messaged me and my stomach knots when I find nothing. I really hope she's okay. I shoot off another text, begging her to call me.

"Let's get you changed," I whisper to Emma. I lay down a blanket and she giggles and fusses as I quickly change her, not wanting her to get a chill. Fortunately, I know how to change a baby. I used to babysit when I was in high school, but the babies were older, which is why I was stressed over a newborn at first. Kace however, he was so natural with Emma. I never thought of him as the kind of guy who'd babysit, but I guess that's kind of a sexist thought. He has a younger sister. Maybe he had a lot of responsibility for her. They are close, and honestly, it's adorable how he calls her Sis.

I start to hum to Emma and she seems to like it. Knuckles rap on the door. "Is it okay if I come in?" Kace asks.

"Yup, we're good."

The door creaks open and I glance up, and when his eyes land on Emma, and a smile touches his mouth, my heart wobbles in my chest. Okay, wow, what is it about the tender way he looks at Emma that gets to me in the strangest ways?

"Have a good sleep?" he asks his eyes lifting to mine.

"Yes, thanks for that." I'm about to snap the pants together on the onesie but stop. "Did you get the clothes?"

"Got everything. The seat is secure in the car, and her clothes are all in the wash."

"Right," I agree. "Good thinking." I snap the legs on her onesies. "You're better at this than I am. I didn't think about washing the clothes first."

"That's because I had a little sister."

I stand up and hand Emma over, and I nearly lose all ability to remain upright as he cradles her against his chest and lightly rubs her back. I inch back until my legs hit the bed and I place my hand on the footboard to steady myself. "You were a good big brother." A statement, not a question.

He shrugs. "We should get her bottle ready."

"Right." He turns and I follow him out of the room. Downstairs, the washer hidden behind folding doors tumbles away as we walk to the kitchen. On the table, I find formula, bottles and brushes to clean them, and some stuffed toys.

I pick up a white bunny. "This is so cute. I didn't see this in the bundle of stuff."

He shrugs again. "Brynn had a little white bunny when she was a baby. It was her favorite. I thought Emma might like one."

"You bought this?"

"Yeah, is that okay?"

"You don't have to spend your money on Emma, Kace."

He hands Emma to me, and I sit at the table. "It's just a bunny."

It is just a bunny, but it's the sweet gesture that's messing with me. If I'm not careful, I could fall for a guy who doesn't really like me very much. Maybe I shouldn't have come here. I frown and look at sweet Emma as she squirms in my arms. We could have gone to a shelter, I suppose. I could have gotten good help there. Would that have been better for Emma? Honestly, what do I know about taking care of an infant? I'm going to mess this all up, scar her for life.

"Jemma," he says, and I lift my head to find him staring at me with those dark intense eyes that seem to hold a lot of knowledge, and pain.

"Yeah?"

He holds my gaze for a second. "It's going to be okay."

"Okay," I breathe out, wishing I could believe that.

"I'm going to help you. You're not in this alone." He pulls a bottle of water from the fridge and pours it into a baby bottle. He removes the plastic lid off the formula and dips in the measuring scoop.

"Why?" I ask quietly.

His shoulders tighten like he carries the weight of the world on them as his hand goes still inside the tub of powered formula, and I can't help but think I've hit a sore spot. I'm about to say never mind, and just thank him, but he speaks before my words reach my lips. "Because Emma should never feel like she's not wanted."

His voice is low, and the pain behind his words match the pain I spotted in his eyes earlier. My throat tightens, and even though he's not looking at me, I nod and let it go. He warms the bottle and hands it to me, and my stomach growls as I feed her.

"I grabbed us some chicken when I was out. Is that okay?"

"That's more than okay." He pulls rotisserie chicken pieces from the fridge, and a box that likely contains taters. "I'm so hungry I could eat the box."

"Wait. Shit, I never thought. Are you vegetarian? I have salads too." Dammit. I am. Or at least I used to be since moving into the sorority, but the chicken smells so good and I'm starving. "You don't have to eat it."

"No. It's good. I promise."

"Okay then, no eating the box." He places the chicken pieces on a tray, drops the taters beside them and puts them in the oven to crisp up. "I would have cooked us something, but I didn't figure there'd be time after all my running around."

"If I'm going to be staying here, I can cook for us."

"We'll figure it out."

"Do you like to cook?" I ask.

"I find it relaxing, actually. I wouldn't say I was a chef or anything."

"So that's what you do for fun?" I ask.

"During hockey season, there isn't a whole lot of time left for fun." His dark eyes leave mine and go to Emma. "Now there's going to be even less time for fun." Guilt grips my stomach and he holds his hands up. "Don't. I'm not blaming you."

Dammit, the man is very good at reading me. "I'm sure I'll hear from Krista soon."

His phone rings and he pulls it from his pocket. He slides his finger across the screen. "Hey sis." He grabs some plates from the cupboard. "Yeah, they both had a nap and we're just eating now. No, nothing yet." A beat and then, "I'll ask." He looks at me. "Okay if Brynn comes over?"

"Of course."

"There's plenty of food. I put a chicken in the oven." A pause as Brynn says something to him. "I know, I know but I have salads, too. Come eat with us."

I take the bottle from Emma's mouth and put her over my shoulder to burp her. What I failed to do however is put a blanket over my shirt. The next thing I know, warm milk is seeping through my sweater and sliding down my back. I groan and Kace ends the call and takes Emma from me.

"I got her." With a nod, he gestures toward the hall. "You go get changed. You have time to take a shower if you want. The food will take time to warm and we're waiting for Brynn anyway."

"I'll be fast."

I turn to leave, and Kace asks, "Do you want something warmer to wear?"

I gather my wet hair in my hand and pull the elastic off my wrist to tie it up. Something soft moves over Kace's face as I secure the ponytail. "I think I have another sweater."

"Go in my closet. There are sweats if you want them. The nights are getting colder and with rain coming, the house will feel damp." He walks to the thermostat and toys with the dial. "It's still early in the season, but I can turn the heat up. I could even light a fire, if you want."

"That actually sounds nice," I tell him as the milk cools on my back and my teeth begin to chatter. I hurry up the stairs and go straight to Kace's room. I glance at his desk and notice the doodles. I grin. He must doodle when studying. I nervously look over my shoulder to make sure Kace isn't standing behind me as I creep to his desk and take a closer look. His doodles are actually pretty good. Most of them have to do with hockey. Maybe he's drawing out the plays. Wait, is this a dragon? I glance at the drawing. Kace draws dragons when he doodles?

A door clicks in the hall and I hurry to the closet and pull out a pair of sweatpants and a big hoodie. He didn't say anything about a hoodie, but I don't think he'll mind. I hold the clothes for a second. I'm a country girl pretending to be a puck bunny. Would a puck bunny be caught dead in sweats? I don't know, but I'm cold, dammit, and I guess a bunny would wear her guy's clothes in a pinch. Not that Kace is my guy. No, that's not a path we're going to go down. Kace likes bunnies, just not *this* bunny.

Are you really going to continue with this bunny farce now, Jemma?

While it does seem ridiculous, how can I just drop the act? I'd be a laughingstock and likely exiled from the dorm. It's not quite what happened to my sister back in high school, but what she went through from the fallout was bad enough. How could I have ever thought this was a good idea? I'd gotten top grades all through school, won nearly every award at graduation. I was a bookworm and used to think I was smart, but there's nothing smart in pretending to be a puck bunny. Now it feels like I'm caught between a rock and a hard place, or rather, a puck and a book.

FML.

I hold the clothes out so I don't get milk on them, and head to the bathroom. The door is cracked so I push it open, only to come face to face—okay, face to chest—with none other than a naked Sebastian. I gasp and turn around.

"Sorry. I didn't know you were in here." I keep my eyes closed, even though I'm facing the other way. "The door was cracked. I should have knocked. I didn't realize you were home."

"It's cool," he laughs, his voice filled with amusement. "I was just about to shower. I'm used to leaving the door open. It's usually just Kace and me."

"I was going to shower too. I'll wait."

"You could join me."

"No, I'll wait," I say again.

His chuckle fills the space between us. "It's not like I haven't seen you naked before."

What the hell? When did he see me naked? Was he behind the picture of me? My lids fly open and I come face to face with Kace. He looms over me, his body big, tall...tight. I gasp again.

"I heard a scream. Is everything okay?" he asks.

God, what did he overhear? Should I correct him, let him know Sebastian didn't see me naked?

"Fine, you can go first," Sebastian says. I hear a rustling sound, and Kace puts his hands on my arms and moves me into the hall as Sebastian walks around me, a towel knotted at his waist.

"I'll be fast," I tell him.

"Fast. Slow. It's all good, baby."

Kace's hands tighten on my shoulders. "You good?"

"I should have knocked. I didn't know he was going to be in there, naked."

He arches a brow. "No?"

"No," I say firmly and pull away from him, my nerves as frayed as my shorts. What the heck? Does he think I was trying to see Sebastian naked? How freaking rude. Then again, sneaking a peek might be something a bunny would do —so maybe I shouldn't be as offended as I am. "It's not like it was you," is something the new, fake Jemma would say to any player other than Kace, because he dislikes me, and the only reason I'm here is because of the baby. The corner of his mouth twitches. Wait, did I just say that out loud?

Ohmigod, no!

KACE

I step from the bathroom to give Jemma her privacy and I lean against the wall for a moment. Jemma Maloney is a conundrum for sure and no, I do not believe she was trying to catch a glimpse of a naked Sebastian. I think I only asked to get a reaction from her, which when it comes right down to it, wasn't a nice thing to do. But I suspect she wasn't putting on a show or pretending to be something she wasn't when she answered.

Does Jemma want to see me naked?

Maybe, maybe not. All I know is I don't want to see her naked, and she's here because of Emma. I probably wouldn't have let her inside my place otherwise. I hurry back downstairs, to where Emma is in her bassinet on the kitchen table. I secured her in her bed after I heard Jemma scream, and bolted up the stairs as fast as I could. She's asleep now, after her bottle, and I go check on the food in the oven.

The front door opens and in walks my sis. I make a mental note to keep it locked. Now that Jemma and Emma are staying here, I can't just have any of the guys coming and going as they please.

"Hey, sis," I call to her as she comes into the kitchen, her face tight, worry in her eyes. She spots Emma asleep in her bed.

"Where's Jemma?"

"She's getting cleaned up. Milk accident."

She crinkles her nose. "How are you?"

"I'm okay." I pull the tray of food from the oven and when her hand lands on my back, I suck in a breath.

"Kace."

I set the tray on the stove and turn to her, doing my best to keep my shit together. When she gets quiet and vulnerable like this, I get so worried about her. She might handle life better than me, but Dad's betrayal hurt her too.

"This is really nice of you. Thanks for always being there for me. I know Jemma really appreciates this."

"I'm sure her sister will come to her senses. Who can leave a baby..."

I let my words fall off, because we both know the answer to that. Sure, Dad came home, once in a while, and his absence was so hard on Mom. Sometimes I wonder if she knew, considering the amount of time she spent alone in her bedroom, leaving her very young son to run the show around the home.

"Yeah, well, not you," she says, and rubs my back. "Saving the world, one baby at a time."

My chest tightens, and breathing comes rough, but I snort out a laugh. "Not what I'm doing," I tell her. She eyes me, seeing deep into my tortured soul. I try to hide it from her, I want to be the guy she can count on, her rock, but she sees it because she's almost as fucked up as I am.

"Oh, sorry, am I interrupting something?" Jemma asks, coming to a halt in the doorway. My gaze takes in her freshly scrubbed face and I think this is the first time I've seen her without makeup. Her wet hair is tied back, and there's such a sweetness in her as she stands there in my big clothes.

Brynn laughs. "Didn't you pack any clothes or makeup?"

Her eyes jerk to Brynn, and for a brief moment I spot the vulnerability before she blinks it away. "I must look horrible."

"You look fine," I say, before I can catch myself. Her big blue eyes hold a new kind of warmth to them without all the makeup. As a matter of fact, her effortless beauty gives her the whole girl next door vibe, and I like it. A lot.

Instead of commenting, she turns to Brynn. "I was in such a panic." She nods toward the baby. She starts folding the sleeves. "These are warm and comfortable." Just then thunder rumbles overhead and the lights flicker. "Besides, Kace is going to light a fire later."

Brynn eyes me, and my heart jumps. "You're lighting a fire?"

Jemma folds her arms, obviously picking up on the shock in Brynn's voice as she makes her way to the table to peek at Emma. "Yeah," is all I mumble and quickly change the subject. "White or dark meat?" I ask as I slice the chicken.

I hold a big slice of white on the end of the knife and wait for an answer. "I'm fine either way," Jemma says.

"You're eating chicken?" Brynn blurts out.

"Kace went to the trouble," she answers, her voice a little unstable. Is she worried Brynn is going to judge her choices? "I'm just going to have a little piece."

Didn't she just say she was starving? I glance at Brynn over my shoulder. She only became a vegetarian when she moved here, and had more control over what she ate. Mom wasn't a great cook, but when she cooked, no matter what it was, we were expected to eat it. "I can't tell you how many times I've watched Brynn scarf down a bacon cheeseburger, but she always seemed to love it." I hold a piece of chicken over one of the plates. "Going once...twice..."

Brynn inhales. "Well, maybe I'll have a little slice of white, since you went to all the trouble."

The two girls smile at each other, and Emma lets out a big burp in her sleep. Laughter follows as I plate up the food. "I'll get the salads," Jemma says and hurries to the fridge. She bends, and while my clothes are huge on her, I'm not sure she ever looked better.

Brynn clears her throat and my gaze cuts her way to find her with an 'I told you so' grin on her face. What she told me was that Jemma and I would hit it off, and she was wrong about that. Sure, she just caught me checking her out, but that doesn't mean we're 'hitting it off' by any means.

I plate the food and set it at the table. Jemma opens the salads, drops a spoon into each plastic container and adds them to the table. As we eat, Jemma tells Brynn about the goods we got for Emma online.

"We're going to have to put a schedule together," Brynn decides. "Figure out how we can all go to our classes, practices, games and work, and still watch Emma." She bites into her chicken, and I don't miss the small moan. "Jemma, you and I share a lot of the same classes, so we should be able to trade off and share notes. A lot of classes are online, too. That might be hard with a baby, but we'll figure it out." I smile at my younger sister. This whole take charge attitude looks good on her.

Jemma goes quiet for a moment, and when I think she's going to protest, I catch her eye and give a small shake of my head. She briefly closes her eyes and is probably rolling them. It's hard for her to let us help her.

"I can cut my hours at the coffee shop to one afternoon a week."

"No," Jemma rushes out. "I can't ask you to do that."

Brynn glares at me, and through tight lips, she snaps, "If you'd just take the money."

"Sis," I warn through equally tight lips, and stare at her. This is not the time or place to discuss our father's financials and how I refuse to touch a penny of his money.

"What…money?" Jemma asks, tentatively, her eyes big.

"Nothing," I answer quickly. Probably too quickly, judging by the way Jemma's head just reared back like I'd slapped her. "I'll cut my hours, and we'll see how that goes. Games and practices are set in stone. I won't be able to do any shifting there." I reach across the table and give her hand a squeeze. When she glances at it, I pull back. "But I'll be here, Jemma. As much as I can. I just have to work around hockey."

Jemma nods in agreement. "Of course, you do." One hand flops over on the table—the hand I'd just touched—as she points a finger at Brynn. "You can go to the games, obviously. Kace is *your* brother and it's important for you to be there."

"We can take turns." Brynn crinkles her nose like she'd just eaten something offensive, and it's not the chicken. No, she scarfed that down like it was gourmet cooking. "Trust me. I've spent a lifetime watching him."

"No, seriously." Jemma waves Brynn's protests away. "You go."

"He's not that good anyway," Brynn adds playfully.

"Not that good." Jemma's jaw drops. "He was drafted by Edmonton." She looks aghast, as she comes to my defense. I guess she doesn't realize Brynn is playing with her. "He's damn good. Best on the team, Brynn."

My chest puffs up a bit, even though I'm not sure I can claim that title. But Jemma thinks I'm good? The best on the team? I suck that up for a brief second and then shake my head. Jesus, why do I care what she thinks?

"He's okay," Brynn counters, with a grin, like she'd just accomplished something very important—like getting Jemma to realize how awesome I was. I shake my head at her—a relationship is not happening here. She ignores me as per usual, and continues with, "But like I said, we can take turns."

I drop my fork down and the clang draws their attention. When both sets of eyes are on me, I shake my head. "Look at you two, bickering over who *doesn't* have to watch hockey. Careful," I joke, "Or you'll have to turn in your *bunny* cards."

A beat of silence and then Brynn laughs. "Please, big brother. You guys would be lost without our support and companionship. And don't say bunnies like you don't love them. Players and bunnies all serve a purpose and we're all getting something out of it. Isn't that right, Jemma?"

Brynn and I are pretty close and always open about everything, so talking about sex with her isn't weird. But suddenly it feels very personal with Jemma sitting at the table. What was that she said earlier when I joked—sort of—about her trying to peek at Sebastian.

It's not like it was you.

Right. On that note, I stand. "Jemma, I have lots of meat if you want a bigger helping." Brynn giggles with the maturity of a twelve-year-old boy, and I can almost hear Jemma's throat as she swallows. Fuck. After talking about sex, maybe that didn't come out right.

"I'm, uh, no. I'm good thanks."

Thunder booms again, and Emma starts fussing. "Can I hold her?" Brynn asks.

Both Jemma and I look at one another. As we wait for the other to answer, Brynn stands. "I know how to hold a baby," she points out with a huff.

"Yeah, of course," Jemma says and I agree. It's not that we don't trust Brynn. It's just that for a moment there, we weren't sure who should answer.

"Still nothing from your sister, huh?" Brynn asks as she snuggles Emma.

Jemma pulls her phone from her sweats and frowns as she stares at it. "Nothing." She sets it down. "I'm still trying to figure out whether to call home or not."

"Tough call," I say.

"What's a tough call?" Sebastian asks, sauntering into the kitchen. "Hey Brynn." He turns to Jemma. His gaze rakes the length of her. "Want to come up to my room and get into my pants?"

"What the fuck?" I set the knife down and crack my knuckles as Jemma pales.

Sebastian laughs. "I'm just saying. Yours are kind of big on her. Mine might fit better."

That's not at all what he was saying and yeah, I get it, they've been together. I don't need the constant reminder.

"Sebastian, don't be such an asshole," Brynn grumbles. "There's a baby in the house."

"What does that have to do with me?" He walks to the fridge and pulls out a water bottle. "She's not mine." Brynn hands the baby to Jemma. "Come on, give me a ride home and watch a movie with me. You haven't yet told me how awesome you were at last Friday's game."

I hate the idea of her hanging with Sebastian, but she's a big girl who can make her own decisions, and when she gives me a wink, I realize this is her way of handling the situation, and getting Sebastian out of the house before I punch him. She's pretty good at reading people and situations. It makes me wonder, though. Could she not see through Jemma the same way I could?

"Fucking asshole," I mutter under my breath as I pick up Brynn's plate.

"How did you two end up roommates?" Jemma asks.

"Convenience," I answer. "I'd prefer to live alone, but sharing the costs worked better."

"I like having a roommate, and being surrounded by friends."

I put the dishes in the dishwasher. Over the years, I've seen the competitiveness at their sorority. She might be careful who she calls friend. Brynn, though, I know she can count on her.

"Brynn's a good roomie?"

"She's the best. She brought me right in to her circle."

I grin. That doesn't surprise me. Brynn builds communities, while I like to be on an island alone. It's just the different ways we process trauma.

"She was always popular?" she asks, and I catch her biting her lips.

"She had lots of friends." The girls who pledged at Brynn's sorority are mainly party girls. That's what their sorority is known for. Popular partying puck bunnies. Jemma would have known that when she pledged. If that's not who she was, she should have chosen differently.

Ah, but that's who she wanted to become, dude.

At the reminder that she's a fake, a chair scrapes across the floor, and with the baby in her arms, Jemma carries her plate to me. "I got that." I take the plate from her, and our hands touch. A strange wave of heat moves through me. I push it down and move around the kitchen, efficiently cleaning up. "It'll only take me a second to straighten up."

"Is there anything I can do to help? I feel a bit useless."

"You have a baby in your arms. You're doing enough. Why don't you two get comfortable in the other room and I'll be right in to light the fire." She hesitates, and I narrow my gaze in on her. "What?"

Worry moves into her eyes as she glances at Emma, and brushes her nonexistent hair from her little forehead. "We don't have to have a fire." I harden myself, pushing down old memories as they grapple for purchase, and I'm about to tell her it's fine, when she adds, "I get the sense you don't really like it."

Fuck.

7

KACE

"It's not," I begin, and stop myself. I am not going down this road, not with Jemma—not with anyone. "You're cold, so we'll have a fire. It will be nice for Emma, too." She stands there rocking the baby in her arms, her body tight, her eyes hesitant as they search my face for answers she'll never find. I keep what she's looking for deep down, where no one can see. "Maybe you should run up and change her first." I gesture toward the hall with a nod. "I bought more diapers."

She gives a fast nod, and walks away. My chest is tight, like there's a belt wrapped around me constricting my air flow as she disappears. Hell, it's not like the fireplace is a campfire, down at my favorite fishing spot. It's fine. Everything is fine. I'm fine. As soon as I convince myself of that, I go back to cleaning the kitchen. Once I'm done, I switch the baby clothes from the washer to the dryer, and step into the living room to find Jemma on the sofa, telling Emma a story.

I stand there for a minute, and listen to her tell tales of whales and fishes and octopuses with twelve arms. It's a large tale of underwater antics, and I lean against the doorway, admiring the animation on her face as she dives deeper into her story. After a long moment, Jemma's head lifts, as if finally sensing me there, and when our eyes meet, I push off the wall, noting the sudden pinkness in her cheeks.

"Sorry, I didn't mean to interrupt," I whisper, as I step toward them.

She stands and holds Emma to her chest. "I was just running a story by Emma."

"From the way she's swinging her fists, I'd say she likes it."

Jemma laughs and dips her head, and that's when Emma's tiny fist hits Jemma in the eye. She winces. "Ow." I hurry to her and take Emma's tiny fingers into my hand. "For a little one, she sure packs a punch."

"Are you okay?" She keeps blinking, and water fills her eye when she tries to open it wide.

"I think her nail might have scratched me."

"Here let me have her. Why don't you go get a cold compress?"

Jemma puts her hand over her eye. "I had no idea babies were so dangerous."

I check her nails. "You know, when Brynn was a baby, Mom used to bite her nails instead of clipping them." My mind goes back in time, to when there were happy memories. "But I did pick up some things at the pharmacy, and there were clippers in the case."

"I'll grab them."

She disappears into the kitchen, and I walk around the room with a wiggling Emma. I move to the window and when thunder rumbles, her body goes stiff and she stretches out her arms. "It's okay, little one. Nothing is going to hurt you." I hum to her, and move around the room, her body so tiny in my arms. I never much thought about having kids. What if I'm a chip off the old block, like my old man and can't commit to one person? Hell, what am I even saying? There's no one I'd ever trust enough to commit to them.

"Are you humming one of Taylor's songs?"

I spin to face Jemma. "What, no."

A laugh bubbles up in her throat. her. "I think you were. Ohmigod, you're a Swiftie, aren't you?"

"No, I think it was Shaggy, and don't go spreading rumors and shit through your sorority."

"Language, Kace."

I change the subject, because yeah, it's possible I'm a Swiftie. "Did you get the clippers?" She holds them out. "Your eye is better?"

She blinks a couple times. "I think she just poked me. I'm good."

I sit on the sofa. I examine her tiny fingers. She squeezes one around my index finger, and every protective instinct I possess comes out full force. "I think this might be a two-person job."

"Maybe we should wait until she's asleep."

I exhale. "Actually yeah, maybe we should."

"I wish I could call Mom for advice," she says with a sigh.

"Yeah," is all I answer. She doesn't need to know that my mother mentally checked out many years ago. "Maybe we should bath her and when she sleeps, we can do her nails."

"Good plan. Wait, what do we bathe her in?"

"A small little tub that came with the stuff." We both walk to the kitchen, look at the tub and look at each other. I see the hesitation in her eyes, the lack of confidence. "How hard can it be?" I finally ask.

"What if she slips, or I don't know? What if we don't get the water temperature right. I babysat before, but this is way out of my wheelhouse. How about a sponge bath for tonight?"

I nod as we walk back into the living room. "So, what was the title of the story you were telling Emma?" I ask. "The ogre in the kitchen?" Which of course, could only be about me.

Her eyes light up. "Ohmigod, Kace. That is a great story title."

I laugh at that. "You're kidding me, right?"

"No, actually, I had this incredible visual as soon as you said that." She shakes her head, a smile touching her face as she glances down, her mind obviously filling with ideas.

"You should write that. For Emma." I put Emma in her bassinet, drop to the floor, and adjust the damper on the fire. "This hasn't been lit for a while, but when I moved in, the owners told me it still worked."

"I love a fire," Jemma says. "Back home we have a big back-yard, and we often had fires and marshmallows."

"Sounds nice." I crinkle up some old papers, toss them in, and strategically place small twigs on top of it. Once I get it lit, I add more kindling, and when I get it burning, I toss in a few small logs. It flares to life and I adjust the damper again.

"You grew up in Shelburne, right?" I ask.

"Yeah, middle of nowhere, I know."

I shrug. "Nothing wrong with the country."

"Says the city boy."

I laugh. "I might have been a country boy at heart. Growing up I loved to climb trees, and we even had a tree f...fort..." My words hitch as my mind races back to that fort I loved. I take a fast breath, to pull myself together.

"A tree fort in the city. I didn't know it was possible."

I snort out a humorless laugh. "Lots of things are possible. Things I didn't even know were possible." Like a man having a second family in Cape Breton. Although they now all live in the city, not too far from me, actually.

"Such as?"

I cross my legs. "Like pulling a speckled trout out of the Sackville River."

"You must be joking. I heard it was completely overfished."

"Nope." I hold my hands out. "It was like eighteen inches."

She narrows her eyes as she sits on the floor with me. "I'd say that was about twelve, Kace."

I laugh. Hard. "Are you accusing me of telling tall tales?"

She tugs her bottom lip into her mouth, and her cheeks turn pink again. "Maybe men and women perceive size differently," she shoots back, and almost looks embarrassed at her joke.

"Hey," I blurt out. "I have pictures."

"I might have to see these pictures."

"Fine. I can dig them out."

"Speaking of jokes and tall tales." She sighs. "How do you get an English Lit major off your front steps."

I angle my head, not sure where she's going with this. "I don't know, how?"

She grins. "Pay for the pizza."

I stare at me for a moment, my brain trying to figure out what she's talking about, and then it hits me. "Oh, you're the pizza delivery person."

"Right."

I grab a pillow from the sofa and lightly hit her with it. She grabs it from me. "Stop. I heard your story. You're going to be a great writer, just don't become a stand-up comedian."

"You didn't think that was funny."

I snort. "Maybe a little."

Her lips quirk. "Right, because it's true."

"I'm sorry." I bump her knee with mine. "It's a tough career, huh?"

She nods. "I can always teach, and there are other jobs out there."

"I heard the story you were telling Emma." I shrug. "I don't know much about children's books, but it sounded pretty good to me. Like I said, we can always reach out to Brandon."

A long quiet—yet comfortable—moment passes between us. "You like fishing, huh?" she asks, changing the subject. I nod. "You really were a country boy living in the city. But that's not a bad thing. You had access to some great hockey coaches here that you might not have had elsewhere."

"True."

"Was your dad into hockey? Is that how you got into it? Following in his footsteps?"

"No," is all I say, and maybe a little too harshly.

"Right." Her eyes go wide, and she gives a fast shake of her head. "Sorry, I didn't mean..."

Now it's my turn to change the subject. "You had a big backyard where you could daydream and make up stories?" She frowns, and I'm about to press when she speaks.

"We should probably get her bathed and to bed. I'm still tired, even after that nap."

Okay, clearly she doesn't like to talk about her childhood either. "Agreed. Why don't you grab the bag of things in the kitchen? I'll carry her up." I pick up the bassinet and head upstairs. I set it on the bed, and Jemma comes in behind me. She dumps the contents of the bag, and I pick up the soap. "You get her undressed and I'll get a soapy cloth ready."

I disappear into the bathroom and come back with two cloths. One for soaping, and one for rinsing her clean. "I'll go get the clothes."

I go back downstairs, and exhaustion overtakes me as I gather the clothes from the dryer and carry them to Jemma's room. I stand at the door for a second as she tells Emma another story. Her back is to me, so I can't hear what she's whispering.

"Hey," I murmur to announce my arrival.

She turns and smiles at me. "You can drop the clothes on the bed. I'll fold them once she's asleep."

I begin to fold them, putting them in neat little piles. I catch the way Jemma is smiling at me. "What?"

"You're like a natural born daddy. What was it you said Olivia and Ally were saying, something about calling you daddy?"

"Ah, I don't quite think that's what they meant, Jemma. Remember they talked about spanking too."

She eyes me for a second. "Oh, right. Of course." Her cheeks turn that pretty shade of pink that's growing on me, in the strangest fucking way. Honestly though, who would have thought sex talk could make a bunny blush? She should probably learn to play the role better.

"I'm a big brother. I spent a lot of time taking care of Brynn."

"Really, how come?" She dabs the cloth on Emma's body to wash her. "I don't ever remember my sister having to take care of me." Her brow furrows thoughtfully. "Where were your parents?"

My gut tightens. "Dad was away a lot for work. Sales," I explain. "Mom, well. Mom and Dad divorced when I was twelve." I don't bother telling her their relationship was dead long before the divorce.

Her hand touches my arm. "I'm sorry, Kace. That couldn't have been easy."

After she finishes cleaning Emma, I put on a new diaper and a clean sleeper. "It was a while ago."

"Does your mom still live here in the city?"

"Yeah, not too far from here, actually. Brynn and I will be having Thanksgiving dinner with her." We'll do most of the cooking, because she'll be busy staring down at the bottom of a wine bottle. The look on her face when the truth came spilling out all those years ago still hurts my heart. I wish she could let it go, move forward and find happiness, instead of holding a grudge.

Yeah, you're one to talk dude.

"Does your dad..." she asks tentatively, and I give a fast shake of my head.

"He's nearby, but I don't see him," I answer my voice a little rougher, deeper than I intended. But just thinking about him angers me. "I hate lies and liars," I snort out before I can stop myself.

"Okay," she murmurs and I'm grateful when she doesn't question me on that.

"Will you be going back to Shelburne for Thanksgiving?"

She sucks in a fast breath and lightly wipes the towel across her forehead. "Ohmigod, up until this moment, I just assumed I would be, but now..." She grips the cloth in her hand. "How can I, Kace? I can't take Emma home. How do I explain that Krista just left her on my doorstep? I had no idea she was pregnant, and I'm one hundred percent positive Mom and Dad didn't either. I'll have to make an excuse."

"I can take Emma home with me."

"No, I can't ask you to do that." She frowns and shakes her head. "I'd love to go home, though, and just feel my parents out. See if they know where Krista is and if she's okay."

"I can take you on the weekend if you want. I have a game Friday night, but we could go Saturday. We don't have to wait until Thanksgiving. We could always get Brynn to babysit. She's in this as much as we are."

Her gaze latches onto mine, and she almost looks like she's going to cry as she searches my face. "Why are you helping me, Kace?"

"I told you. You're Brynn's friend." Once again, my voice holds that edge that warns I don't want to go down this path. "Think about it. Let me know. We should get Emma to bed." I take the clothes from her and toss them into the hamper in the bathroom. I walk back to Jemma's room in time to hear horns blare as cars race down the street.

"Freshmen. Fucking annoying."

"Hey, I'm a freshman," she says with a laugh, and it lightens the mood around us. "I always dreamed about living in the city."

I pick Emma up, hold her to my chest and rub her back. "Is it all it's cracked up to be?"

She goes quiet for a moment, her brow furrowed, a pained look in her eyes. My heart thumps as she crinkles her nose and her freckles bunch together. There is way more to this woman than she lets on, and right now as I take in her freshly scrubbed face, her alluring girl next door look, I can't help but want to get to know her. As if someone flicked a light switch in her brain, her demeanor changes and she starts coiling her ponytail around her finger, and that's when I realize puck bunny Jemma just made her appearance. What the fuck? Just when things were nice between us.

"You don't have to do that you know," I tell her, my voice holding a measure of annoyance.

"What?" she asks.

I inch back, putting a measure of distance between us—physically and emotionally— as old painful memories claw their way to the surface and remind me I can't trust anyone. "Pretend to be something you're not."

8

JEMMA

My stomach is nothing but a tight ragged knot as I lay in bed, embarrassment flooding every inch of my body. I had a feeling that Kace could see through me, see the book nerd beneath all the skimpy clothes and glitter. The look on his face said it all, he hates pretenders as much as he hates liars. I'm both. God, why did I think I could be something I wasn't? And honestly, playing the role of carefree, playful puck bunny who has casual affairs and takes her top off for naked pictures isn't all it's cracked up to be.

What if he tells everyone I'm a fraud?

Will I be the laughingstock of the sorority, ostracized and overlooked and left home while everyone is out partying? Oh, wouldn't that be lovely. That thought makes me laugh. Seriously though, I really like Brynn, a lot, and don't want to lose her as a friend. The other girls have all been nice and inclusive too, and that's what I really wanted when I came here. To be included.

I roll over, and the light shining in through the crack in the curtains falls over a sleeping Emma. Jeez, here I am feeling sorry for myself—upset by Kace's cold, abrasive, accusatory words, despite the fact that they were accurate—when there's this tiny, abandoned baby beside me. My problems are minuscule and ridiculous compared to hers. What will happen to her if Krista doesn't come back? How long am I supposed to —can I possibly—take care of her, and still go to classes and pass?

I realize it can be done. People have had babies in college before. Maybe they weren't left on their doorsteps, but still, and I'm getting help from Kace and Brynn. I groan as I think about how Kace and I left things after he called me out. I just sort of stood there staring at him, my mouth hanging open, my words stuck in my throat. He left and went to his own room, and I'm sure he must think I'm ridiculous.

I pinch my eyes shut to push all thoughts of our conversation away. I can't dwell on it. I have more important things to figure out. I reach out and lightly touch Emma's small hand and my heart aches as she closes her tiny fingers around one of mine. When she did that to Kace, I swear to God, my ovaries went into overdrive. Exhaustion pulls at me and I close my eyes, and quiet my mind. The next thing I know movement beside me is pulling me awake, and my lids fly open to find a big looming figure on the other side of the bed.

It takes me a moment to figure out where I am, and that the big figure picking up a crying Emma is Kace. I sit up and I'm about to turn the lamp on when Kace stops me.

"Leave it off," he whispers, his voice deep but low. "I don't want to hurt Emma's eyes."

"Right," is all I manage to get out. How am I so bad at this, when he's so good? Feeling stupid, I sit up as really I don't need the lamp to see his nearly naked body. The rays of early morning light shining in are helping with that. He cradles Emma against his bare chest as my gaze drops to note he's only in a pair of boxers. Okeydokey. I guess he was in too much of a hurry to pull on clothes. Does he sleep in boxers? Why the hell do I even care? The man hates me and while he gives off warmth with Emma, there's a definite chill between us.

I rub my eyes, not just because I'm sleepy but because I need to erase the perfect, alluring image before me from my brain. "How long was she crying?"

"Not long."

"I can't believe I didn't hear her. I'm not usually such a deep sleeper. I just had a hard time falling asleep last night." God, stop rambling already.

"I'm sure you would have woken up, but I came and got her because I don't want to disturb Sebastian's sleep. I'm sorry about rushing in when you were sleeping."

"It's okay. I appreciate it. Sebastian is good enough to agree to this, so I don't want to bother him. I can take her now."

He pats her bottom. "She needs to be changed and needs a bottle."

I push the covers off, and dressed in my pajama shorts and T-shirt, I cross the room and hold my arms out.

"Which do you want to do?" he asks.

I stifle a yawn. "I can do both."

"Pick," he orders, the tone of his voice letting me know it's not up for negotiation.

I watch the play of his muscles as he rocks Emma and paces the floor. "I'll change her."

He hands her over, and walks toward the door. "I'll be right back."

He opens my door wider and turns on the bathroom light. It spills across the hall and helps me better see what I'm doing. I hum quietly to her as I quickly change her and get her dressed again. When she starts to cry, I grab her soother and pace.

Kace comes back with the bottle. I reach for it. "I can feed her if you want," he tells me.

"No, you've done enough. Go on back to bed, and get a few more hours sleep. No sense in us both being up." I walk to the bed, position myself against the headboard, and cradle her in my arms as I feed her. She gobbles it quickly. Poor little girl is starving and I slept right through her cries. Some mother I'll be.

I glance up, and meet Kace's dark stare as he watches me. Does he not think I'm capable? Well, he's probably right. Surprising me, he comes closer and the bed dips as he sits on the edge. "How come you couldn't get to sleep?" he asks.

"I was just thinking. Worrying about Emma."

He nods, and doesn't say anything, but we both know I couldn't sleep because of what he said to me. Does he feel guilty about that? Did he really have a right to call me out? Judge me? I guess not, or maybe he did have a right because he's helping me out. God, I don't know. But what I do know is that he has no idea where I'm coming from or the reasons behind my actions. Just like I don't know the real reason he's so eager to help out with Emma.

I'm guessing, from the new kind of coolness about it, confessions are not going to be in our future. Which is fine with me.

"If you got this, I'll go get some sleep," he murmurs.

"I got it."

He nods and stands, and his perfect ass in those tight boxers hold my attention as he walks to the door, stopping to look back one last time, like he has something on his mind. A few seconds tick by and then he turns back around and disappears. I wait for his bedroom door to click shut, but it doesn't.

I take the bottle from Emma's mouth and put her over my shoulder to burp her. "Oh God," I murmur when hot milk spills all over me. When will I learn to put a blanket over my shoulder? I shift as it soaks the sheets.

"Everything okay?"

I gasp, and nearly jump up as Kace comes back into the room. "She spit up. Poor thing. I think all this disruption is messing with her little belly."

"Babies spit up." He crosses the room and takes Emma from me. "Go get cleaned up."

I put my hand on the sheet to push out of the bed, and it lands in milk. "I think I need to change the sheets."

"Shit," he murmurs.

"What?" My heart jumps. "Is Emma okay?"

"Yeah, it's just, we don't have any more sheets. Our spare set is on this bed."

I stare at the bed. "Oh."

He jerks his head toward the door. "Go get cleaned up and you can sleep in my room."

"No, I'm not going to take your bed." I work to stifle a yawn. "I can wash these and just wait. No big deal. Tomorrow I'll get a set from the sorority."

"Jemma, it's fine. We're adults and we all need sleep, and while this might not be ideal, life with kids can get messy and we all have to make sacrifices."

Yeah, okay, I get it. Me, in his bed, is a sacrifice.

"Okay."

I grab a clean shirt and shorts from my bag. "Besides, it's not like we haven't slept together." His voice is low, allegation hidden in the depts of his words. Does he know we slept together but nothing happened? Of course, he does. He's on to me. Is he waiting for me to admit it? My blood drains from my cheeks and my throat thickens as I think about how horrible it was not to correct him. I'm a bad person and I can't blame him for hating me. I hate myself. Damned if this week isn't just getting better and better.

I hurry to the bathroom, and since I don't want to turn on the shower and wake Sebastian, I use a cloth and contort my body to wash up. I finish up and quietly open the door. I walk by my room to see the sheets have been removed from the bed. In Kace's room, I find Emma in the middle of the bed, pillows all around her.

"Sheets are in the wash," Kace whispers as he steps in behind me, his body brushing mine as he crosses the room and slides in beside Emma. I guess this won't be so bad with a baby between us. I act casual—like Kace said, it's not the first time we've been in bed together—and crawl in on the other side.

I roll, and inhale. The sheets smell nice. An enticing blend of fabric softener and Kace. I close my eyes, willing my body to relax and go to sleep, but I spend most of the next couple of hours tossing and turning and having disturbing dreams about the man in bed with me.

His feet hitting the floor pull me wide awake, and I open my eyes. I'm instantly greeted by his gorgeous, cut body, and my gaze lingers on the bulge in his boxers.

"Morning," he says and my eyes lift quickly to find him watching me.

Busted.

"Morning," I shoot back.

"Did you get back to sleep?" he asks, and even though he's being nice, there's still a coolness about him.

I nod. "In and out. You?"

"I slept." He runs his fingers through his hair. "I have to get to practice before class. You're okay here with Emma?"

"Yes, and my morning class is online, so I'll try to watch as much as I can. But Brynn is still going to take notes for me."

"I can take over this afternoon." He walks to his dresser and pulls out some clothes. "I'll let them know at the coffee shop that I'm cutting my hours."

I want to protest, but it won't do any good. Kace and Brynn are both headstrong. What was that she said about taking the money? Whatever it was, it upset Kace, and leads me to believe he might be a little more stubborn than his sister. I am curious, though. What money is Brynn talking about?

"I'll grab a shower and put on some coffee."

I glance at Emma. I don't want to come off like I have no idea what I'm doing and I hesitate before I ask, "Should I wake her?"

"Just put her in the bassinet. She'll wake when she's ready. Then she'll need to be changed and fed."

He goes into my bedroom and comes back with the bassinet. I gently pick Emma up and her body stiffens as I set her in the little bed.

"Want me to carry her down for you?" he asks.

"No, you go shower. I've got this."

He scrubs his face, his eyes narrowed in thought, before he finally moves and leaves the room. At the sound of the water turning on, I place my phone at Emma's feet and carefully carry the bassinet downstairs, amazed at how quiet his place is. I could get used to this. No gossiping or hair dryers or girls running around to get ready. I secure Emma on the table and when my phone pings, I read the message from Brynn, checking in with me. I message with her for a bit, then set my phone down.

Wanting to have the coffee ready for Kace—even though he's acting distant with me, but hey, he's still helping me out—I put a pod in the machine and open the cupboards. Great, they put their mugs on the top shelf. Easier for them. They're both over six feet tall. Me, not so much. I go up on my tiptoes and wiggle my fingers, struggling to reach. Just when I'm about to give up and drag over a chair, Kace steps up behind me.

"Let me help."

I gasp as his big, hard body pins me to the counter as he reaches over my head and easily pulls down a mug.

"Thanks," I say, my voice low and breathless. "Top shelf...too high. I like...bottom."

Stop talking, Jemma.

For a moment he doesn't move. Nope, he continues to press against me, holding me hostage between the counter and his hard body, and dammit, I like it.

"You like bottom?"

I swallow. "Yeah, bottom."

God girl, stop saying bottom—it's coming out sexual. At least it is in my brain.

His breath is warm on my neck when he puts his mouth near my ear and whispers, "Bottom it is then."

"Yeah, bottom," I repeat like an idiot. "Not top."

Freaking kill me now.

Okay, so much for that coolness he's been directing my way. As his body presses against mine, everything about him is hot, and as his heat seeps under my skin, I begin to burn from the top of my head to the tips of my toes. I wiggle my backside, needing him to stop pressing against me almost as much as I need him to continue. Did he just groan?

Wait, what is that currently pressing into my...bottom?

KACE

What the hell am I doing?

I don't like this girl. Okay, maybe that's not true. I don't like her when she's pretending to be something she's not, but when she's like this, sleepy, warm, and lacking any kind of façade, everything about her is alluring...sexy as hell.

I back up and set the mugs on the counter, and work to get my erection under control as I try not to think about her bottom, beneath me, between the sheets...right now. Jesus, when I woke up this morning and saw her laying there, her hair sprawled, the sheets around her waist because it was so hot in the house, I nearly brought her into my arms—until I remembered there was a baby between us and I am not getting involved with a girl who lies. No matter how hard my cock was....is.

Fuck me twice.

I clear my throat. "Thanks for starting on the coffee."

"Not a problem." She inhales as she turns to me, her gaze dropping to my T-shirt. Dark lashes fall over blue eyes as she takes me in. "You...smell..."

She stops talking, her words falling off as she briefly closes her eyes and shakes her head. Her hair tumbles over her shoulder, and I barely resist the urge to touch the soft looking curls.

"I smell?" I lift my arm and inhale, getting hits of fabric softener, and eucalyptus from my body gel. "I just showered." Then again, I am sweating—not from last night's fire, but from the sexy sight of Jemma in my kitchen.

She slides a mug into the coffee machine and presses the button. "I...mean...I smell..." She stutters, stumbling over her words, and I sense her distress. "You...you smell nice." She turns back to me, and braces her hands on the counter behind her. She offers me a big smile. "You smell like me."

I shake my head at her. "I don't think I smell like you." Trust me, if I smelled like warm vanilla, I'd have to go have another shower and scrub my skin raw.

"No, I mean..." Flustered, she grips the counter harder. "...I smell like you."

I laugh, because she's clearly not doing a good job of making her point. "Do you need more sleep? Or maybe you need coffee. You can have the first cup."

She finally laughs with me and wipes her forehead with the back of her hand. "This heat is making me delirious. What I'm trying to say is I used the gel in the shower last night. That's what you smell like. Your soap. I smell like your soap." She inhales again. "Eucalyptus. I didn't pack any of mine so I used what was in the shower last night. I hope that's okay."

"Ah, I see and yeah, it's okay." I lean in and put my nose near her neck and inhale, and the second I do, I realize I just made a big mistake. A hard quiver goes through her body, and my cock once again thickens. I inch back, so she doesn't see it. Although it was pressing into her body just a few minutes ago, and I'm pretty sure she was well aware of every inch. But I am not, under any damn circumstances, going to mess around with my sister's best friend, for numerous reasons.

The coffee finishes and I hand her the cup. "You can have this one."

She pushes it back toward me. "No, you have it. You have to leave."

I close my hand around the mug and take a much-needed sip. Maybe it will help me get my brain screwed back on right.

Don't think about screwed.

Jesus.

I grab two slices of bread and drop them into the toaster. Jemma frowns. "What?" I ask.

"I should have gotten up and had your breakfast ready for you. It's the least I could do for letting us stay here."

"You don't have to cook for me."

"Maybe I want to."

Before I can think better of it, I blurt out, "Look at us, like an old married couple after one night." Her eyes go wide, and I silently curse myself for suggesting we're playing house, or assuming any kind of a relationship. "Anyway, if you need anything just text me, okay?"

"Do you have your phone?"

I reach into my pocket and my search comes up empty. "No, what the hell did I do with it?"

"We're going to have to tie that around your neck."

"I'll be right back." I rush upstairs and find my phone on my nightstand. By the time I get back, my toast pops and Jemma is sipping her coffee. I step into the kitchen and take one look at her standing beside the table, her hair a complete mess, her eyes sleepy and warm as she smiles at Emma. My heart pinches tight and for a moment, my lungs constrict. My gaze drops to take in her sleep shorts and long, smooth legs.

"Are you okay?" she asks, as I admire her.

"Yeah, just thinking." About her bottom. But I think it's best not to say that. "I should bounce." I point to the counter. "My car keys are there if you need to go anywhere."

"Thanks, Kace."

My body tightens at the gratitude in her voice. When she drops the act there is something so sweet and vulnerable about her. I grab my toast, drop a blob of jam on both slices and eat as I snatch up my bag and jacket and head out the door. The morning air is cool as I cut across campus. The rink is close enough to walk, and I wanted to leave the car with Jemma.

Coach Jamieson is in conversation with a couple of players by the time I get my equipment on, and hit the ice. I'm early. I like quiet time on the ice before the rest of the team get here, but maybe I should have stayed back and walked here with Sebastian. I really don't like the idea of him and Jemma alone in the house. What the hell is that about? They're both adults and obviously had some sort of relationship. That really shouldn't bother me as much as it does.

I stretch out and by the time Coach calls us all in, I turn and spot Sebastian skating our way. I really don't like that shit-eating grin on his face, and a part of me wants to ask if he bothered Jemma this morning.

I ignore him as he skates up beside me and the coach chats with us all for a moment. Then, for the next hour, we practice, and I try not to slam Sebastian into the boards harder than necessary.

"Something on your mind?" he asks after our last play.

"Nope, you?"

He shrugs. "Nope."

I skate off and head to the locker room. Inside I strip off and take a fast shower, my mind going back to Jemma and how she said she smelled like me. I don't know why I like that, or how I laid in bed this morning, breathing her in as her scent filled my room.

I finish showering and Sebastian is naked in front of his locker. He really likes to show off his body, but now that Jemma is staying with us, I hope he's not going to walk around with half his clothes off—or completely naked. He takes a bite of a granola bar and holds it out. "Bite?" he asks.

"Nope, I'm good." My stomach grumbles, and I remember the granola bar in my own bag.

"I don't mind sharing," he says, and I get it, he's not talking about his bar. He wants to fuck Jemma—again—and thinks I owe him that.

"I'm good." I pull my bag from my locker and get dressed.

He rolls on some deodorant. "How long is that kid going to be at our place?"

I stiffen. "I don't know. Not long. Did she wake you last night?"

"No, I'm good, man. Just wondering."

"Did you ah, see Jemma this morning?"

"Fuck yeah, she was looking hot." I swallow, and try not to react. "I'll be glad when the kid is gone, and we can go back to partying." He makes two fists and bumps them together.

"Yeah."

"Unless you two..."

"No," I answer quickly.

"Hey, like I said, I'm into sharing if you're getting serious about her or something." He eyes me.

"I'm not."

"So, Jemma and I, we can do what we want then? I mean, if you're not into her."

Fucking asshole. I close my locker and pull on my coat. "I'm into hockey and school, Sebastian."

With that I leave the locker room and head outside. I reach into my bag for my granola bar and spot my phone. I pull it out and consider texting Jemma, partly because I want to make sure Sebastian didn't harass her this morning, and partly because I just want to message her.

Before I can stop myself, I shoot off a message.

Me: Hey, how are things going?

I wait a long moment, and when no response comes, I'm about to shove my phone back in my bag, but then three dots appear.

Jemma: Good. Emma had a bit of a crying fit, but she's settled now. I'm just getting ready to watch my class online.

Me: Okay, I won't keep you.

Jemma: No, it's okay. How was practice?

Me: Good. Just heading to class now.

Jemma: It's so quiet here at your place.

I lean against a tall oak tree, enjoying our messages, even though I should be getting my ass to class.

Me: Is that good or bad?

Jemma: Lol, good. I'm used to the sorority.

Me: Sebastian was quiet this morning?

Nice, Kace. Way to be subtle.

Jemma: Well, no. Not really. He's kind of noisy, and um...

Me: Um what?

Jemma: I think we made it too hot in the house last night. He was walking around in his boxers this morning.

I shake my head. Nope, that's just Sebastian.

Me: I'll have a talk with him.

Jemma: No, it's okay. It's his place, not mine.

Me: I'll let you get to your lecture. I'll see you this afternoon. Oh, are you guys warm enough now?

Jemma: It's two million degrees in here. I might have to open a window.

Me: Probably a good idea. Enjoy your lecture and see you soon.

I stare at the phone and wait for a response and it's crazy how disappointed I am when none comes. I drop my phone back into my bag and hurry to the life science building, to the auditorium where my class is held.

I take my usual seat, and pull out my laptop. Unfortunately, I find my mind drifting, my thoughts on Jemma and not on statistics. But I'm good at math, so I should be okay. When class is finally finished, I hurry out and run into Sierra.

"Hey, Daddy," she says and puts her hand on my arm.

I resist the urge to roll my eyes. "I'm not anyone's daddy," I tell her. "I'm just helping Jemma out."

"That's awfully nice of you."

"Yeah, well she's Brynn's friend. I'd do anything for my sister."

"Right and these new sleeping arrangements make it easier for her and Sebastian to be together. You did tell me she liked him, right?"

"Right," I agree, and glance over her head, looking to escape.

"Just be careful, Kace."

"About what?"

"You're looking a bit tired. You don't want a baby interfering with the NHL."

She's right, I can't let anything interfere with my game, but I'll be damned if I ever let Emma feel like she's not wanted. "She won't be there long."

She leans in conspiratorially. "Do you think it's Jemma's baby?"

My head rears back. "What the fuck?" Is that the gossip weaving its way through the rumor mill?

She shrugs. "She could have had her over the summer, and doesn't want anyone to know it's her baby. Maybe she's trying to latch on to a future NHL player. Crazier schemes have happened, and I heard they look alike."

Of course, it's not her baby and they look alike because it's her sister's baby. What kind of person would try to pull off an insane stunt like that.

Uh, didn't your father have a second family, Kace?

Yeah, okay, but come on. It's her sister's baby.

Why won't she call her parents, and is she really trying to call her sister?

As old hurts make me second guess everything I can't help but wonder who would want to have a baby and pretend otherwise.

Someone who lies about who they really are?

But why?

No, this is all just crazy speculation because people like to gossip and I'm not going to stand around and entertain the idea.

"I have to go."

She gives a little wave. "See you later and if you need anything, you know where to find me."

"Right." My head swims with her ludicrous accusations as I cross the street and hit up my favorite pizza joint on Pizza Corner. Yes, they renamed the street because there are three pizza places side by side. It's become an iconic local landmark in the city. My phone buzzes. I search my bag, find it, and my blood rushes a little faster as I read the message from Jemma.

Jemma: Sorry I didn't text back. Lecture started and then Emma was fussing. I'm just getting a second to myself now.

Me: Yeah, it's all good. I'm on my way home. Be there shortly.

Jemma:

I grin and step inside the pizza place. I'd normally just get a couple of slices for myself, but I'm sure Jemma is hungry too so I order a whole pie, as I try not to let the lies going through the rumor mill fuck with me. I make it home and as I search for my key, Jemma swings the door open. A smile lights up her face, like she's super happy to see me and she probably is, not because she missed me—not that I care one way or another—but because taking care of a baby is hard work.

"How do you get a hockey player off your steps?" I ask when she glances at the pizza in my hand. She laughs and the happy sound curls around me.

She taps her chin, pretending she's in thought. "Cut him a slice?"

"Or two."

She takes the box from me and I follow her inside, glancing around. "Emma asleep?"

"She is."

I check the living room as we walk past it and the kitchen is also empty when I enter. "Where is she?"

"Upstairs, sleeping."

"But—"

"There was a baby monitor in the things you got yesterday."

"Oh, I didn't even know. Anything from your sister?"

"No, nothing." With her back to me, I can't see her face, and do I really think she would have a baby, so she could hook up with a future NHL player?

She goes to the cupboard and opens it. I follow her and reach over her to grab the plates and when I do, I once again push her into the counter. Did she just moan?

Fuck me.

"Thanks," she croaks out.

I clear my throat. "Sure. I'll move the plates and mugs onto the bottom shelf after we eat."

"Yeah, bottom," she murmurs, and just like that my double-crossing cock—prick that he is—hardens and rises up for more.

JEMMA

My eyes never leave Kace as his teammate Mason shoots him the puck and he carries it down the ice on the edge of his stick, moving past the Islanders' defense with incredible ease. Beside me, my sorority sister Paige screams and grabs my hand, squeezing it so hard, I'm sure she's going to break a few bones. I react, but not quite as loudly. I don't want anyone thinking I'm hot for Kace or anything. Because I'm not. Much.

Okay, I am a lot.

Oh my God, earlier in the week when he pushed up against me to get the mugs down, I thought maybe I was imagining things—imagining it was his cock pressing into my back. But then, later when he was getting the plates down for the pizza...confirmation. He was aroused. I'm totally sure of it. Or he had a hockey stick in his pants.

But of course, he didn't, which means one of two things are happening. My presence at his house is preventing him from having female companionship in his bed and it's getting to him. Or he wants me. After the way he treated me, all cold and distant, I'm having a hard time believing the latter. Because he accused me of pretending to be something I'm not and it hurt, even though it was accurate.

Wait, maybe there's a third option. He wants me because he's not currently bringing anyone home, even though I told him it wasn't a problem. I had heard any female with a hot pocket would do. Sebastian's words—overheard by me—at our last pool party. Which is extremely disgusting and insulting. How I ever let that guy pour me a drink or put his arm around me is baffling.

Okay, no. Not so baffling. But I can't think about that right now, not when Kace scores fast, and the buzzer goes off. We all jump up and clap, and his gaze moves to the stands—to me specifically. Beside me, Paige notices.

"What was that?" she asks.

I blink, and work to control my racing heart. "What?" I decide to play dumb, but yeah, his gaze was hot, needy and targeted at me. My entire body knows it. It's known it all week, and what a hell of a week it's been with the two of us sharing duties, accidentally touching as we handed Emma back and forth.

My God, I thought I was going to spontaneously combust the other night. But no, I am not going to do anything about it. Not even touch myself to take the edge off. I have Emma to take care of, and to be honest, I'm freaking exhausted. It's been a long week and while I planned to miss this game, Brynn insisted I needed a night out and she wasn't wrong.

My phone pings, and I quickly pull it from my pocket to find a cute picture of Brynn and Emma. I still can't believe I haven't heard from my sister, and at this point I'm worried sick about her. I'd called home, and kept it casual, and asked about Krista. All they said was she was good and I didn't want to press it and make them suspicious. So earlier today, when Kace asked if I'd given a drive to Shelburne anymore thought, I decided it was a good idea. I need to get home to feel my parents out. Heck, maybe Krista is there and something is going on they don't want me to know about. Yeah, well I have something they likely don't want to know about either.

"You and Kace. You snacking on that deliciousness?"

I laugh almost hysterically, which is probably making me look like a fool and raising her suspicions even more. "Ah, no. I'm only there because I needed a place to take care of Emma."

Her brows pull together. "I can't believe a baby was left outside your door."

Yeah, I know. She can't believe it. Most of my sorority sisters can't either, hence the rumors that Emma is my secret baby. Good God. Don't we have better things to do than gossip about our friends?

Are they your friends though, Jemma?

An invisible fist hits directly between my breasts and nearly knocks the air out of my lungs. I thought I'd have so many friends at the sorority, but none of it feels genuine or even fulfilling. Don't get me wrong, I love Brynn and all she's doing for me. She's one of a kind, a real friend. Alison was a real friend too, until we moved to the city. I miss her.

Paige longingly gazes at Kace as the game ends with a win for us, and the guys all cheer. "He seems different lately."

"How?"

"He's always been a little grumpy and gruff, and a bit stand-offish, but it's that attitude that makes him appealing, you know."

"He's not like that anymore?" Okay, so maybe he wasn't just cool with me. Maybe he's like that with everyone and I'm just a foolish girl who assumes the world revolves around her.

"Worse, actually," she answers with a laugh. She turns to me. "If you're not snacking, is he getting laid? Maybe that's what's wrong with him."

I swallow against a tight throat. If that's true, then it is because Emma and I are in his way, messing with his lifestyle. I'm either going to have to move out or have a serious talk with him tonight.

Paige tugs on my arm her demeanor changing after the teams shake hands and skate off. "Come on, let's go get a drink." Her grin turns mischievous and playful "Maybe I'll have to see what I can do about putting a smile on Kace's face tonight."

My heart lurches. God, I don't want to be around for that. Also, I'm so tired I'm sure I'll be asleep at the table after one drink, but I put on a happy face and we file out of the stands and head outside. I, along with about fifteen other sorority sisters, stand at the back door, and while I'm excited to see Kace, I sort of just want to go back to his place, curl up in bed with Emma and read a book.

The guys come out and squeals erupt around me. Tradition dictates we jump on their backs for a piggyback ride to our favorite local pub, but now, after he called me out—and heck the guy has seen me at my worst—it feels wrong. Should I, or shouldn't I, go? I hover back, and the decision is taken from me when someone shoves me to set me into motion. I turn to Paige, but she's running and jumping on Kace's back. He grips beneath her thighs to hold her on, but then I watch him search the crowd, and when he finds me our gazes lock and he crooks his head, indicating for me to come. Tension, heat and want arc between us and I turn before anyone spots it.

My gaze moves to Sebastian, and I note the way Kace follows the direction. Sebastian is talking to a man I can only assume is his father. I've seen him on TV before and know Sebastian comes from a political family. They're in deep conversation, and I notice a few of the other guys have family here watching them too. That's nice for them. I turn back to Kace and he has a scowl on his face. He tears his gaze away and my heart squeezes. He has no family here. Brynn would be but she's doing me a favor.

His mother lives close and she doesn't come watch her son. Heck, if I had a son going off to the NHL next year, I'd be the loudest person in the stands. There's definitely tension in his family, and I don't know what I was thinking when I asked if he was following in his father's footsteps. I should have known better from earlier conversations that family was something he didn't want to talk about.

The crowd moves and I fall in beside Olivia and Ally as we all walk to the waterfront. Olivia nudges me, a knowing grin on her face as she wags her brows. "How's big daddy?"

I snort out a laugh I don't feel. "He's been a great help, actually."

"Any spankings involved?" Ally teases, waving her hand in front of her and shaking her hips.

I know what she's talking about, but I say, "I don't believe in spankings."

Olivia eyes me. "Ha, then that means you've never tried it."

Would I like to be spanked? I nearly swallow my tongue at the thought of Kace's hand coming down on my backside. I wave my hand and laugh it off. "Or maybe I just haven't been spanked by the right guy."

Or any guy.

They both laugh, loving my answer, but pretending to be a puck bunny doesn't feel so right tonight. I glance over my shoulder as Kace walks behind me, Paige on his back. Where she has every right to be. I'd just told her nothing was going on between us, and while nothing is, I can't deny there is a new kind of tension in the air tonight. Kace, with the way he's stalking closer, looks a little bit like a wild animal about to sink its teeth into its prey.

Damn, I want to be his prey.

A shiver goes through me, but it's not from the cool night air. Nope, it's from the way he just let go of Paige's leg and brushed his knuckles against my hand.

Breathe, Jemma, breathe.

Honestly, how am I going to spend the day in the car with him tomorrow, our bodies locked together in a small space as we travel to Shelburne, without wanting him to touch me, to spank me? Ack, I nearly bite my tongue off at that thought.

I pull my phone out and text Brynn to let her know that we won, and that I'll be home soon. She texts back and tells me to take my time, and asks if Kace is piggybacking me. I get a pouty emoji when I tell her I'm walking with friends.

We make it to our favorite pub, and I glance at the guy playing guitar as we all take a seat. Olivia and Ally are on either side of me, and voices are loud and boisterous as Kace takes a seat across from us, Paige plopping onto his lap. Just last week that was me, on a different lap of course.

When she shifts, I take in his hard jaw line. He doesn't look happy at the moment. Then again, does he ever? Numerous pitchers of beer are set in front of us, and I busy my hands by pouring everyone a glass. I slide one to Kace and his hand touches mine as he takes it. My entire body quakes and I shift in my seat to hide it.

"Thanks," he says. I can't hear him, I can only read his lips and now that I'm staring at them, soft and plump, I can't help but wonder what it would be like to kiss him, to have those lips on my body.

I remove my coat, and take a big swig of my beer, needing to cool down my hot body, but someone bumps my elbow and I spill my drink all over my shirt. "Damn, that's cold," I shriek, and reach for a napkin. I dab my white shirt, but all I end up doing is spreading it and staining it more. I have a white lace bra on underneath, and when I hear Sebastian groan and note the way he's staring at me, I'm guessing I could be a contestant for a wet T-shirt contest.

Everything about his stare makes my skin crawl and I push to my feet. "I'll be right back." Ally slides from the booth and I hurry down the hall to the bathroom. I'm about to push open the doors when I hear laughing, both male and female coming from the girls' washroom. Damn, I'm not going in there now.

I walk to the men's and listen at the door. Should I? I push it open and peek in. "Hello." My call is met with silence so I hurry inside, grab a paper towel and run it under the water. I move fast and once I get the stain out, I open the door, and come face to face with Kace as he steps in. I gasp at his presence, and the way it completely takes over the room.

"What are you doing?" I ask.

His gaze moves over the empty bathroom. "I could ask you the same." His eyes drop to my wet shirt. "Are you lost?"

"No, there were some things going on inside the girls' bathroom." I always knew there were hookups after the game, I just never stumbled across one before. "I didn't want to walk in on anyone. I checked to make sure no one was in here before I entered."

"Someone is in here now." He takes a step closer, and I forget how to breathe as the intensity around him zaps my last working brain cell. "Do you need help?"

"Help?" I ask. What the heck is he talking about.

"Getting it out?"

Ohmigod, is he talking about... My head dips to the button on his jeans. Is he asking if I need help getting his cock out? "Um. Kace." I lift my eyes to his and he angles his head. "Are you talking about..." I can't quite bring myself to say it, even though any good puck bunny could.

"The stain," he clarifies, and lightly rubs his thumb over the damp spot on my shirt. Each caress comes closer and closer to my breast, and my damn nipples respond. There is no way he can't see what he's doing to me. But why? Is he playing with me, wanting me to back down, and prove I'm not a bunny once and for all.

Maybe I don't want to. Maybe I want this. Want him. Maybe I'll shock the hell out of him and play along.

"I can't quite get it out. Do you think you could help?" Okay, so this isn't normally like me, but it's a part of me, a confidence deep inside, something that really isn't an act at all. I don't know where it's coming from, to be honest. Maybe it's the hungry way Kace is looking at me. Maybe it's the bulge in his pants. And maybe he just wants me because it's been too long for him and maybe I'm okay with that.

There's no way we have a future together, but this is college and the man I want to give my virginity to is looking at me like he wants to eat me alive.

Let's see where this goes.

KACE

The bathroom door swings open, hitting me in the back and fortunately, knocking some sense into me. As my brain refires, I shake my head. Jesus, I was two seconds from pinning Jemma against the wall and devouring her lips, among other parts of her body.

I glance at Conner as he puts his hands up palms out and I'm glad he stopped this. This act...this isn't Jemma and I'm not going to encourage her lies and fake behavior. But there was just something about her this week, all warm and real and vulnerable when she was taking care of Emma, that totally drew me in.

"Sorry," Conner blurts out and begins to back up, hauling the door with him.

"No, it's okay. We were just leaving."

"Dragon, no. don't let me—"

"We were leaving," I say again, my voice firm and holding an edge of anger...at myself. What the fuck was I thinking?

"Girls' bathroom was busy, and this stain," Jemma explains weakly. I reach behind, take her hand in mine and pull her into the hall with me.

I run agitated fingers through my hair. "I'm going to get out of here."

"I should go too. I'm wet."

Fuck me twice.

"My shirt, I mean."

"I know what you mean."

She stares at me, hurt in her eyes, and can I blame her? One minute, I'm cold and distant. The next I'm ready to ravish her, only to turn cold and distant again.

"I should probably go back to the sorority to get more clothes. I've been washing the same ones every couple of days and need more. I didn't bring a lot." She shrugs. "I guess I thought I'd be long gone from your place."

I put my hand on the small of her back and give a little nudge to set her into motions. "I'll go with you."

"It's okay."

I don't answer. Instead, we stop at our table and I reach for her coat. She tugs it on as I pull mine off my chair and I don't miss Paige's pout.

"You're leaving?" she asks, even though it's obvious.

"Jemma is wet." Fuck. "She spilled beer on her shirt and I'm going to walk her home."

Her eyes skirt to Jemma and for a second I think I spot anger. But she quickly blinks it away. "I'm around later if you want to do something."

"Probably going to call it a night. The baby is up a lot through the night."

"Right." She shifts on the chair. "Night, Daddy."

I ignore that, and follow Jemma out into the night. It's only early October but the weather is changing fast. "You warm enough?" I ask, when Jemma wraps her arms around herself.

"The wind is cold with a wet shirt."

"Then zip up your coat." I put my hand on her arm to stop her and her arms fall as I reach for her zipper, pulling it to her chin. I stand back and take in her thin coat, which barely reaches her waist. I guess it's for style, not comfort. "Here."

I take off my coat, and drape it over her shoulders.

She tries to shrug out of it, but I stop her. "I'm not taking your coat."

"Leave it," I command in a soft voice. She looks like she's about to protest so I say, "If you were Brynn, I'd make you wear my coat."

Her nose scrunches up. "Oh, so I'm like a sister to you."

"Yes," I lie. Nope, not like a sister at all. For a second, I think she's going to call me out on the heat arcing between us a couple minutes ago. Nothing happened, so if she does, I'll play it off as just trying to be helpful. Our feet slap against the pavement as we walk, and voices and music can be heard from all the downtown pubs.

The noise dies down as we get further away, and up ahead, the sorority comes into view. We both remain quiet, lost in our thoughts and I'm happy for the cool air on my body. It helps keep my brain working.

"I can run up," she suggests when we enter the big house. "I'll just be a second."

"I can help." She hesitates for a moment. Yeah, okay, maybe she's getting some sense back in her brain too and realizes what almost happened in the bathroom was a mistake.

"Okay."

I follow her up and she opens her door. I've been in this room before—heck, I've slept in Jemma's bed—but I've never really paid much attention to its furnishings, or the unopened box in the corner beside her bed.

I walk to the box as she pulls clothes from her closet. I reach for the flaps. "You need help unpacking?"

"No," she says quickly, alarm in her voice.

I tug my hand back fast and spin to see her. "What, do you have a dead body in here or something?" I'm joking...I think.

She laughs, but it's humorless. In fact, she seems agitated. "Just some things from home. Nothing important."

"If it's not important, why did you drag it here just to take up space?"

"It's just books."

"We can put them on your shelf."

"No, it's okay."

Why is she acting so strange? I know she wants to write children's books. She told me that. "You have children's books in here."

She nods, but it's easy to tell she's lying. I wish she'd quit it. Christ, I'd seen her at her worst this week and vice versa. Is there really any need for lies between us at this point? "Can you grab that bag from up high?" She points to the shelf at the top of her closet, and I get it, she's dragging me away from the box. What is it she doesn't want me to see?

She could have had her over the summer, and doesn't want anyone to know it's her baby.

As Sierra's words come back to haunt me, I quickly dismiss them. No that's ridiculous, and that box isn't full of baby things. Nevertheless, whatever she has in there, she doesn't want me to see.

I reach for the bag and hand it to her. She stuffs it with clothes and zips it up. "I'm ready." She's about to hike the heavy bag over her shoulder when I take it from her. I wince as it digs into my shoulder.

"Are you okay?"

"Fine, just took a hit tonight. Sore muscles."

"I can carry the bag."

"I got it." I open her door, and wave for her to exit. I follow behind, and she locks up. Wind blows outside, and a few leaves fall at our feet. Soon enough, winter will be here. "Do you get a lot of snow in Shelburne?"

"We're right on the water, similar to Halifax, so it was mainly wet and cold." She laughs like she's remembering something. "One winter, though, remember that year we had white Juan?"

I laugh. "White Juan. Yeah." Juan was a hurricane that tore through the province, then when winter came five months later, we were hit with a Nor'easter nicknamed 'White Juan'. It shut everything down—including our power—for over a week. "Fun times."

"We actually did have fun. My sister and I..." She begins and then swallows as if current memories are plaguing her. "Well, there was this building, and we were jumping off the roof, into the snow. The snow almost reached the roof." She casts a glance my way. "Do you have any fond memories?"

"I just remember cleanup. So much shoveling."

She squeezes my bicep. "Is that how you got all those muscles?" My gaze cuts to her, and her eyes go big. "I'm just kidding. Must have been a lot of snow for you to shovel."

A beat of silence. "Dad was supposed to be home that weekend."

"You had to stand in, huh?"

I nod and glance up at the sky. Why the hell am I talking about this. Are the planets all misaligned or something?

"Brynn is lucky to have a big brother like you." She bangs against me as we walk. "I like how close you are."

"I take it you and your sister aren't close. You didn't even know she was pregnant."

She takes a deep breath. "We were really close as kids. Best friends, actually. That sort of thing happens when you grow up in the middle of nowhere, where houses are far apart."

"When did you grow apart?"

"High school. She kind of dumped me...she became popular... until..." She swallows and stops talking, like she'd said too much.

"Until what?"

"My dad is a minister," she blurts out but that didn't really answer my question.

"Oh, shit."

"Oh, shit is right. I don't think this is going to go over so well with him, but...I'm really worried about Krista's state of mental health right now. I thought getting away—Montreal College—would be good for her." She toys with the zipper on my coat. "A clean start," she adds so quietly, I'm not sure I heard her correctly.

"And now...you don't think getting away was good for her?" She shakes her head, and something in me softens at the concern on her face. She really cares about her sister, and I appreciate and respect that. If it was my sister, I'd scour the earth for her. "It's a thirteen-hour drive to Montreal. Should we go this weekend?"

We walk under a lamp pole and her smile is soft and appreciative. "No, that's too far. I could always fly up, I guess. Not that I have time now."

"Can you call her friends?"

She looks away fast. "I...don't know any of her friends." I eye her and she hurries on with, "It's just that she's been at Montreal College for a couple years. I'd never been there. Her friend group from back home would have changed, right? Everyone is gone their own way now."

I shift the bag on my shoulders and try not to wince. "You could always try."

"No, I don't think so."

I let it go as we reach my place, and find a light on in the living room. I flick the light on in the hall, and spot Brynn on the sofa flicking through the channels. She glances up. "I heard it was a great game."

"Sorry you missed it," Jemma tells her.

She waves the remote. "Don't be. Emma and I had a fun night. I gave her a bath and she babbled and told me this whole big story," she says with a laugh. She checks her phone. "She went up to bed about thirty minutes ago.

"Thanks so much, Brynn. I really appreciate it."

"Thanks, sis."

"With any luck she'll sleep through the night," Jemma says, and puts her hand over her mouth to stifle a yawn.

"I should get out of here."

I set Jemma's bag on the floor. "I'll walk you home."

"It's okay. I can use my campus security app." She gives a playful wink. "There's a cute guy working security. Besides, you guys look exhausted." She opens up the app, shows it to me before she punches in her information. Once finished she stands and stretches. "What time are you leaving in the morning?"

"Not early," I tell her. "After lunch." I glance at Jemma to confirm and she nods.

"Okay, I'll come before that."

Jemma puts her hand on Brynn's arm as she steps into the hall. "Thank you again."

"Not a problem. Emma is adorable. Tomorrow I'm going to take her for a walk on the waterfront."

"Don't get too used to it," I warn.

"Don't worry, big brother. I don't plan to have babies for a long time." She laughs. "But wouldn't it be funny if I ran into Dad. Give him a real shock."

"Sis..." I warn. "Don't start trouble." The last thing I want is for my father to be calling my mother. She's unstable enough as it is.

"Yeah, well he'll get his when you start playing for Edmonton."

"Right,'" I agree, not wanting to talk about this.

She brushes my shoulder, as if to remove the chip there. "Then maybe you'll move on and think about having a family of your own."

This whole time, Jemma stays quiet, her gaze going back and forth between the two of us as she takes it all in. I put my hand on the door and hold it open for her. "See you tomorrow."

"Night," Jemma and I say as campus security shows up.

Brynn leaves and as I lock the door behind her, Jemma points to the stairs. "I...uh...should get up to bed."

I pick her bag back up, and my shoulder twinges. "Same."

We head upstairs, and I follow her into her room to find Emma asleep in her bassinet. I smile at her sweetness, even though my heart aches for her. Hopefully tomorrow we can get some answers.

"Night," Jemma says and opens her bag after I drop it on her bed. I nod and go to my room. I head to the bathroom to brush my teeth and wash up. Back in my bedroom, I roll my shoulders out, and do some stretches before stripping down to my boxers to climb into bed.

I toss and turn, falling into a fitful sleep filled with visions of Jemma and what we nearly did in the bathroom at the back of the pub. A noise or something wakes me, and I shift to check the time. When I do, my shoulder screams in protest. Fuck. I listen for sounds of Jemma or Emma. All is silent. I get up and make my way to the bathroom in search of my anti-inflammatory cream. I don't bother turning on the lights in the hall. The light in the bathroom—which we've been using as a nightlight if we need to get up with Emma in the middle of the night—gives enough illumination to lead the way.

I reach the bathroom, push open the door and when I realize I'm not the only one occupying the small space I inch back. But not before my heart squeezes so tight in my chest I nearly drop to the floor. This...everything about this unadulterated display of honesty and vulnerability I see before me is going to lead me down a path that can only end in trouble... and pain.

12

JEMMA

It's not the movement at the door that has me closing my mouth and lifting my head. No, it's the strange, strangled noise crawling out of Kace's throat that forces me to turn my gaze from Emma, and end the made-up story about mermaids that I was telling her. My gaze meets with eyes full of tenderness and something that looks like a mixture of want and fear.

I gulp and my heart jumps in my chest as Kace stands there, his body eating up the doorway and overwhelming every nerve in my body. "She spit up a lot after her bottle," I tell him quickly, unable to hide my breathlessness. "I had to clean her. She's good now. We'll get out of your way." With Emma in my arms, I gather her soiled clothes and toss them into the laundry bin. I take two steps toward Kace, but he straightens to his full height and continues to block my exit.

"Jemma," he murmurs quietly, zero hardness in his voice as I cradle a sleeping Emma against my chest.

"Yeah."

He lightly touches my wet hair. "You need to get cleaned up, too."

Warm knuckles brush against my neck and my knees nearly go out from beneath me. "I know. I'm just going to get Emma back to bed first."

He nods and stands to the side as I push past him and cross the hall to place a freshly washed and changed Emma in her bed. I glance back over my shoulder and his big body continues to hover at the bathroom door, which automatically takes my thoughts back to the pub, when I thought he was going to ravish me in the men's bathroom. Everything about that would have been wrong. I'm still not even sure he likes me. But none of that means I don't want him.

Oh boy.

I take my time gathering up some clean pajamas, giving him time in the bathroom alone, so he can be gone by the time I return. But he hasn't moved. He continues to stand tall, looming in the doorway. Maybe we woke him, and he was just checking on us. With my clothes in hand, I inch past him, our bodies brushing, and I reach for a facecloth from the small cabinet and run it under the water. I catch his eyes in the mirror as he stares at me, completely silent and unmoving.

"I'm good," I say, and force a smile. "You can go back to bed."

He rolls his shoulder. "I was actually looking for some ointment." He lifts his arm and his bicep flexes as he points to his shoulder.

"Still hurting?"

"Yeah, hurting. Need to rub..."

He quickly stops talking, and I can't help but think I'm hurting too...and need a rub. Just not on my shoulders. Is that why his words fell off? In his head did it sound sexual, too? Or am I just tired, my mind going down a ridiculous path?

I move to the side to give him access to the cabinet, but in a very deliberate move—at least I think it is—he steps up behind me, and presses his groin against my back as he reaches over my shoulder, opens the medicine cabinet and pulls out a tube of ointment.

I hold my cloth under the water and work to regulate my breathing as he keeps me pinned, like he's in no hurry to leave. "Here," he says, his voice deep and raspy, his breath hot on my neck as he sets the tube of ointment down, and closes his hand over mine to take the cloth from me. He squeezes the water out, and examines my hair.

Oh my God, what is happening...

He takes a few strands of my hair into his big, rough palm and begins running the cloth over them and I grip the sink to keep myself upright as he gently cleans my hair. *Breathe, Jemma breathe.* Honestly, I have never, ever in my life been treated with such care and delicacy. It's messing with my ability to think with any sort of clarity.

Big fingers part my hair and he goes to work on another section. His gaze meets mine in the mirror as his cock grows and presses against my back. "I don't think this is working," he grumbles.

It's working for me...if he's trying to turn me on that is.

"No." God, why do I sound like I just strained all my vocal cords? Actually, I screamed quite hard at the game tonight—

not has hard as some—but I don't think that's what's making my voice raspy.

"I think you might need to rinse off." I follow his gaze in the mirror to the shower.

"Probably, but I'm tired, Kace," I say. "I don't think I have the energy to stand that long."

"I can understand that, but I can help you, if you want." I stand there, confused, as he reaches into the shower and turns on the water, leaving what happens next in my shaky hands.

"Kace…" I stare at him. What the heck is going on right now? He inches back, and tugs off his boxers, no shame about him as he releases his hard cock. Shocked at his lack of modesty— the man should be proud of his body—I stare, a little gasp catching in my throat.

"Yeah?"

"I thought they called you Dragon.... because of your doodles."

He stares at me for a second, and then, when understanding hits, he laughs. "They do." He points down. "You thought…"

I nod and stand still, trying to wrap my brain around the fact that Kace Andrews is standing before me naked—and we're about to shower. Am I dreaming? If I am, I don't want to wake up. My eyes gobble up his rock-hard cock, a little frightened of its length and girth. But there's another part of me that wants to touch him, to see if his smooth stretched skin is as velvety soft as it looks. Something tickles the side of my face. Am I drooling?

"Hey." That one word snaps me out of my reverie and my gaze jerks to his. He gives me an adorable, crooked grin that might as well be a long hot, caress to my clit. "I mean, it's not like I haven't seen you naked, right?"

He hasn't. Well, okay maybe partially. He did, after all, return that half naked picture from the locker room, but my God, we didn't sleep together. He wasn't between my legs. He has the right to know that before we do anything here, I think.

"Kace," I start my voice breaking as I begin to shake with embarrassment. How do I do this? Will he laugh at how desperate I was to fit in, and walk away, telling the others? I don't want this to end like it did for my sister. "I...we..."

"Babe." He lightly touches my face, running his thumb over my cheek in a soothing manner. His eyes narrow, real concern dancing in their dark depths. "Do you want me to help you?" I blink as his gaze moves over my face. "It's a simple yes or no answer."

For a brief second, I don't know what to say, because there is nothing simple about this. I shouldn't be getting mixed up with a guy who confuses the hell out of me, might not even like me, and is only doing me a favor because of his sister.

Why not, Jemma? Why not, just once, be with the one guy you want to be with—the one guy you've wanted to lose your virginity to. Do the reasons driving his behavior, and what this is really all about to him, have to matter tonight?

No, they don't, and nothing about this is long term. It's just two people enjoying each other and letting off steam, which is why I say, "Yes."

His shoulders relax, his eyes dimming with desire as they focus in on my mouth. "Okay." He reaches out, touching the hem of my damp T-shirt. "Let me help you out of this." I lift my arms, making it easy for him to peel it over my head.

"Ugh, it got on my face."

As I wipe the back of my hand over my face, he chuckles slightly and it helps ease the tension inside me. "Are your shorts dry?" He grips the hem of my pajama shorts as his gaze moves over my face.

God, he has no idea just how wet they are, and not from spit-up. "Um, no," I answer honestly.

"Wow, she really did a number on you."

"They're uh...not wet from the formula," I admit, and he angles his head. I swallow and continue with my honesty. "They're wet because of..." I pause and poke him in the chest.

"Jesus," he curses under his breath as he sinks to his knees, dragging my shorts down with him. I lift my legs, one at a time, allowing him to take them off me. His fingers trail up my inner thighs as he stands, and a hard quiver goes through me, my body now alive, exhaustion from earlier no longer mattering.

His hand finds mine and he gives a little tug. I follow him into the shower, and he puts me under the spray, turning me so my back is against his hard chest. His heart pounds rapidly against me, as does one other part of his body.

"Want to smell like me?" he teases, his chuckle vibrating through my trembling body. I laugh with him, and he fills his hand with his body gel and starts at my throat. He lathers me for a moment, before his hand trails lower, sliding over and under my breasts. I groan and let my head fall back against his chest. My nipples pucker under his ministrations, and he brushes the rough pads of his thumbs over them.

I move my body, rub against his erection, and soft curses fill the shower. He might be using me for sex, and I've concluded that I'm okay with that, but damn, I love the way his body is reacting to mine.

His hands go over my belly, and lower, and I suck in a breath. I'm a goddamn virgin. The only fingers that have even been between my legs are my own. I stiffen for a second. Will he know? Will he put an end to this? I was, after all, pretending to be a sexed-up puck bunny.

Ah, but he called you on that, Jemma.

Still, will he want to be with a virgin? Will he be disappointed that this book nerd has no idea what she's doing? I mean, I sort of built a fictitious sexual history with my actions and words. Should I tell him? I can't help but feel a little embarrassed that I'm still a virgin—a girl no guy ever wanted.

"Jemma," he murmurs into my ear. "Are you okay?"

I try to relax as I put my hand over his, and lace our fingers. "I'm okay," I try to assure him. The truth is that I want this. The second I set eyes on Brynn's older brother, I knew he was the guy I wanted to be my first. That's partly why I tried to be the kind of girl he gravitated toward. A man like him would never look at a nerdy book worm. Although when I'm at my most vulnerable, well, those seem to be the moments when he's drawn to me.

I push those thoughts aside as I guide his hand down, and he puts his foot between my legs to spread them. God, that is so arousing. I swear to God, I'm going to climax the second he touches me. Which, I don't want to, because then he'll know too much about me. More than I want him to know.

"Please," I say, even though I have no idea what it is I'm begging for.

He presses a wet kiss to my neck. "Need this." One thick finger slides into me, and I am sure I've never felt anything quite so incredible before. I move my hips and then, with his finger still deep inside me, we both go still when Emma cries out. I suck in a breath and hold it, praying she goes back to sleep. Sometimes she cries through the night, for no apparent reason. Although maybe the reason tonight is a sign that I shouldn't be messing around with a guy I've been lying to.

She quiets down and we both relax. "Thank fuck," he murmurs, and I don't know why, but it brings a laugh to my throat.

"Agreed."

He begins to move his thick finger in and out of me, and I rock into him as his palm presses against my clit. "God..." I cry out like some virgin who's never had her clit played with before.

Hashtag, true story.

I laugh again, but it quickly turns into a moan as he pushes a second finger into me for a deliciously snug fit. I put my hands on the wall in front of me and claw at the tile as his thick pistoning fingers fill me and take me higher and higher.

He groans against my neck. "You are so tight, babe. I can't wait to put my cock in you."

I gulp. He truly doesn't know the half of it, and I hope he doesn't figure out I'm a virgin. When it comes right down to it, that's no one's business but my own, right? His free hand cups my breast and he plays with my hard nipple. I lift my face and let the warm water run down my body as he fingers me, and rubs my clit.

"Do you want that?" he asks, and for a second it doesn't register what he's asking until he jerks his hips forward, massaging his thick cock against the small of my back.

"Yes," I answer quickly. "I want you to put your cock in me."

His teeth scrape my neck and when everything he's doing to my body becomes too much, I cry out and wiggle against his cock. His grunt of pleasure pushes me over the edge and every muscle in my body tightens as hot, powerful pulses begin in my core and spread onward and outward. The world around me fades as the pleasure centers between my spread legs.

"Kace...oh, yes...Kace."

"Fuck, yeah," he grunts as I come around his probing fingers. I squeeze them as liquid heat pours from my body and drips down his hand. He keeps his fingers inside me, and I move my body, riding his fingers without shame, and wringing every ounce of pleasure I can out of my orgasm. Honestly, I've pleasured myself in the past, but what I was doing...can I even call it pleasuring myself? This...this orgasm he just wrung out of me...umm, more please.

Wait, there's going to be more tonight, isn't there?

I finally stop spasming, and his deep voice reverberates through my body, arousing me all over again, when he puts his mouth to my ear and says, "I want you in my bed, legs spread."

All righty then. Apparently, there *is* going to be more tonight. I resist the urge to yelp with excitement, and while I'm terrified that his big cock might ruin me—in many ways—I'm also incredibly excited.

Okay, here goes nothing…and everything.

13

———

KACE

———

I reach around her and turn the water off as she leans against me, like her legs are of no use. I chuckle and keep one arm wrapped around her waist as I guide her from the shower. I like her body all warm and relaxed and sated, and the little whimpering sounds she keeps making are curling around my cock and tugging tight.

I grab a towel and wrap it around her, tying another around my waist. We walk quietly, not wanting to wake my room-mate, and head straight to my room. "On the bed," I demand in a soft voice. A hard quiver goes through her as she sits, and I dart back down the hall, into her room. Her eyes are wide and perplexed when I come back. I show her the baby moni-tor, and she nods.

"This way, we can close the door. You know in case you want to scream."

"Maybe you'll want to scream," she counters, her gaze drop-ping to take in the way my throbbing erection is tenting my towel.

"Oh, I have no doubt about that," I answer honestly and let my towel fall to the floor, giving her a clear view of my cock. "You see what you do to me, right?"

"Good, because I want your cock in me." She grins, and her fingers go to the knot on her towel. With a little tug, she releases it, and I damn near swallow my tongue as I take in her flawless body. Jesus, her skin is so soft and creamy. Her breasts are pert and perfect, and the soft swell of her hips are perfect for gripping when I sink into her.

Her breathing changes and her chest rises and falls rapidly as I take a step toward her. What we're doing isn't smart. Hell, I know she's been lying to me and everyone else, but when I walked into the bathroom and saw how real, honest, and genuine—no pretense about her—she was as she told an animated story to Emma while cleaning her up, I was a goner. She has no idea how appealing and irresistible that girl is. Although she might now, after I got naked with her in the shower and brought her to orgasm.

Speaking of orgasm. I believe I want to give her a few more, with my mouth and cock this time.

"Did you miss the part where I said I wanted you on that bed with your legs spread?"

A little whimper catches in her throat as I reach down, lightly running my hands along her arms as I snatch up the damp towel and toss it away.

After she backs up, I climb onto the bed, going up on my knees, my gaze meeting hers, letting her know I'm damn serious. I want her wide open so I can admire every inch of her body, including her soft pinkness.

Her gaze never leaves my cock as she falls onto a pillow. I take it into my hand and stroke from base to crown, and a little puddle of pre-cum pools on my tip. Her eyes grow wider as she adjusts her body, her damp hair splaying over my pillow. As I let my gaze move down her body, her legs slowly, tentatively open. For the briefest of seconds, something niggles in the back of my brain. She's done this before, right? I know she's been putting on a show, but no way is she a virgin.

I hesitate, my gaze zinging back to her face, and I catch the tiniest hint of panic, not to mention the way her eyelashes are blinking rapidly, her throat tightening as she swallows. I inch back, unsure and rake my hand through my hair. "Jemma, are—"

She crooks her finger. "Did you forget the part where I said I wanted your cock in me?" She sits up, takes my cock into her hand as her soft, delicate fingers trace the long length of me, a careful examination, all blood leaves my brain.

What again was it I was worried about? I close my eyes, almost remembering, until her warm lips close around my crown, drinking my pre-cum. As rational thought once again eludes me, I grip her hair and grunt as I move my hips forward wanting every inch inside her mouth, even though it's impossible, but goddammit, it feels so good.

She moans around my cock as I fuck her sweet mouth, wanting to go deeper, but not wanting to choke her. She runs her hands along my length, and slides the other lower to cup my balls. Jesus, the woman really knows how to touch me. She cradles my balls, and I take pleasure in the way my cock stretches her lips as it disappears into her mouth. Fuck, that is nice to watch. My body begins to tremble and I'm so close, too close, I inch back, needing to stop this before it ends on its own.

She frowns as she blinks up at me. "You were going to make me come, babe." Her eyes light up, and I shake my head. "I want to do things to you first."

"Oh, okay. What kind of things?" she asks, an innocence to her words that nudges something in my brain.

Is she teasing or is she serious? She must know what I want to do to her right...unless? My thoughts come racing back.

"You want to kiss me?" she asks and falls back, touching her inner thighs. "Put your mouth on me?"

Okay, yeah, she's done this before.

"I want my mouth right here," I say and lightly pet her sex. She sucks in a breath as I part her wet pinkness, hot and swollen from my fingers. Jesus, her pussy is so fucking pretty all spread out like this for me. "You want that, babe?" I know she does by the change in her breathing, but I just like hearing her say she wants me. That's crazy, I realize. Not to be egotistical or anything, but I do hear that a lot. All elite hockey players do, but I want to hear the words on her lips. Want to know it's what she wants.

"I want that," she whimpers as her hand slides to her sex, once again tangling with mine, like she needs the connection. Does it somehow comfort her? Is she nervous? Or maybe she just wants to guide my hand to where she wants it.

She keeps her fingers locked in mine as I lightly touch her, and her gaze never leaves mine. She moans with pleasure and my cock drips with need. I wet my lips, lightly touch her clit, and move so I can take her hands and put them over her head.

"Yeah, just like that." I drop to my stomach, flat on the bed and slide my hands under her thighs, lifting her gorgeous sex to my mouth. She goes up on her elbows, her eyes wide, her cheeks pink as I lean in and lick her from bottom to top, stopping to swirl the soft blade of my tongue around her clit.

Her body jerks, her pussy hitting my face as a little cry catches in her throat. "Kace," she cries out, sheer pleasure dancing in her voice. "My God, Kace."

I chuckle at her enthusiasm and dive back in, licking, nibbling and sucking until she's a hot writhing mess beneath me. I don't want to bring her to orgasm again, at least not yet. No, I want my cock inside her when she comes, want to feel her strong muscles clench around my throbbing dick when she let's go again.

Her entire body quivers as I eat at her, and she reaches down, runs her fingers through my hair as she takes all I can give. My tongue easily slicks over her sex as she grows wetter and when a keening cry catches in her throat, I ease off and reach into my nightstand for a condom.

She watches in total fascination as I rip into it and quickly sheathe myself. "Kace," she murmurs, a new kind of softness in her voice.

"Yeah, babe."

"This is..." I angle my head, as she wets her dry lips. "This is going to be good."

I fall over her and press my lips to hers. "Yeah, babe, this is going to be very good."

I press hot, opened mouth kisses to her neck and take her puckered bud into my mouth for a second and I work to get my shit together. I'm so goddamn aroused, and she's so damn slick and ready, I'm afraid that I'll detonate the second I enter her.

I take a couple of fast fueling breaths, and angle my body, taking my cock in my hand to position it at her opening. She sucks in air and holds it.

"Hey, you have to breathe, babe."

She laughs. "Right. I'm just, excited."

"Me too." I tell her. I move my hips, inching my crown into her, and she's so tight around me I wonder how much of me she can take. Her hands clasp together around my back, and she squeezes her eyes shut.

"Am I hurting you?"

Her lids open. "No," she answers quickly.

I study her face for a second, and when I spot the need growing, I give her a little more. Fuck, she feels so good, it's insane. "Bend your knees." She does as I ask, and her thighs squeeze my body as the position allows me to slide in a bit easier. I find her mouth again, and kiss her hungrily as I go deeper and deeper, her body opening to mine as I push.

"Kace," she murmurs, her voice shaky and breathless. "You're inside me."

Is she asking a question or making a statement?

"I'm inside you, babe." I meet her shiny eyes, and brush her damp hair back from her forehead. "Feel good?"

She nods, very enthusiastically and it makes me laugh. "Does it feel good for you?" she asks in return.

"Fuck yeah, it does."

That makes her laugh. I start moving, slowly, wanting to draw this night out, since it's probably going to be our first and last, and I don't know why that thought bothers me. I don't do relationships. Sex is for recreation, to blow off steam. Women know that before ever getting involved.

Jemma knows that too, right? She would have heard all about me at the sorority house. What if she doesn't know? Maybe I should tell her, just to be sure. I open my mouth, but my words stall. Why the hell can't I seem to tell her?

Oh, maybe because you might want more.

Nope, nope, nope. This is not about more. Not with Jemma. As pleasure tears through me, my thoughts fail, and I fill my lungs with air and hold my breath as I concentrate on the need building.

"I want to see," she says, a new kind of shyness about her as she nibbles her bottom lip.

"You want to watch my cock slide into your hot pussy, Jem?"

She nods, and goes up on her elbows as I shift to the side. "Fuck, that is hot," I say as I sink into her body.

"Yeah..." Her response, combined with the dreamy look on her face makes me think she's experiencing this for the first time. I push a little deeper as she stares, transfixed and my pelvis bumps against her clit.

"Kace." Her eyes go wide. "Ohmigod, yes, just like that."

"That's what you like?"

She nods. "Can you do that again?" Instead of answering, I pull almost all the way out and slide back in, and really grind against her clit this time. "Like that...more...please..."

I do as she asks and at first, my movements are slow and steady, hitting her clit with laser precision, but it's hard to maintain control when she's so damn wet and tight and moaning my name—like this is the greatest moment of her life. I just want to go caveman on her, and fuck like a wild animal. She tosses her head from side to side, and it's obvious I'm not the only one coming unglued.

Her hands move to my shoulders, and she holds me tight as I pound into her, picking up the pace and clenching down on my jaw to keep myself in check.

"I never knew it would be this good," she whimpers.

I slow my rhythm. "What?"

"I mean...you...uhh..." Her eyes widen, and her mouth drops as she fumbles to find her words. Did she just say something she didn't mean to? "With you," she finally manages to get out. "I never knew it could be this good with you."

"Why is that?" I ask, as my cock throbs for release.

She gives a fake laugh, and the rumble goes through her body and squeezes my cock. Jesus.

She blinks rapidly. "From what I hear everything you do, you do fast. But you're not fast tonight, right?"

Again, is that a question or a statement?

I don't know and I'm too goddamn aroused and my brain clearly isn't working at the moment. "Maybe it's too early to call that, baby." I let loose a deep, guttural grunt as I inch out and push in so deep I hit her cervix. She whimpers as pleasure spreads across her face. "You're fucking killing me," I groan. "Trust me, it's all I can do not to come."

"Are you doing math?" she asks and I raise my brows. "At the sorority house, I heard you guys do math to keep it in check."

"I can't do math. I can't even figure out what one plus one is right now."

Her laugh is light but also laced with pleasure. "Right now, one plus one is one."

"Okay," I say, believing her.

"The two of us, joined like this." She glances between our bodies. "We make one."

"Yeah, we do," I respond, and hope my smile isn't as ridiculous or goofy as I feel right now, because I like her math and way of thinking.

"Oh, and I want you to come. How about a power play?"

I grunt. "Do you even know what a power play is?"

"When someone scores...fast."

"No, Jemma," I say and as I change the pace, her mouth forms an O. Knowing I've got her just where I want her, I pump into her, and her body quivers, her hands squeezing my shoulders as an orgasm takes hold.

"Kace..."

Her muscles squeeze around me and I grit my teeth at the pleasure tearing through me. I go still inside her and push my pelvis against her clit. As she rides out the waves of her pleasure, I lose complete focus, drowning in sheer ecstasy.

I'm going to lose it. I'm going to fucking lose it.

As her pulses slow around my cock, I flatten myself on top of her, find her mouth and explode high inside her. She gasps. "I feel you."

I grunt as I deplete myself, and put my arms around her, holding onto her like my life depends on it. "Babe," is all I manage to get out as the world around me spins out of control. I fill my lungs and exhale heavily as I bury my face between her shoulder and neck. I kiss her lightly as her tight sex squeezes every last drop of come from my body.

Her heart pounds against my body, and mine pounds against hers, as we stay like this, one plus one, equaling one. I chuckle against her flesh, and a quake goes through her. It takes all my strength to lift my head and she's smiling as my eyes meet hers.

"You good?" I ask.

She brushes my hair back. "I am, are you?"

I grunt my response, and slowly inch out of her, even though I'd like to stay buried in her all night. But I need to get rid of the condom. A little whimper catches in her throat as I leave her body. The room is dark as I take off the condom and wrap it in some tissues. I drop it into my trash can, and make a note to dump it tomorrow.

I stand, and glance at Jemma as she pulls the blankets up to cover her body. It confuses me. A minute ago there was nothing shy about her, now she almost looks like a deer in the headlights.

"Hey," I begin softly, walking around to her side of the bed, and lightly touch the bedding. "Everything okay?"

"Yes," she answers quickly. "Just got a chill."

"It's only a million degrees in here."

She shrugs. "Go figure."

"I'll be right back. I'm going to wash up."

I pick my towel up and wrap it around my waist. Unlike Sebastian, I don't walk around the place naked. I hurry to the bathroom, wash up and grab a cloth to clean her. By the time I get back to the bedroom, Jemma is standing there, the towel covering her body, and the bedsheets bundled in her arms.

What the fuck is going on?

14

JEMMA

I roll over in my bed, and find the other side empty. My heart jumps, but slows when I hear Kace's voice in the bathroom, along with a babbling Emma. Last night, when he went to get washed up, I checked the sheets and found a bit of blood. In a panic I stripped the bed, which is why we both slept in my room. After lying and letting him believe we'd slept together the other day, it seemed wrong to blurt out that I was a virgin. Well, I'm not anymore, so I can put that behind me.

I sit up, and my heart wobbles as he talks to Emma. I can't believe how good he is with her. But it appears, not that he talks about it, that he had a lot of responsibility for his younger sister growing up. Dressed in a T-shirt and sleep shorts, which I climbed into last night after pretending I was cold, I push to my feet and start toward the door. It opens wider and in comes a half-dressed Kace, Emma in his arms.

Dear ovaries: Cool it.

"Sorry, didn't mean to wake you. This little peanut decided I had enough sleep."

I grin. "You didn't wake me. Brynn will be here soon anyway."

"Right."

My heart flutters at the way Emma looks up at Kace with love in her eyes. My throat tightens. What will become of her? Does she have a father that wants her, doesn't want her, or even knows about her? I have so many questions for my sister. None of this is right, and a child deserves to know their parents. I can't imagine not growing up with a mother and a father.

Is this why Kace is so taken with Emma? He grew up without a man in his life, from what I understand, and maybe he hates the idea of it happening to anyone else. It's not my business, but I can't help but want to know more about him, especially after last night.

Not that it meant anything other than what it was—sex. If I keep telling myself that, will I eventually believe it? It's crazy really, because I used to think of sex as losing my virginity. I wasn't any kind of loser last night. Nope, I was the winner and gained a lot, like pleasure, intimacy, comfort, and tenderness.

It was just sex, Jemma.

Lord, I never thought I was going to be the kind of girl who fell for the first man she slept with. Wait, no, I'm not falling for him. I'm just being a silly, emotional girl because last night was my first time, and even though it was sex, it's going to hold a special place in my heart forever.

My voice is raspy when I whisper, "Here, let me take her so you can get some more rest."

"Nah, I'm awake now. What I need is coffee. How about it?"

"A bucket full please."

Chuckling I hold my hands out for Emma, and as he places her in my arms, he catches me off guard by leaning in and giving me a kiss on the forehead. I must look completely stunned when he pulls back, because he angles his head and says, "Oh, sorry."

"No, you don't have to be sorry. You just surprised me."

"I thought after last night." He holds his hands up. "I shouldn't assume anything. I mean, it's not like we're a couple and I'm allowed to act on compulsion."

"Right," I agree, liking that he acted on his compulsion. "What we're doing here." I look around the bedroom. "This is all just playing house."

He gives a curt nod. "Yeah. I'll still make you a bucket of coffee, though." He's about to leave, but stops and lightly touches my arm. "Last night, Jem. That was..."

"Really nice," I say.

"Yeah." He smiles and my heart thumps. "Really nice."

I swallow. "We probably shouldn't do that again though." He narrows his eyes, like he's not sure if I'm asking a question or making a statement. "Right?" This time I really am asking, although I'm not sure I'm getting that point across.

"Right," he agrees and turns. I stare at his cute backside, snug in his boxers as he leaves the room, and I exhale, glancing at the baby in my arms.

"What is wrong with me?" I ask her. "Never mind. Don't answer that. I make bad decisions for all the wrong reasons.

Let's hope you don't take after me. Or your mother," I add. "After a stunt like this..." Truly though, I am so damn worried about Krista and I hope my trip home will shed some light on her situation.

I hug her too me and step into the hall, coming face to face with a naked Sebastian. I quickly avert my eyes. "What, it's not like you haven't seen a naked man before."

"The baby," I say.

"She's too young to know better." He steps around me and heads to the bathroom, not bothering to shut the door. I don't say anything else. This is his place and we're the ones who are invading.

At the top of the stairs, I glance down and find Kace staring up, his face a bit harder than it was earlier. Did he overhear Sebastian? Does he still think Sebastian saw me naked? That I saw him naked?

I head down, and Kace waits for me. "Everything okay?"

"Everything is fine. Or at least it will be when I get some coffee into me." He nods and I follow him into the kitchen. I set Emma into her car seat and give her a little toy, which she immediately starts chewing on.

"When do they get teeth?" I ask. Kace grins as he puts a big, glorious cup of coffee in front of me. I grab my phone, and do a quick search. "Three months. So soon." It breaks my heart a little to think down the road my sister might actually be sad that she missed this time with Emma. Does that mean I think I'll have her for another month? I begin to hyperventilate.

"Jemma," Kace says his voice cutting through my thoughts. "It's okay."

"I just…have a lot to learn."

He lightly touches my face, his thumb sweeping across my cheek in a soothing motion. "Let's see what we can find out today and go from there, okay?" I nod. "Now drink."

I gulp the coffee, and when the front door opens, I jump up. Kace eyes me. "It's my sis," he says.

I shake my head. I have no idea why I thought it could be Krista. She doesn't know I'm not at the sorority anymore.

"Good morning." Brynn's voice is cheerful as she comes into the kitchen and sees us. She goes still for a second, no doubt sensing the tension inside me. "Everything okay?"

"As good as can be expected," Kace says and hands her a coffee.

She warms her hands on the mug. "Thank you, big brother. It's chilly out there this morning. How's peanut?"

I grin as the brother and sister before me call her peanut. "Peanut is teething," I announce.

"Cranky," Kace adds.

When Brynn winces I begin, "Are you sure you're—"

Brynn holds her hand up to stop me. "I got this. Mommy and Daddy need a break. Isn't that right, peanut?"

We're not Mommy and Daddy, we're only playing at it, but for the briefest of seconds, something about that completely terrifies me, and yet warms me in the strangest ways. My gaze goes to Kace, and I take in the way his back muscles play as he drops toast into the toaster. I stare, remembering those big hands on my body last night. A burst of heat weaves its way through my body.

Kace opens the fridge and that's when my brain registers the sound of the dryer. "Kace's sheets are in the dryer if you want to take his bed," I inform Brynn.

She gives me a knowing grin, like she knows why the sheets are in the dryer. I just roll my eyes at her. I'm not sure why she likes the idea of Kace and me together. He's off to Edmonton next year and I'll still be in college. Nothing about us works, if you ask me.

Oh, except in the bedroom. We worked there. We also work in our joint efforts with Emma. But other than that, nope.

The toast pops and Kace asks, "Jam or butter?"

"Jam is good, thanks." He goes to work on my toast as Brynn plays with Emma. Kace hands me my toast and I bite into it, ravenous.

"Were you able to catch up with all your classes?" Brynn asks.

"Yes, thanks to your notes and online."

"What about you, big brother? You still on track, and down to one day at the coffee shop?"

"Uh huh," he grouches and I guess he's warning her not to talk about the 'money' again. Whatever that means. He certainly won't tell me but I get the sense he doesn't have to work but chooses to.

I finish my toast quickly. "I should shower so we can get out of here."

Brynn waves me away. "I'll watch Emma. You go."

I stand and put my dish in the dishwasher as Kace takes the seat I just vacated and falls into easy conversation with his sister. I really do love their relationship. I dart upstairs, pausing at the top to listen for signs of Sebastian. When my ears meet with silence, I grab clean underwear, my yoga pants, and a shirt. I hurry to the bathroom, locking the door behind me, and jump in the shower. Even though I brought my own body wash, I decide to use Kace's. I like his smell on me.

The warm water falls soothingly over my body, and while I should hurry, the second I run my soapy hands over my curves, the familiar scent of Kace in the air, my eyes slip shut, and I touch all the deliciously sore spots that Kace caressed last night. My clit swells as I stroke it, and I begin to burn from the inside out.

A groan crawls out of my throat and I shake my head to snap out of it. I finish quickly, and step out, double checking that the door is locked. I don't need Sebastian bursting in on me. I dry my hair and dress and by the time I finish in the bathroom, Kace is coming up the stairs to get ready. He slows in the hall as we pass, and suddenly things feel a bit awkward.

I gesture toward my room. "I'll just gather up some clothes for the night and I'll be ready."

He nods toward the steamy bathroom. "I won't be long."

Oh, I guess he doesn't plan to touch himself in the shower, like I just did. Of course, he doesn't. He's sated from last night and not thinking about more. Note to self: Get it together, girl.

I hurry to my room, throw one night's worth of clothes into my bag, and toss it over my shoulder. Twenty minutes later, I'm in Kace's car, a knot in my stomach as I wave to Brynn and Emma at the door.

A big palm lands on my leg and squeezes. "She's going to be okay."

"I know," I answer quickly. "This is all just surreal."

"That it is," he agrees and backs out of the driveway. I stare straight ahead, and as we drive past the playground at the commons, and I see the dragon sculpture, I turn to Kace, not wanting this drive to feel as awkward as our passing in the hall.

"Do you draw anything else, besides hockey rinks and dragons?"

He shrugs. "I do, but it's just doodling."

"Actually, they're quite good for just doodles. Maybe I could hire you to illustrate my children's book."

His laughter fills the car. "I'm not that good." He grins at me. "Do you think I'm that good?"

"Look at you, fishing for compliments. I heard that hockey players were all like that."

"I don't know about the others, but the only fishing I do is in the lake." A strange sadness comes over him, as he takes the corner. Was it something I said?

"Do you miss fishing?"

"I miss a lot of things," he mumbles, and for a moment, I'm not sure his words were for my ears.

"I can show you some good fishing spots at home. It's never really been my thing, but I know where to go."

"Yeah?" He smiles. "That would be cool. If we have time. I can teach you."

For some reason, oddly enough, if it's important to him, it feels important to me. "We can make time. Brynn was telling me that Liam Dunn's family owns a fishing conglomerate in Lunenburg."

He nods. "Why were you guys talking about him?"

"I don't know. He just came up." I eye him. What, is he jealous? No, of course that can't be it. Maybe the guys have history. I let it go and stare straight ahead.

We reach the highway and he flicks on his signal and passes a couple out for a leisurely Saturday drive. I glance in and smile when I see the elderly couple. Will I ever grow old with someone I love?

"What's the story we're telling your parents?" Kace asks pulling my thoughts back.

"About?"

"Us?"

Us...

Funny, I like the sound of that.

"We're traveling back to your hometown together." I take in his firm jawline, as he negotiates traffic with ease. I really can't believe I slept with Kace Andrews—dragon. My body still tingles with the memories. He looks at me, his brow raised. "They're going to have questions. Are we going to pretend we're a couple?"

I toy with the zipper on my jacket. "I don't know. I know you hate deception."

He goes quiet for a long second and then, "I do, but it seems odd if we don't. They might wonder why some strange guy from college is driving you home for the weekend. If you don't want them to know we're looking for information on Krista, we're going to have to come up with a cover story."

I nod, and check my phone. Still nothing from my sister. "You're right." He nods and goes back to negotiating the highway. "Kace?"

"Yeah?"

"Will you be my pretend boyfriend for the weekend?"

He chuckles. "What's in it for me?" I open my mouth about to ask what he wants, but he narrows his eyes and casts me a playful grin. "How about a weekend with all the benefits of being a boyfriend."

My pulse races. Does this mean he wants to have sex again? Do I dare hope? Although I shouldn't want that again—considering I foolishly thought I couldn't fall for the man I gave my virginity to—but dammit I do. Right now, I wish I could be like the girls in my sorority, and not fall for the first guy who's nice to them.

"My father is a minister, Kace. You're not getting near my bedroom."

He shakes his head. "A minister's daughter. You know what they say?"

"That they're shameful? That while her father is addressing his congregation, she's out involved in debauchery to shame her parents?"

His lips flatline and he goes quiet, staring straight ahead at the long string of traffic before us. What is going through his brain now? That I'm not shameful, and that it's possible he slept with a virgin last night—a girl who's been acting like a sexualized puck bunny for weeks now. God, I don't want to talk about this. It's so embarrassing.

"It wasn't like that," I say quietly.

"I know."

I realize he knows, a little anyway. But he has no idea just how much of a nerd I really was—am—shunned by the popular kids. At least I wasn't preyed on like Krista. A hard quiver goes through me as I think about how cruel people can be. I don't want my friends turning on me like that. The picture in the locker room was hard enough to swallow. I can't imagine what they'd do if they found out I was fooling them all. The less Kace knows, the better, which is going to make a trip to my hometown of Shelburne a tricky one.

15

———

KACE

———

Jemma shameful, out doing debauched activities. I don't think so. I grip the steering wheel tighter as my thoughts return to last night. There were so many times I thought she was a virgin, but then she'd do or say something that eased my concerns. Was she faking it? Fuck man, what if she was pretending to be experienced when she wasn't?

Did I take her virginity?

That can't be right. Sebastian told me he'd hooked up with her. Then again, he is an asshole and I'm not sure I believe anything that comes out of his mouth. I should come right out and just ask her, but then it would make this whole trip awkward, and right now I have Emma to think about. I'm doing this for her. Okay, I'm doing this for Jemma too, because there are so many things I like about her—the real her.

She checks something on her phone and when a song comes on she likes, she nudges the radio up a bit. I stifle a yawn. "I can drive if you want to have a nap," she offers.

"I'm okay. It's not that far. Why don't you tell me a story to keep me awake?"

"You mean like a children's story?"

"Sure, one that you wrote."

She crinkles up her nose. "I think it might put you to sleep."

I laugh at that. "Is that what your stories are supposed to do, put children to sleep?"

"No, not really. I want them to be fun and exciting and for them to learn something. But you're an adult and they'd bore you. Although with the right animation, it could really help bring my stories to life."

"Tell me about one. Let me see if I can figure out how to draw the characters."

"Okay." She flips through her phone, and pulls up her notes. "This one is about a little boy named Jack who starts school and he's shy and fearful, completely out of his comfort zone, so he pretends to be a dinosaur, big and strong and confident. He roars at everyone. But instead of making friends, the kids are all scared of him."

"Is he going to be okay?" I ask, completely serious.

She stares at me for a second and then her hand lands on my arm. "He's going to be okay, Kace."

"Thank God."

She laughs, hard. "You know, maybe you should have gone into social work. You really care a lot about kids."

I shrug. "Hockey is my life."

"Do you want kids someday?"

"I don't know. I never gave it much thought. I'll be on the road a lot."

"Players make it work, though, when it's important enough to them."

I snort. "Yeah, when it's important enough, you can make anything work, even a double life." Fuck, why the hell would I blurt that out? I stare straight ahead, not wanting to see Jemma's expression, or the plea in her eyes for me to explain. She's heard enough tidbits about my life, that she knows something shitty went down, and I don't want anyone's pity. Unable to help myself I cast her a fast glance, and when our gazes collide and hold, I don't see pity on her face. What I see instead—the understanding and sadness for a childhood lost—wraps around my heart and squeezes tight.

"Your father," she begins cautiously, her voice soft and low, and compassionate. "He had a second family, didn't he?"

I'm about to tell her I don't want to talk about it. It's not something I talk about with anyone.

Then why did you just mention a double life, Kace?

Do I want to talk to her about it? That doesn't make sense, considering I don't even trust her.

"It's okay, Kace. You don't have to tell me anything."

Everything from the way she's not pushing, to the gentleness in her touch and compassion in her voice—she really is a sensitive person at heart—has me blurting out, "Yeah, he did. He was an asshole."

"He sure sounds it," she shoots back without an ounce of hesitation.

My gaze flies to hers and I can't help but smile as she sides with me, no questions asked. "Asshole with a capital A."

She gives a curt nod in agreement. "Asshole times a million, plus infinity," she tacks on and I laugh.

I hold my finger up. "Plus one."

"Yeah, of course." She holds two fingers up. "Plus two, even."

Unable to help myself, I reach out and take her hand in mine. "Asshole with a capital A times a million, plus infinity, and add two. Thanks for the help in summing that up."

"Anytime."

We both go quiet for a long time, and it's so odd, the invisible band that's always been tight around my chest is suddenly looser. "He would go away for weeks at a time for work," I say, my words spilling out. "Sales. I think my mom knew. They would fight a lot when he came home. I could always hear the muffled sounds." A beat of silence and I add, "She started spiraling when we were really young."

"Which is why you had to pick up a lot of the slack with Brynn."

"Sis was younger, and it affected her too of course. I tried to shield her, which is why I don't think she hates him quite as much as I do."

"I think he lives rent free in her head too, Kace. I just think she just deals with things differently. You know, like taking the money for college when you won't. Maybe it's her way of making him pay for what he'd done, and this way she gets an education out of it."

"Wow, figured that one out fast, I see."

"The tumblers are clicking into place." She gives my fingers a squeeze. "I'm sorry, Kace. That was a really shitty thing to happen to your family. I hate your father as much as you do right now, but hate." She gives a low, slow whistle. "It's a lot to carry around and you know what they say…"

"There's a fine line between love and hate," I answer.

"Yup, but indifference…not caring one way or the other. Now that's when you know you really moved on." She clicks her tongue. "Not easy to do, but doable." As I consider that, she continues. "At the end of the day, though, does one really want to be indifferent and have zero concern for someone?" She goes quiet for a second and adds, "Like I always say, hurts from your past aren't your fault. But you're responsible to heal from them."

"Wow, deep and smart. Do you follow that philosophy?"

The honesty in her eyes wraps around me. "Sometimes I fail," she admits.

I nod, totally understanding that. "Dad loved hockey but was never good enough to make the NHL."

"I know you're not killing yourself on the ice to make him proud, Kace," she says, once again surprising me with her astuteness. She's really fucking smart.

"No, you're right. It's almost like I want to rub it in his face. I want…I want to say fuck you. Look what I did, despite you." I glance at her and my stomach is tight, the whole idea of shoving it in his face suddenly making me ill. "Do you think that makes me a shitty person?"

"No." There's nothing in her expression to suggest she thinks otherwise.

"Sometimes, when I have hateful thoughts like that, I worry that I'm no better than him," I tell her, and that's not something I've told another soul, but it's a deep-down worry that scares me. "I look like him. What if I turn out like him? A chip off the old block. Unfaithful, and uncaring. Hurting those I was supposed to love and protect."

"You won't," she says with confidence. "Trust me, I see the way you care for Brynn, and for Emma. I'm sure you treat your mother the same way. You don't hurt people, Kace. You're a good person, and a nurturer at heart. I don't know if that comes from the environment you were raised, or if it was something you were born with. Either way, you're a good guy."

"I never want Emma to feel unloved," I respond, my voice tight as I shake my head. "What kind of man does something like that, though? Why weren't we enough for him?"

"You were enough. This is on him, not you. He's the one who abandoned his family."

"Abandoned? I don't know, he always came back. Until Mom finally had enough."

"It's still abandonment. That's hurtful, and I guess one of the big reasons you don't do relationships?"

"Trust," I admit. "It's hard for me, you know." She fidgets under my stare. Is she going to tell me why she lies about what type of person she really is? I give her a second, but when she goes quiet and toys with her zipper, my gut tightens. I guess she doesn't trust me enough with her secrets, and that's okay, I don't trust her either.

Then why did you tell her your deepest, darkest hurts?

I squeeze the steering wheel. "I'm tired of him living rent free in my fucking head."

"Then let's try to do some fun things this weekend. We're both exhausted from school and taking care of Emma and even though we're on a fact-finding mission, it doesn't mean we can't do something for ourselves."

"I think that's the best idea I've heard in a long time."

"Really, because I actually think, last night when you suggested I shower to get the spit up off me was the best idea I've heard in a long time," she teases with a grin.

My dick jumps. "Okay, my mind is no longer on my father."

She laughs. "Mission accomplished."

"But wait, you liked that, huh?" I resist the urge to adjust my cock as it sits up, wanting a front row seat for this conversation.

"Um, yeah. Wasn't it obvious?"

"So maybe…" I shrug and crush my lips together, like what I'm suggesting is no big deal, but something inside me tells me it just might be. "We could maybe recreate that?"

"I mean, I can't make Emma spit up on me on a whim." She's joking. I can tell by the playfulness in her eyes and I really, really like when she's real like this. "I guess I could always shake her after a feeding, and while I don't know much about babies, I'm pretty sure that's frowned upon."

I laugh hard. "Fuck, Jemma. If the only way I can get you naked again is if someone spits up on you, I'll down a gallon of milk myself, and do fifty push-ups. That ought to do it." The air around us grows lighter as we both laugh. "Okay, tell me about Shelburne and what we can do there."

"You've never been?"

"No, it's in the middle of nowhere. Buttfuck nowhere, I believe it's called."

"True," she says with a laugh, but then raises her brow playfully. "But there are some hidden gems known only by the locals."

I arch a brow, intrigued. "Tell me."

"Nope." She lifts her chin. "I'm not sure you deserve that after calling my hometown buttfuck nowhere."

"Ah, come on, you agreed it was in the middle of nowhere, and I can be nice."

Her laugh is cynical. "I can probably put a petition together tomorrow, signed by hundreds who think otherwise."

"I can be grumpy too," I agree and of course we can't forget about that chip on my shoulder weighing me down. That would make anyone grumpy, right?

I wink at her. "If I say pretty please?"

"Maybe if you say pretty please."

"Okay, pretty please tell me."

She inches her chin up. "Nope."

"Hey."

She laughs. "Maybe I just wanted to hear you say pretty please."

"Now who's not the nice one?"

She slumps in her seat. "Fine, but how about I show you instead. I think you'll really like it, actually. It's somewhere I used to go and read for hours on end."

She stiffens like she didn't mean to tell me that—I have no idea what's wrong with reading for hours on end—but I decide to keep the conversation playful. "Show and tell, I like that. Wait, it's not anything scary, is it? Like a haunted house."

"What?" Brows pulled together, her gaze goes up and down my body. "A big strong guy like you, afraid of a haunted house?"

I straighten my shoulders. "No, it's just that my buddies Dane and Jesse went to this haunted house in the valley last year. They were never the same."

She whacks me. "Oh, stop."

"Let's backtrack. You think I'm big and strong."

"Oh, puleeease, Kace," she shoots back and rolls her eyes.

I chuckle. "Am I going to meet any of your friends back in Shelburne?"

Her laughter stops and her body goes stiff. "No, probably not. Most people my age are gone. It's a very aging population. My best friend Alison, actually, she goes to the Academy?."

"Oh, is she in the sorority house?" I wrack my brain but don't remember meeting an Alison.

"No, the sorority wasn't for her. She's sharing an apartment with some other friends." I want to ask more, like why I've never seen her around, but Jemma glances out the window, and I sense it's a conversation she doesn't want to have. Did they have a fight?

"What kind of guys do you usually bring home? Are your parents going to hate that I'm a jock'?" I do air quotes around the word, jock.

"My father is probably going to lose his mind, actually. He loves hockey."

"What's his favorite team?"

She crinkles her nose in thought. "Pittsburgh, I think."

"He's not rooting for a Canadian team. I'm going to have to have words with him."

She chuckles. "I don't think that's a good idea."

"Why not?"

"The man is a minister. He'll lecture you for hours on end. I hated doing anything wrong when I was a kid. The lectures were too painful."

"I don't want that." I stare straight ahead. "I really hope we can find something out about Krista."

"Me too."

I cast a fast glance her way. "You might have to tell them."

She winces. "I don't want to. Krista asked me not to, and ugh, I just don't know what to do, Kace." Her eyes are narrowed and worried as she looks at me.

Maybe she doesn't want to tell them because the baby is really hers.

I push that thought from my mind. I have enough people living rent free in my brain. Sierra shouldn't be one of them, but I can't stop thinking about the rumors.

They're rumors, Kace. Nothing more.

I check the time and we're still a long way out, so I settle back. "You were going to read me one of your stories."

"Right." She wakes her phone again and I listen to the story about Jack, the boy who pretended to be a dinosaur. As she reads the story, a part of me wonders if she's the dinosaur, acting like something she's not, because she's afraid no one will like her. My heart softens a bit as she finishes on a happy note.

Her gaze is hesitant and nervous as she sets her phone down. "You need to get that published."

A smile touches her lips. "Do you really think it's good?"

I wink. "Hey, I thought you said fishing wasn't your thing. But seriously, I do like it, and like I said, I can put you in touch with my buddy, Brandon."

"I wasn't fishing for compliments, much," she says with a laugh. "But I might take you up on meeting Brandon. Do you think my story is something you'd like to animate?"

"I could give it a try, and I won't be offended if you don't like it, much."

She laughs and points. "Oh, take this exit. Let's take the secondary highway and go by the water. It's really pretty."

"Yeah, really pretty," I agree, but I'm not talking about the scenery. I'm talking about the sweet, caring, book reading girl beside me.

JEMMA

I enjoyed the drive with Kace far more than I thought I would, and taking the scenic route might have been more about spending time with him than my fear of going home and finding out something bad was going on. I can't believe how much he opened up to me. Brynn doesn't ever talk about her father. That couldn't have been easy on either of them, and Kace is always guarded and hard. But in that moment, when he shared his deep pain, it meant something to me, and I could almost feel our bond growing.

But I'm not sure he felt the same way, especially when I closed up and shut down, keeping all my secrets inside, where they belong.

"It's that house right there," I tell him. "Just up on the left."

He nods and turns on his signal light, even though we're the only car in the street. "Nice place," he says, and I try to see the old house with the fading cedar shingles through is eyes. It's big, with a huge corn field and equipment in the back. I'm guessing his house in the city was much smaller than this, with far less land.

He kills the ignition. "I know you mentioned a farm, but I didn't know it was a corn field."

"Yeah. Most of it will be harvested by now. We can still walk the field if you'd like to explore."

"Sounds fun." He grins at me.

"What?"

"Not only are you the minister's daughter, you're also the farmer's daughter."

"And what do they say about the farmer's daughter?" I ask, even though I know the stereotype.

"Desirable and naïve."

"I guess I'm a lot of things."

"Yeah, but you know. I like you best when you're not *trying* to fit in to any kind of stereotype."

His eyes bore into mine, and my heart lurches. Partly because he just said he liked me, and partly because he's calling me out on not really being a bunny.

I reach for the door handle. "We should get inside," I say, needing to talk about something else.

He exits the car and I climb out and follow him to the trunk to get our bags. He looks around. "It's so quiet here."

"It's a good place if you want to be left alone with your thoughts."

"Or a good book," he adds, and I can't help but think he's feeling me out.

"Right. Let's go say hello."

"They're going to be okay with us just showing up?"

"I'm their daughter, they'll be happy to see me. You, maybe not so much," I tease.

He takes my bag from me and carries it to the door. I turn the knob and slowly open it, not wanting to scare my parents if there just on the other side.

"Hello? Hey, Mom and Dad. It's me, Jemma. I'm here with a friend."

Mom comes around the corner, her blue eyes wide. The second she sees me, she spreads her arms. "Honey, what a surprise. What are you doing here?"

"We thought we'd get out of the city for a few days."

"We?" Her gaze turns to Kace as he comes in behind me. A little smile touches her lips as she takes in the tall, handsome man beside me. "Oh."

Yeah, oh. That was my reaction a few weeks ago too.

"Mom, this is Kace. You remember me telling you about Brynn. This is her brother. We're, uh..." For a brief moment, guilt grips me and I can't find my words. I don't like lying to my parents. That thought almost makes me laugh, hysterically, considering all the lying I've been doing since moving to the city.

"I'm her boyfriend," Kace explains with zero hesitation and holds his hand out to Mom. She waves it away and pulls him in for a hug, and at first, he stiffens, no doubt surprised by the warm display of affection. I cringe at the way Mom is hugging tight and he's uncomfortable with it, but it also makes me a little sad to know he didn't grow up with love and warmth. I don't think he's used to this kind of affection, but my parents are huggers. Sunday congregations are full of love and hugs. He eventually relaxes and when Mom pulls back, he says, "It's nice to meet you, Mrs. Maloney." It takes me by surprise because I don't ever remember telling him my last name. I guess Brynn must have when I wasn't around.

Maloney Baloney.

Yeah, kids are cruel.

"Call me Jenn," Mom says and he nods.

"We're going to spend the night," I begin. "I was thinking Kace could take Krista's room. Unless, of course, she's home for the weekend." I try to sound casual, not at all like I'm seeking information.

"No, she's not and of course Kace can take her room. Why don't you two get settled, and I'll call your dad in from the field. We can have coffee out on the back deck and you can tell me all about college." Kace picks the bags up, and Mom studies them. "Are you just here for the night?"

"Yes, we have to be back tomorrow."

"Well, you must be a very special man in Jemma's life if she brought you home to meet us. She's never brought a guy home before."

Ack. "Mom," I say quickly, a little embarrassed, and not wanting Kace to know too much about my past. How did I think bringing him home with me was a good idea? "We're just...dating. It's no big deal. We thought we'd get out of the busy city for the night."

"Of course, dear."

"Come on." I say to Kace and he follows me through the big old house and up the stairs. The old wood creaks under his impressive weight, and he stays quiet behind me as I lead him down the hall. He stops to look at childhood photos of Krista and me. He grins as he examines them.

"You guys were cute." He winks at me. "Well, you still are." He turns his attention to a picture of Krista and me in front of the Christmas tree. I was thirteen and Krista was fifteen. "If there wasn't a height difference here, I'd think you two were twins."

"We used to get that. Come on, I'll show you to your room."

We walk by a bedroom and he slows. "This is yours?"

"Nope, Krista's."

He steps in and drops the bags on the floor. Turning back to me, I note the mischievous grin on his face and brace myself. "So, you never brought a guy home before, huh?"

I groan. "Kace."

"I had no idea I was so special," he teases, and cups my elbow, bringing me close. His head dips, and his eyes are dark and hungry. God, I want to kiss him right now, to feel those soft lips on mine, devouring with want, much like he did last night.

"Stop," I say, and reluctantly inch back. I glance out the window. "Dad is on his way back, and if he catches us like this, we'll have an hour-long lecture on the birds and the bees."

A cute little grin tugs at his lips. "We're in Canada. Here the lectures are on the beavers and the geese, or is it gooses?" I burst out laughing at that. I had no idea he could be so funny.

He gives me a look that suggests he's completely outraged. "Come on, what kind of children's author are you going to be if you don't know that?"

"My God, Kace. That would be such a funny book. Do you think you could illustrate that?"

"I could try."

"I'm sure you've seen enough beavers in your life," I point out. "They're everywhere." Of course, we both know I'm no longer talking about Canada's sovereign animal, and maybe I don't want to be reminded about all the women he's been with.

I force a laugh—I don't want him to think it bothers me—but it dies an abrupt death when his big hands span my hip and pulls my *beaver* against his long-necked *goose*. All righty then. Heat barrels through me, as his hardness presses against my softness, and it's all I can do not to wrap my legs around his waist and beg him to take me.

I pull back before I do just that and put my hands to my cheeks. "Great, I'm going to be flushed when we go back down."

"Sorry," he murmurs, even though he doesn't look it. "I couldn't help myself."

I reach for my bag, but he picks it up and holds it out of my reach. "Nope, you're not getting off that easy. You saw my bedroom, now I get to see yours."

"I didn't see your *childhood* bedroom."

He shrugs. "No, but you will. When you come for Thanksgiving dinner."

"I didn't know I was actually doing that?"

"Under the circumstances," he says quietly. "You can't really come home, unless the truth comes out this weekend."

"Right." I turn and head to my room, and Kace is tight on my heels. My body quivers as his heat reaches out to me and overwhelms me in the craziest ways. "This is me." I announce and stop just inside the door, but he's not having any of that. He puts his hands on my hips again, lifts me up and easily moves me to the side like I'm a marionette and he's the puppet master.

I swallow against a tight throat as he drops my bag onto my bed, and moves around my room, his fingers brushing over my furniture. Jeez, who knew I'd be jealous of my dresser. "Nice room," he murmurs and glances at me. He pauses by my bookshelf. It's mainly empty. I've taken most of my books with me. There aren't many pictures on my walls, but my comforter is still the pink flowered one I've had for years. It gives the whole room an innocent quality.

He eventually drops to my bed, and glances at my window as he tests the mattress. "You've never snuck a boy in?"

"No, have you?"

"No, I've never snuck a boy into my room." I roll my eyes at him. "Have you ever wanted to?"

"I guess, sure. I mean I was a normal teenager." Normal, meaning I wanted what all girls wanted—attention, love, a hot boyfriend. And I did have a hot boyfriend, he just lived between the pages of a book.

"Hmm," is all he says and jumps to his feet when the back door downstairs slams shut. "I guess we should go see what's what."

He moves past me, purposely brushing up against my body, and I feel the caress deep between my legs. Yeah, bringing him here was definitely a bad idea.

"Kace," I say and he turns. "Did you ever sneak a girl into your room?" I ask, curiosity getting the better of me.

"No, actually," he tells me with a frown as he scrubs his chin, the hairs making a rustling sound. "Things weren't good at home. I just tried to keep it calm."

I nod, and my heart goes out to the little boy whose father abandoned him, forcing him to become a responsible man long before his time. But if you ask me, he's doing the best he can with what he has, and deep under the gruff exterior, I've glimpsed another side of him, and dammit, I like that side. And while he knows I'm pretending to be something I'm not, he's been getting glimpses of the real me, and I'm beginning to believe he likes what he sees—which is surprising, considering I've seen the girls he gravitates toward.

Although maybe he gravitates toward them because it's easier to keep it casual.

But if he digs deeper, uncovers more layers and discovers I'm an unlovable book nerd, shunned by the popular crowd—his crowd—would he like that girl or would he tell the others I've been deceiving them? Honestly, I really don't even know anything about hockey and almost blew it when I talked about a power play.

"Coming?" he asks at the door, his eyes narrowed.

I force my legs to work and follow him out. We head down the stairs, and voices rise up from outside. Dad pulls himself up to his full height, a big smile on his face as he greets Kace. Dad is a kind man who only wants what is best for everyone.

Will he like Kace, think he's good enough for his daughter? My gut tightens, but not for me. No, it tightens for Krista and for Emma's father, and how hiding all this is going to hurt my parents.

"Kace, so nice to meet you."

"Nice to meet you too, Mr. Maloney. I've heard a lot about you."

Dad gives me the side eye. "Funny now, we haven't heard anything about you?"

Ugh.

Kace laughs it off. "I think Jemma didn't want to influence your opinion of me. She wanted you to like me all on your own."

Dad laughs at this. "Come, sit down, son. Let's get to know one another."

"Dad," I begin. "Kace has been drafted by Edmonton."

"Is that right?" He pours Kace a coffee as Mom smiles at me, obviously congratulating me on my choice of men. "Have you thought about Pittsburgh?"

Kace laughs and takes a drink of coffee. "I heard you were a fan."

"Best team in the league," he says without hesitation.

"Yeah, you say that now, but with due respect, just wait until I'm playing for Edmonton. I bet I can get you to change your mind."

Dad grins and turns to me. "He doesn't lack confidence."

He doesn't lack anything.

I don't say that, instead I say. "I've been going to the games. He's really good, Dad." I smile at Kace and spot pride on his face. He thanks me with a warm look in his eyes.

Dad nods and takes a sip of his coffee. "Maybe I'll have to get into the city to see one."

I smile at Dad. "That would be great." Honestly, Kace would probably love my father's support, considering the situation with his own father. But that's not going to happen. What we're doing here is fake, and I appreciate Kace helping me, knowing how much he hates fake. It's a little sad though, that he's never going to experience my father's true kindness. Guilt eats at me, because I suddenly feel like I'm dangling something in front of Kace that he can never have.

"Is Krista coming home for Thanksgiving?" I finally ask.

Mom frowns. "Unfortunately, no. She said she's so busy with school and a thesis, she can't find the time."

"I'm sorry, Mom."

"It's okay. She seems happy. We all want that and she deserves it." There's a vulnerability about Mom when she speaks about Krista. From what I hear, when a child hurts, a parent hurts, and Krista's last year in high school was painful for us all. I'm surprised she talked about Krista's happiness, actually, but I assume she thinks Kace is my boyfriend, and I told him all about Krista's trauma.

I pick up my coffee and catch the way Kace is watching Mom. What does he see? I casually sip it. "I guess that's why I haven't heard from her in a while. She's so busy. When was the last time you guys talked?"

"Oh, we try to video chat every Sunday," Dad pipes in.

"Really?"

"Yes," Mom says. "Although, like you said, she's been so busy, so the last month has been difficult to connect. Before that, her video wasn't working so we just talked. I like seeing her face, though. It's much more personal."

My stomach tightens and as I catch Kace's glance, I try not to jolt upright. "You'll be chatting with her tomorrow?"

"That's the plan," Dad says. "What time do you have to go back to the city? Maybe it can be a family chat. I bet Krista would love that, too."

My brain races. I don't want to put Krista on the spot by jumping in on the chat, but I really, really need to talk to her, and see if she's okay. "What time will you be talking?"

"Normally around two our time, after my morning sermons."

"Will we still be here?" I ask Kace.

He nods. "Sure, we're only a couple of hours from the city. We can leave later in the afternoon."

My stomach churns, the coffee I managed to swallow threatening to make a second appearance as I mentally prepare for tomorrow's conversation. I grip my thighs and squeeze.

Kace must sense my apprehension, because he reaches beneath the table and lightly brushes my fingers. I take a breath and try to relax.

"Are you two staying for dinner?"

I check my watch, and set my cup down. "Actually, I have a little adventure planned for Kace."

17

KACE

Back in the car, we wave to her parents at the front door and tug on our seatbelts. "Where to?" I ask.

"It's a surprise."

I laugh. "I can't drive there if I have no idea where I'm going."

She taps her chin like she's thinking about that. I arch a brow and wait for instructions. I can't help but smile, loving this alone time I have with her. While I normally hate surprises, since they've never been good in the past, I'm looking forward to whatever it is she has planned. Will it involve us getting naked? That thought makes me laugh. While I like the idea of it—hey, I'm a red-blooded man—I like spending time with her outside the bedroom too.

"Fine," she finally says. "At the end of the driveway, turn right. I'll give instructions when you need them."

"It's going to be like that is it?"

"It is. Are you hungry?"

"The surprise involves food?" I ask. Food is in my top five favorite things in life.

"It can."

"Then yes."

I turn right at the end of the driveway and meander along the winding street. "It's kind of nice here. I'm not sure I could get used to this kind of quiet, though." We pass a brew pub, and I spot numerous people on the deck. "That looks fun."

"That's new. Honestly, there wasn't much here when I was young." She points. "Take a right, we're going down by the water."

"Are you going to make me swim in these cold temperatures?"

"Nope," she says with a laugh, and then goes quiet.

My chest tightens, and a new kind of heaviness envelopes me. "Are you worried about tomorrow?"

She sucks in a breath. "Oh yeah. I mean, how is Krista going to react when she sees me? I don't want to put her on the spot and upset her, but I need answers, Kace. I'm just suddenly not sure this was the best way to go about it."

"I understand." I cast her a quick glance as she fusses with her zipper, a nervous habit I'm becoming accustomed to. "Can I ask you something?" Her brow furrows as she glances my way, uncertainty in her eyes. "You don't have to answer if you don't want to." She nods. "Something about what your mother said about Krista being happy."

"Yeah." Her entire body tenses and she slides her hands under her legs and leans forward a bit, like she has a stomach ache.

"Is she okay? Like did she have mental health issues in the past that may have resurfaced? I've been trying to figure it out. There must be something going on with her if she left her baby outside your door, right?"

"I'm worried she's unwell."

"Okay," is all I say, sensing she doesn't want to talk about it. We drive toward the shore and seagulls squawk overhead. I roll my window down to breathe in the salty air as we pass a building that says, Shelburne High School. "Is that where you went to high school?" She nods, her body tight and I understand the reaction. "No one liked high school, Jemma."

Her eyes widen, somewhat surprised by my statement. "You didn't?" She stares at me, disbelief on her face.

"No."

"But...you were popular, weren't you?"

"What does that matter? High school sucked for popular kids too."

A frown mars her pretty face, and she glances down in thought. "Yeah, I guess," she agrees after a while, although she looks like she's still conflicted. Is that what all this pretending is all about with her? She thinks life is easier for the popular kids and wanted to be a part of that? She's mistaken if she thinks the popular kids didn't have their problems too.

"Did you get picked on?" she asks quietly.

My heart thumps. Jesus, did she get picked on? Suddenly I want to hunt down those who hurt her. I grip the steering wheel tighter. "No, but there were pressures, and trying to keep shit together at home and play hockey, and be the best."

Her voice wavers a bit when she whispers, "That's hard."

"Were you picked on?" I ask carefully, not wanting her revisiting painful memories, but wanting to understand her better.

"Krista was," she answers quietly. "I was just sort of left alone."

Left alone, as in unpopular and ignored? I don't ask that. Instead, I go quiet and wait for her to continue.

"This one guy, he was such an asshole. God, what he did to Krista." She shakes her head, past pain and trauma tightening the muscles along her jaw. "I'd like to have five minutes alone with him."

"Oh yeah?"

"Yeah."

"Is he still here in town? Maybe we can pay him a visit." Hey, she jumped in and took my side when I told her about my dad. The least I can do is talk to this asshole with my fists.

A garbled laugh crawls out of her throat. "I'm not going to involve you in something that could get you in trouble. He's not here anyway."

"What did he do, Jemma?" I ask quietly.

She stares straight ahead for so long I'm not sure she's going to answer, but then she starts with, "Krista was shy, quiet. She liked to read a lot and kept to herself." She shakes her head again. "God, this story is so cliché it's ridiculous." She runs shaky hands over her legs, as if to wipe the moisture away, and I get it, this is hard for her. I don't want to make anything hard for her, but sense she wants to talk about it.

I stay silent and she continues. "Anyway, this guy was a stupid bully. He started hanging out with her, and she sort of pushed me out of her life at the time. He eventually invited her to one of his parties, and she thought he liked her, and she was excited to go, to be involved and liked by the cool kids, but he was just fucking around. He slept with her and told everyone he gave Maloney Baloney, his baloney. Ugh. Everyone laughed, and shamed *her*, of course. She was embarrassed and ashamed, and I was really worried about her. Mom and Dad got her counselling, but the whole thing really destroyed her confidence, you know."

My knuckles turn white as I continue to grip the steering wheel. "Fuck."

"Messed up, yup. She went to Montreal College to get a fresh start, and away from those mean kids, but now I'm worried she's unwell again." Her lashes flash rapidly as she stares at me. "That something really bad happened."

"I can understand that."

"We all just want to be liked and accepted," she says quietly, and my heart thumps in my chest as the pieces of the puzzle known as Jemma fall into place. She was just like her sister, a girl the mean kids called Maloney Baloney, and when she came to the academy, she saw it as an opportunity to be with the in-crowd, thinking life was better in that clique. My chest tightens as hurt for the girl who was always outside looking in, squeezes the air from my lungs. Fuck man, I hate that I was mean and distant with her. She didn't deserve that from me, when she was only trying to find her place at college. I have to say, she's wrong about one thing, though, no matter what clique we're in, we all have our own demons. The grass is not always greener on the other side.

"Pull into that parking lot," she eventually says, and turns from me. I can't see what she's doing, but I think she's wiping her eyes, and it hurts my heart so much I could sob for the little girl who simply wanted to be liked.

"What's here?" I ask, trying to keep my voice level and strong. I don't think she wants sympathy from me at the moment and I want to be her strength.

"Food truck. Best fish and chips in town. You like fish and chips, right?"

"Of course. I live in Nova Scotia, don't I?"

"Kace," she says, going quiet again. "I don't know why I told you all that. I wanted us to have fun tonight."

"I'm glad you told me." It gives me much better insight into her and her motivations. But she doesn't have to pretend with me. I like Jemma when she's not putting on a show. When she's just being Jemma, the girl who wants to write children's books, goes makeup free, wears my too-large sweats and knows how to drive a tractor.

"Tomorrow is going to be a hard day," I tell her. "How about we put that out of our minds tonight, and you show me around your old stomping grounds. You said you wanted to have some fun this weekend, so let's have some fun."

Her smile is warm and genuine. "I'd like that."

"Okay, now let's go get some fish and chips."

We step from the car, and delicious smells reach my nose as I read the menu written on a chalkboard sign. My stomach growls, and Jemma laughs. "You should get the seafood platter. That way you get to try everything."

"Yeah, that sounds about right. I don't have practice tomorrow, so maybe we can find other ways to work off all that food." I wink at her, and I can't deny that after discovering the horrible things that happened to her sister, there's a new kind of closeness between us. Her body brushes up against mine, and I slide my arm around her shoulder. She cuts me a glance, a shaky, questioning smile on her face. I give a casual shrug. "Boyfriends do this."

Her wobbly smile turns into a laugh and her eyes shine as she gazes up at me. Gravel crunches behind me as a car pulls into the lot, but I don't turn. I just want to take in sweet, real Jemma.

"What are you going to get?" I ask.

She turns back to the truck to read the menu. "Hmm, I think maybe a two-piece fish and chips." Voices can be heard coming up behind us, so I move to the window and put in our order, grabbing a couple of water bottles as well. I'm given a slip and told it will be about five minutes.

"Jemma, hey," someone calls, and I turn and spot two girls walking toward the food truck. "I thought that was you."

Jemma shifts from one foot to the other, and I note the way her shoulders sort of curl in on her. Fuck, were these some of the girls who ignored her?

"How's the city?" the other girl asks, making polite conversation. I don't sense a closeness between them.

"Good."

"Hey," I inject and step up to Jemma, putting my arm around her, and the girls stare at me, their jaws hanging open.

"Um, this is Kace Andrews," she explains. "My boyfriend."

"Holy shit," the taller girl whispers as her gaze rakes over me. I might be used to that kind of reaction, but it doesn't mean I like to be looked at like I'm a piece of meat. Unless of course, it's Jemma doing the looking. I'm man enough to admit that I like being admired by her.

I hold my hand out. "Are you two are friends of Jemma?"

"Ah, yeah, we go way back." The taller girl puts her hand in mine, and gives it a little squeeze as she steps closer to me, like Jemma is invisible. That's fucking rude. "I'm Blake, and this is Brit." I nod, and pull my hand back.

"What are you guys up to?" Blake asks, suddenly more interested in Jemma.

"We're just—" Jemma begins and points to nowhere specific.

Blake cuts her off, and it pisses me off. "We're home from Acadia College for the weekend. It's Grant's birthday, so we're partying at his place." Blake's eyes remain locked on me when she twirls her finger in her hair and says, "You should come."

"You look familiar?" Brit says.

"Hockey fans?" I ask.

"Yes, huge," Blake answers her eyes going wide. She's obviously trying to place me.

"Then if you guys go to Acadia College, you might have seen me there. I play for the Storms."

"Ohmigod, I knew it," Brit says as her gaze slides to Jemma, a hint of curiosity and jealousy in her eyes. "Come tonight. It will be fun."

As Jemma's body tightens, I put both arms around her and pull her back to my chest. I lightly nuzzle her neck. "Actually," I begin. "I've been looking forward to having Jemma all to myself tonight. Unless of course, you want to go, baby?"

She falls back into fake Jemma. "We do have plans."

"Yeah, I can't wait to see the surprise you have for me tonight."

She puts her hands over mine. "I know you're going to love it."

"I love everything you do, baby." Blake and Brit's gaze goes back and forth between the two of us, and I can't help but think they look like a pair of bobble heads. "And remember, we need to find a way to work off all these calories before my game Monday."

She giggles and wiggles against me, and dammit, even though we're putting on a show, I'm getting a boner. The number on my receipt is called, and I inch back. "Looks like our food is ready. Nice meeting you both. Ready, baby?" I ask Jemma. She nods and we grab our order and Blake and Brit continue to stare as we head back to my car.

"Not friends of yours, huh?"

"We go way back, but we've never been friends," she says honestly. "They sure seemed to like you."

"What's not to like, babe," I tease, and she laughs.

"Kace?"

"Yeah?"

We climb back into the car, and she takes the bag from me, setting it on her lap. "Does it make me an awful person to say that was fun."

"Putting a couple girls in their place for ignoring you through high school, and only inviting you to a party tonight because you're with a hockey player?" I eye her and wait for her to contradict me, but instead she just nods and answers.

"Yeah."

"It's no different than me wanting to rub my success in my father's face. But what was it you said. Indifference?"

"I know you hate pretenders and liars, and what we just did…"

"What did we do that was fake, Jemma?"

"Well, I mean, you're not really my boyfriend."

I shrug. "Okay, so for this weekend, I am your boyfriend. A real one. Not a fake one."

Her head rears back. "What, why?"

"Why not? I don't like fake, so let's not fake, and you did say you had a surprise for me tonight. That was true."

"You said you were looking forward to having me to yourself tonight."

I bite back a grin. Is she checking to make sure that is true too? "Not a lie."

Her eyes brighten and she draws her bottom lip between her teeth. She likes that. She taps the food bag. "And that we had to find a way to work off these calories."

"Again, not a lie. So, let's eat, and then get to work on that." I'm about to rip into the brown bag when her hand closes over mine.

"Not here."

I glance around the parking lot but don't see any picnic benches. "What do you have in mind?"

"Take a right when we leave this parking lot."

"So cryptic," I tease and start the car. I follow her instructions until we're at a beach, a lighthouse not too far from shore.

"When the tide is out, we can walk out to that lighthouse. It's where I wanted to take you tonight," she says, her voice animated, and excited. I love that something so simple as a lighthouse makes her happy. "It's really cool, actually."

"And what happens if the tide comes in?"

"We'll have to swim to shore, but we have time to sneak in and eat up there." She points to the high deck, painted in red.

"Sneak in? Maybe I wasn't so wrong about the minister's daughter."

She laughs. "We don't get many tourists this time of year, and there's no other cars around, so we'll have the place to ourselves."

I angle my head and wag my brows. "Which means we can also work off the calories in the lighthouse." A fine quiver goes through her. "Have you ever done that, Jem?" I ask, even though I'm sure I already know the answer.

"Maybe," she hedges and opens the car door.

"Hey, I'm your boyfriend. We're supposed to share things like that."

Boyfriend.

Crazy, that sounds kind of nice.

"Come on, time is of essence when you're dealing with tides, especially in Nova Scotia." She glances at me over her shoulder, and it doesn't go unnoticed that she hasn't answered my question. "You can swim, right? You know, just in case the tide comes rushing back in."

I catch up to her and my feet sink into the wet sand as I take the food bags from her. "You're kidding me, right?"

"I don't know, boyfriend. Am I?"

God she's so much fun when she's real and relaxed. I seriously love this Jemma.

Love?

No, no, of course not. I just love being around her. She's smart and fun and spontaneous, and life hasn't always been easy for her. It makes me want to help her, take care of her. Not that she can't take care of herself and she's doing such a great job with Emma. I snort out a laugh. For the first time in a long time, anger and hate aren't driving me, and my father's hurt is fading into the background in my brain. How can I be thinking about past pain when there are just so many other things to be thinking about?

Indifference, yeah, I kind of like that.

Do you though, Kace? Do you really not want to feel anything at all for your father?

"Everything okay, Kace?" Jemma asks, as I snort for no apparent reason.

I glance around. "Did you hear that?"

She follows my gaze, and stares out into the Shelburne Harbor. "What?"

"I don't know it sounded like a whistling sound, or howling." I consider it for a second longer. "Maybe like putting a shell to your ear. That kind of sound."

"Oh, that. It's nothing," she says and hurries off again. Why is her body shaking? Is she laughing?

"Hey." I rush to catch up to her, and love the big smile on her face. I eye her suspiciously. "What's going on?"

"I'll explain once we're inside. Our food is getting cold."

We reach the tall, tapered wooden lighthouse, and I see the big lock on the door. "How are we getting in?"

"Follow me." She circles it, and grips a panel, easily pulling it off. She gives me a warning glare. "Tell no one."

"Who am I going to tell?" I follow her in and she puts the panel back in place. "What happens if we get caught?"

"We won't. I've spent a lot of time in this lighthouse. It was my go-to place."

"For reading?" I ask, curious about her.

"Yes, and for when I just needed some quiet time."

"We're in Shelburne, everywhere is quiet time," I joke and dip my head, my gaze scanning her face. "But seriously, am I invading your secret, quiet spot?"

"Actually, no." She cocks her head and smiles. "It's something I want to share with you."

My heart does a stupid little tumble, but the truth is, I like that she's sharing this, and parts of her past that were painful, with me. Nothing about us is pretend right now, and I like it. Maybe a little too much. Who knows what will happen after we talk to Krista. Maybe she'll come running back for the baby. While that's the best thing, it also means Jemma can move back to the sorority. Damned if that doesn't leave me feeling a little hollow inside.

What the hell is happening to me?

18

JEMMA

"**F**ollow me," I say to Kace as I begin to climb the winding stairs leading to the turret at the top. I hold onto the metal rail and glance at him over my shoulder. "Do you need help with the bags?"

"Not the first time I've climbed stairs," he shoots back, and I laugh at his witty comeback.

"I'm sure you haven't climbed twisty ones like these before."

"I'll be fine, Jemma," he grouches and gives my ass a little tap to set me into motion, but holy hell, the second his hand connects with my backside, it takes me back to our talk about spankings.

I gulp and grow breathless as we ascend, and it's not from the steep climb. I've done it numerous times. No, it's from visualizing his big palm coming down on my backside. Would I like that? Oh God, it's possible I would. As we near the top, I check on him again. He's tight on my heels and I'm surprised he's not even breathless. Then again, he's in top notch shape, and I very much appreciate the work he puts into staying that way. All this fried food is going to play havoc with his diet.

Ah, but you're going to work it off, right, Jemma?

My body warms at the thought and I lift the latch to step out onto the red upper deck. I lift my face to the wind and breathe in the ocean, a sense of peace coming over me the way it always does when I come up here. Kace moves in behind me, his big, warm body close to mine in the tight space. I love everything about this.

"I hope you're not afraid of heights," I say, my voice coming out a little raspy. "I probably should have checked first."

He glances over my head at the wide expanse of harbor. "I'm not, and Jesus, this is amazing. No wonder you spent so much time up here."

I take in the childlike enthusiasm shining in his eyes as he turns to absorb the beauty around us. I love how he can see what I can feel in this spot. "Right," I say, my voice low and wistful. Catching me by surprise, he bends and kisses me, a long leisurely kiss full of warmth and happiness—if a kiss can actually hold happiness.

"Thanks for bringing me here," he says as he inches back, and I stare up at him, breathless, my hands still on his broad shoulders. "It's one of the nicest places I've ever been. I'm so glad we broke in," he teases.

I beam, thrilled that he likes it. I walk to the side of the light-house that overlooks the harbor, and not the sandy shore. Up here, where it's private, it's like nothing exists, except the two of us and while we have problems to figure out, tonight, atop this gorgeous lighthouse, it's easy to let the world melt away, for a little while anyway. I drop down, rest my back on the wooden slats and stretch my legs out.

I pat the deck, wanting him close. "Come, sit."

He drops down beside me and when he stretches his legs out, his feet dangle over the side. He lets loose a long breath. "Sis would love it here."

I love how he thinks about Brynn. "Let's send her a picture."

He sets the paper bags down and reaches into his coat. "Where is my damn phone?"

"What is it with you and your phone?"

He searches his other pocket, but his hand comes out empty. "I don't know. When did I have it last?"

"I'm not sure. It's probably in your bag back home." I pull mine out and punch in my code. "Use mine, and I can airdrop them to you later." He holds my phone out and snaps a bunch of pictures, then turns the camera and takes a couple of us.

He hands it back. "I'll send them to Brynn," I say. "You want to get our food out?"

I shoot off the pictures as he delves into the bags, handing me a water bottle and setting his beside his thigh. "This looks so good." He places the cardboard container with the fish and chips on my lap, and does the same with his seafood platter. "Where do I even start?"

"With the scallops, of course."

I tear open a ketchup package and drown my food. "Are you going to have some fish and chips with that ketchup?" he teases.

"Stop."

He holds a scallop out to me. "Here."

I don't want to eat his food, but scallops, yum. "You sure?"

"Open," he commands in a soft voice that sends shivers through my body.

"Bossy."

"Open." I open my mouth and moan as he slides the scallop in. "That good, huh?"

"See for yourself." He plops one into his mouth and his eyes go wide as he stares at me, like he'd just won the lottery.

"Jesus, Jem. That's the best scallop I've ever had."

"Everything is better when you eat it outdoors."

"I think what you really mean to say is everything is better deep fried," he corrects and we both laugh.

"Truth." We take in the views and sit in comfortable silence, our legs touching every now and then as we eat.

After a while, he asks, "Do you miss it here?"

"I like the city. I'm enjoying my classes."

"That's a no?"

"I miss places like this, but I was happy to get out of Buttfuck nowhere where everyone knows you."

"Maybe it's nice to start new, huh? No one putting you in a box." My gaze moves over his face, and there's a new kind of softness there, and maybe even something that resembles understanding. "I move to Edmonton next year. Big city. A lot bigger than Halifax."

"Are you excited?"

"Yeah, I enjoyed it when I went to camp there." A moment of silence is followed by, "I'll miss Sis, and Mom and...people."

"People?" I laugh. "They have people in Edmonton."

He nudges me with his leg. "You know what I mean."

"Yeah, people. We all need people." I think about Alison. I miss her, but I'm not even sure she likes who I've become after I decided to change to be able to fit in with the popular crowd. "You'll make friends fast," I tell him. "You'll have your teammates too."

"Brynn said she'd come visit." He tosses a crispy French fry into his mouth, and it crunches as he chews. "Maybe you could come too." He gives a casual shrug, but nothing about this feels casual. It feels intimate, and nice. "If you're interested in seeing Edmonton, I mean."

Did he just ask me to visit him in Edmonton?

I try for casual and say, "Yeah, that would be fun." Although I have no idea where Emma will be then. But I promised not to worry about things tonight.

"Did you hear that?" A haunted look comes over his face as he turns to the right, craning his neck, trying to see around the turret. "There it is again."

I listen to the howling sounds swirling around us. "Oh that."

"Tell me what that is." He eyes me. "You know, don't you?"

"Yes, but I'm not sure I want to tell you." I make a hissing sound, to add to the drama. "I know you're afraid of haunted houses."

"Shit, Jem. Is this lighthouse haunted?"

Ohmigod, could he be any more adorable than he is right now?

I cringe, and crinkle my nose for added effect. "I'm afraid so."

He shifts closer to me. "Like, it has a ghost?" I don't answer, I just open my eyes wide and he continues with, "A ghost lives here?"

I take in the worry in his big, dark eyes. How can a man, as big and strong and powerful and protective as he is, be afraid of ghosts?

"Legend has it, one night, long ago a woman waited in this lighthouse for her husband to return home from the seas. It was dark and foggy, and she paced for hours. When the ship never returned, she stayed in this lighthouse, and eventually died here. Now, on nights when the water is calm like this, her cries of sorrow can be heard for miles."

Eyes as big as saucers, he says, "No way."

"No, Kace. No way." I laugh. "It's just a legend. I don't think it's true."

He relaxes a bit. "What's making that sound then?"

"Look over at the dock over there." I point. "It's probably just breaking waves."

"Then why are you telling scary stories?" he accuses, looking like a sullen child.

"Storyteller at heart." I throw my hands up. "What can I say?"

"You tell stories like that to children and you'll be out of a job."

I wave my hand. "Pfft, kids love scary stories. So, Edmonton," I begin, bringing the conversation back to his big move, a little excited that he asked me to visit and unable to stop playing that scenario out in my brain. I uncap my water and take a long drink. "You're going to get to see a lot of places in the NHL."

"I'm going to get to see a lot of locker rooms and ice rinks," he corrects, with a smile. "Halifax will still be my home base, though."

"During the off season?"

"Yeah, I'll always come back. Are you going to stay in the city?"

"I don't know. If I become a big, well-known author, I might have to move to Hollywood or New York or somewhere where famous people go and tour and sip champagne and wear feather boas." He knows I'm teasing because I can't keep the goofy grin from my face.

"Well, I'll have to go with you. If I'm illustrating, I'll have to go on tour, too. I'm not wearing a feather boa, though."

"No, I think you would be so adorable in one. Pink, maybe. That might be your color."

"Pink, my favorite color," he says, something in his voice changing, deepening, as he places his empty container back in the brown paper bag and takes a big drink. Why do I get the feeling we're no longer talking about boas? I swallow the last of my food and wash it down with a drink as he gazes at me, a new kind of hunger in his eyes.

"Do you have any idea how much I want to push you up against these wooden slats and fuck you right now?"

All air leaves my lungs. "I...we just ate. Don't we have to wait like twenty minutes or something?" What am I even saying? I want this, but we're outside, and it's so risky...so exciting.

That brings on a laugh. "We're not going swimming, babe. We're going to have sex, and I swear to God, if you make me wait another twenty minutes, I might throw myself off this lighthouse."

"Well, I can't have that. I need a ride home tomorrow. Unless, you know, you want to give me your car keys."

"There's something I want to give you, Jem, and in a way, you can ride it."

"Look at you. I'm the writer, but you're the one who has a way with words."

He laughs, finishes off the water in his bottle and pushes to his feet. That's when I realize if I go up on my knees, I'd be face to face with the growing dragon between his legs, or rather, goose neck.

Deciding to do just that, I shift, and his growl curls around me. "What the fuck," he grumbles, as I drag his zipper down and slip the button through the hole. He grips on to the wooden rail behind him as I tug on his pants and free his engorged cock.

"If you jumped, I don't think you would have drowned."

"No?"

"This..." I say, taking his elongated cock into my hand. "This wood would have kept you afloat."

"Jesus, Jemma."

"Not funny?" I ask, as I lick his crown, and he groans.

"I might find it funny later. Right now, I'm fucking hurting."

"Is this what you're hurting for?" I lean into him, and take his cock all the way to the back of my throat, and his hand goes to the back of my head. He follows the motion as I move back and forth, pleasuring him with my mouth and loving the way he's coming unglued under my ministrations.

I breathe in the scent of his skin, as his body begins to shake. "Babe," he grunts. "Babe." He twirls my hair around his fist and I glance up at him, meeting his dark eyes as they watch me take him to the back of my throat. He grows thicker in my mouth, and I lap at the pre-cum dripping from his tip. So tangy and delicious. Who knew I'd like it so much?

"Mmm, I love the taste of you."

"Fuck me." I don't even recognize his voice as he curses. He tugs on my shoulder. "I need you to stop."

Ignoring him, I take him deeper than I have yet, and hold my breath as he slips into my throat. "Jem," he moans, my name garbled and labored. "I can't…"

He tugs me off him and pulls me to my feet. His breath is hot on my face as he struggles to fill his lungs. "Oh, sorry," I tease. "You wanted me to stop?"

"You know I did." He grips me, and turns me until my hips are pressed against the wooden slats and the view of the harbor is laid out in front of me. He gives my ass a little slap. "You chose to ignore me." I gasp and he puts his mouth near my ear.

"Who me?"

"Don't play innocent." He slaps my ass again and I yelp. He puts his big palm on my throat and pulls my head back until it's extended. It's damn sexy. "I nearly came down your throat."

"Maybe I would have liked that."

"Yeah, but then I'd never get my cock in here." He dips his hands into my pants and slides into my damp panties, running the rough pad of his thumb over my slick clit. "Seems to me, you really want me in here."

"I do, I do."

His chuckle reverberates through me as he groans and pushes a thick finger inside me. "Oh my God, that feels so good." I rock against him, and grind as I jam his hand between my body and the wooden slats. He fingers me and I grow wetter, needier. A keening cry catches in my throat.

The next thing I know, my yoga pants are at my knees and he's standing behind me putting on a condom. I take a gulping breath and hold on as he slides his thick cock inside me, his thrust wringing a cry of pleasure from my lungs.

He leans over me, his chest to my back as he puts one arm around my waist and holds on. My God, I'll never look at this lighthouse the same way again, and I kind of like that. I spot a boat in the distance, and I really hope they don't have binoculars.

"Babe," he whispers against the back of my neck, his lips nuzzling me. I move against him as he goes still. "Yeah, that's it. Ride me."

He gives the side of my ass a light slap, and I can't believe how much I love that. I move quicker, chasing my orgasm as he lowers his hand and runs his thumb over my clit.

"Kace," I murmur, as pleasure builds, coming to a peak. My body breaks around his cock, and a hard tremble goes through me as I climax. His hands move to my hips and he drives in deep, his cock pulsing hard inside me.

"Babe…"

He breathes hard against my neck, and I rest my arms on the wooden slats and lay my head down on top of them. His big fingers trail over my back as he pulls out and I whimper at the loss. I grow sleepy as he removes the condom, and then he's behind me again, whispering in my ear.

"You're not nearly as wet as you're going to get."

Since my brain is still on hiatus, I can't quite understand what he's saying. My thighs quiver, as my release drips down my legs and tickles. "Why would I get wetter?" I murmur. Chuckling he lifts my head, and I look out over the water. "Oh, shit."

19

KACE

I stand on the edge of the river casting my line out, as I watch the rushing water pull my bobber out deeper. The morning air is warm and it's so quiet here in the middle of nowhere, I could practically hear Jemma's dream last night. Not that I slept with her. That's a no-no in her parents household and I totally respect that. You'd think that after sex at the top of the lighthouse I'd have been sated, and in a way, I was, sexually at least. The truth is, I wanted to hold her again, wanted her beside me when I fell asleep and when I woke.

I chuckle as I think about last night. After we had a cold swim to shore in our clothes, getting in my car soaking wet, we hurried back to her place. Her parents had a good laugh at the pathetic sight we made, and after a warm shower, I crashed in her sister's room. I still can't believe we lost track of time and the tide started coming in. Nevertheless, it was a lot of fun and I'd do it again in a heartbeat.

Sitting beside me on the grassy embankment, Jemma exhales slowly, and I turn to her, taking pleasure in spending quiet time with her. "Bored?"

As she lowers her pen, a mixture of emotions play across her pretty face. While I've been fishing, she's been busy writing, but I know her mind is on other things.

"No, just thinking about talking to Krista later. I've got a giant knot in my stomach." She's definitely dealing with a lot and I wish there was more I could do to help her. "Are you having fun?" she asks and plasters on a smile. "Still haven't caught anything, I see. Some fisherman you are."

I chuckle at that despite the wave of nostalgia and sadness washing over me. "It's been a long time since I've been fishing."

"I'm sorry, Kace. I didn't mean—"

"No, it's okay." I frown and glance into the water, the weight of old memories haunting me. "I stopped fishing after Dad...I guess I hated doing anything that reminded me of him, reminded me that we weren't enough for him." She opens her mouth and I cut her off and I quickly shift my focus. "I know, it's him, not me." I grin at her, and thread my fingers through hers. "I like making new memories with you, Jem."

She gives me a big smile, leans over and presses her lips to mine. "I'm glad." A small chuckle rumbles in her throat. "We made some good memories last night at the lighthouse."

"That poor old lighthouse." I briefly close my eyes and shake my head. "The things it had to endure." She laughs. "And if it really is haunted, we might have frightened the ghost away."

"Unless she's a voyeuristic ghost. Then she'll never leave, waiting for us to come back."

"Let's do it," I blurt out, only half teasing.

"While that sounds amazing, can I get a rain check?"

I nod in agreement, although I'm not sure I'll ever be coming back to Shelburne with her. I'm headed to Edmonton at the end of the school year. We don't have a chance at a future, do we? Is that what I want? What does she want? I drop back onto the grassy embankment and stare at the sky, an ache in my chest. Jemma's phone pings, interrupting the quiet, and she reaches for it.

"It's a pic of Brynn and Emma, both wearing daisy sunglasses." She falls back beside me and holds the phone up for me to see.

A strange sense of longing for my new, found family brings a smile to my face. Do I want a family of my own? After what my father did to us, I swore I would never get married. "They're having fun."

"I still can't believe any of this is happening."

I put my arm around her and bring her to my chest. "Hopefully we'll get some answers today." We both fall silent, listening to the rushing water and the birds chirping in the trees around us. I close my eyes, and just breathe. "Are you sorry you missed the party last night?" I eventually ask.

She chuckles. "I didn't miss any party, Kace." I laugh at that.

"We were the party," I tease.

"Can I ask you a question?"

I glance at her. "Sure."

"Did you ever...meet your father's other family? Does he have kids your age?"

"I saw them once. They were all out at a restaurant. He has two boys, younger than Brynn. I went the other way."

"Do they know about you?"

"I don't know. Probably."

"Are you curious about them?" She shifts, puts her hand on my chest, and rests her chin on it. "I bet they'd love to meet their big brother who's going to play for Edmonton next year."

"I might be a little curious about them, I guess. What my father did wasn't their fault, and they're just as much victims as Brynn and I were. I wonder if they play hockey." I go quiet for a moment as she watches me. "Dad still tries to call me. I don't answer. Every now and then, Brynn fills me in on things happening in his life, and I'm sure she fills him in on things happening in mine."

"I can understand not answering his calls. But, like I said before, holding on to all that hate, it's hard, Kace."

"I—"

"I'm not saying you have to forgive him, or even that you should. Don't get me wrong. I just don't like seeing you hurting. Maybe meeting your brothers would help you find some sense in all this and pave a way to healing."

I swallow against a tight throat. "In the end, he chose them."

"Right, and you have choices too. Like finding a way forward without carrying around all this anger and hurt." She pokes me. "It's your responsibility to heal, Kace."

She's not wrong. I shake my head and grin at her. "Are you sure you're a literature student and not a psychology major?"

"My father," she says and throws a hand up. "I listened to a lot of his lectures over the years, about love, forgiveness, and healing."

I bend forward and kiss her, this new closeness between us wrapping around me and hugging tight. "I like you like this, Jem. Real and honest." She tightens in my arms. "The girls would have liked you like this too, you know."

A sad, tortured moan whispers from her throat. "Kace...I..." I brush her hair back and take in the tears forming in her eyes.

"You never had to pretend. Not with me or anyone."

"You don't understand. You were popular, and had lots of friends. I just wanted to be accepted, to fit in." She pulls back, and I sense her struggles. "If you say anything..." She sniffs. "What if they hate me for pretending? I don't want to be a victim, or bullied. My sister..."

"Hey, it's okay." I pull her back to me and hug her. "I just want you to be happy."

"I'm happy, here with you."

"I'm happy here with you too." I hold her to me, and her racing heart pounds against my chest. I smooth her hair down and she melts into me. I'm not sure what will happen when we go back. Will she fall back into her role of puck bunny, or will she come to understand that she has value and worth just the way she is, and if people can't see that, then are they really the friends she wants?

After a long while, she shifts. "We should get back. It's nearing two." She stands and I sit up, grab the rod and reel in the line. "Sorry all that fishing was a bust. I thought you might have caught something, even something small."

I push to my feet, hook my finger into the band of her yoga pants and pull her to me. "Look at that, looks like I caught something after all."

She grins and goes up on her toes to kiss me. "Yeah, so what are you going to do now that you caught me?"

"How about anything I want?"

"How about a rain check on that?"

I glance up at the blue, cloudless sky. "Please rain."

She gives me a shove and laughs. "Let's get out of here." I pick up the tackle box and follow her out to the clearing where we parked. I drop the gear in the trunk, and notice the tightness about her as I slide in next to her.

Her smile is a bit wobbly as she aims it my way and I take her hand in mine and give it a kiss. "It's going to be okay."

I start the car and we head back to her home. When we reach her driveway, her parents' car is there. I kill the ignition and open my door, but Jemma doesn't move. "Coming?"

She shifts uncomfortably. "Maybe I shouldn't surprise her like this."

"She's not answering your calls and you need to talk to her. I don't see any other way. At some point, she has to expect that you'd talk to your parents."

"Maybe I should have flown to Montreal to see her. I can't really talk about this with my parents in the room."

I eye her. She's really second guessing her own decisions suddenly. "Flying to Montreal would be a surprise too, wouldn't it? And you can gauge her reaction in front of your parents. Maybe this is an opportunity to open up and tell your parents what's going on. They're good people, Jemma. They'll be there for her. I'm sure of it."

"I'm sure of it too. They'll be hurt at first that she didn't come to them, and left her baby with me. But hiding the truth is never the answer." Her face pales a bit as she says that, because that's what she's been doing since moving to the city.

"This could be the help she needs."

"I just...don't know."

I stand there, and wait for her to decide, even though I think she has to have a conversation with her sister and this seems to be the only way. We came here for information, and this is her chance. Why the sudden change of heart?

She could have had her over the summer, and doesn't want anyone to know it's her baby.

No, no, no. That is crazy. She's not hedging because the baby is actually hers. She's just worried about her sister.

"Jemma," her mother calls out from the door. "Hurry, Krista is about to call."

When she still doesn't move, I touch her lightly. "Jem?"

"Yeah, okay." She hurries from the car and I empty the trunk, leaving the fishing gear at the front door, before heading inside. Jemma is standing there waiting for me. "You should uh...maybe wait in the living room."

She doesn't want me to hear, and I suppose that's fair. This doesn't involve me. Not really. Okay, maybe a little since she's staying with me and I'm helping. Jesus, why is this bothering me. Oh, probably because it feels like she's shutting me out, that I'm not needed, and it's a familiar feeling that I don't like. Hell, I was never enough for my father, so how could I be enough for anyone. I shut that thought down. That's not what's going on here.

"Okay, sure." I walk into the living room, plunk down on the sofa and reach for the remote. I flick on some old sitcom and numbly stare at it.

After a few minutes, I stand up and head to the bathroom, but as I walk down the hall, I can't help but hear the conversation happening just a few feet away in the kitchen. What I overhear has my steps slowing and my heart racing. It appears Krista is absolutely thrilled that Jemma is in on the call and she's apologizing profusely, not for dropping a baby off at her doorstep, but for not returning her calls. Apparently, she's been swamped with schoolwork and her thesis. I glance into the kitchen and what I see is a perfectly happy family. Christ, either her sister is a great actress, great at pretending, or the baby really isn't hers.

What the hell is going on here?

JEMMA

I steal a glance at Kace as we approach the city. "Are you okay? You seem like you have something on your mind?" I ask him—something other than what I'd told him about my conversation with Krista. Maybe he's thinking about hockey, or Edmonton, or how we talked about him visiting his brothers.

"Yeah, good." He scrubs his face. "I'm having a hard time wrapping my brain around what you told me about Krista. She really acted like nothing was out of the ordinary?" I nod. "Are you sure it was your sister who left Emma, or maybe it was someone else, and they just pretended it was Krista's baby, knowing you'd take care of her."

Unease works its way through my body. "I can understand why you'd consider that scenario. I'm grasping for answers too." I frown and search my brain for answers. "Her behavior was so strange, which really leads me to believe something is really wrong."

"But do you think Emma is hers?"

"You've seen Emma, and you saw pictures of my sister. They look a lot alike."

"She looks a lot like you too."

I eye him as he clenches down on his jaw, and stares straight ahead. I'm not exactly sure what he's trying to say, but I answer with, "Krista and I look a lot alike. You said so yourself."

"Yeah, that's true." His shoulders relax slightly. "It's just all so confusing."

"I'm guessing she's been avoiding video chatting with my parents because she was trying to hide the pregnancy, and then nothing the last month, because she's not been well."

"You said she sounded well."

"Yeah, I know. It's all messed up." I play with my zipper. "Maybe I really should fly to Montreal." I crinkle my nose as I consider the logistics. "No, I can't do that. I don't want to take Emma on that flight."

"Sis and I can watch her, if you think you should go. You have to figure this out, or you're going to end up raising Emma yourself, and eventually you'll have to explain that to your parents anyway, right?"

He drives through the city and it's a little after dinner time by the time we pull into his driveway. "Home sweet home," I say, wanting to lighten the tension inside him.

"Yeah," is all he says and kills the ignition. I glance at the front window as the curtain moves back and find Brynn standing there with Emma. She has Emma's hand in hers and is waving to us with it. My heart pinches tight. What will become of Emma if Krista refuses to care for her? I'm really not equipped for this and I can't stay at Kace's forever. None of this is right and I don't know what the solution is.

I step from the car as Kace gets our bags, and I follow him to the front door. Brynn opens it, a hopeful look on her face. While we were driving I'd phoned her to let her know how things went, but maybe she thinks something new developed.

"Nothing," I say. "Thank you again for watching Emma." I reach for Peanut, and Brynn hands her over.

"She was an angel." She stifles a yawn. "We had fun, didn't we, Emma?" Emma drools a little, and Brynn produces a tissue from her pocket and wipes it away. "I made some pasta for you guys. It's in the fridge. Emma's had her dinner already."

"Thanks, sis. Much appreciated," Kace tells her while he pulls her in for a hug.

"I'm going to take off." She shoves her laptop into her back-pack. "I have some reading to do before class tomorrow."

I nod. I'll be doing some serious cramming this week, after spending the whole weekend away. Will I ever get caught up?

"I'll drive you," Kace offers.

She waves her phone. "Did you forget I like to use the campus security app?"

"I can walk you," Sebastian says, coming down the stairs. At least he's fully dressed. He wags his brows. "I'm on my way to the sorority anyway."

"Fine." Brynn gives in reluctantly and snatches her coat from the closet. She shoulders her backpack. I note the look Kace casts Sebastian's way as he heads to the door with his sister. He clearly doesn't like the idea of the two of them together.

"Wait, I have to get my overnight bag." She darts upstairs, leaving the three of us in the hall.

Sebastian casts me a glance. "Unless of course you want to hang out tonight. I can stay home."

"No, I have Emma," I say, jutting my hip out as I slip back into bunny mode, like I tend to do around the hockey players. Shit. I take a fast look at Kace and he's eyeing me.

"So did you find your sister?" Sebastian asks. "Is she coming for her baby?"

"We're working on it," Kace answers, his voice tight as he talks between clenched teeth.

"Good. I'll be glad when things get back to normal, baby." He gives me a wink and it sort of makes me nauseous. Why did I ever cozy up with him, or want to be the kind of girl the guys hook up with when the mood hits? He pouts like a child. "I'm losing my patience."

From the look on Kace's face, it looks more like Sebastian is going to lose his front teeth.

Sebastian ignores it and says, "If you want to catch up later, just text me, or if it's really late, you know how to find my room."

I open my mouth to tell him that's not going to happen when Brynn comes racing back down the stairs, and says, "Let's go."

They head outside, and Kace turns around. "I'll go heat us up some pasta," he says and I stare at his broad back as he walks down the hallway. He clearly has a lot on his mind, but he knows I'm not going to be sneaking into Sebastian's room, right? Maybe he was hoping our baby issue would be solved and he'd have his place back to himself.

I snuggle Emma and carry her to the kitchen. I put her in her little seat. "How can I help?"

He puts a container in the microwave and hits a couple of buttons. "Want to grab the plates?"

Since he put them on a lower shelf, it's much easier for me to get them. I reach into the cupboard, and before I can turn, he's pressing against me, his hard body pinning me to the counter. I take a fast breath.

"You okay, Jem?" he asks, his mouth close to my ear.

"I...I don't know. Should I go?"

"Hey." He turns me, puts his thumb under my chin and lifts it, until our eyes meet. "I told you, you and Emma are welcome here. What's going on with you?"

"I just...I know the rumors, Kace."

"People like to talk." His gaze moves over my face. "As long as you're honest with me."

"I am. I have been." He arches a brow. "Well, I am now."

He smiles, dips his head and plants a soft kiss onto my mouth. The microwave beeps, and he says, "Let's eat and then maybe watch a movie."

"I should be studying."

"Yeah, me too. How about we take tonight off and really dig in this week?"

"Okay." He grabs a dish towel, and takes the big container of pasta from the microwave, and I plate it up for us. "I'll check out flights to Montreal for next weekend."

"I can't go with you," he tells me.

"I know. It's okay. You don't need to go. We're monopolizing enough of your time and space as it is."

"I would go Jemma but I have a game. Maybe Brynn can go to support you."

"I can do this on my own. It might be easier facing Krista that way. Besides, I need to ask Brynn to watch Emma again. You can't. You have a game."

"Okay, babe." He kisses me and picks up the plates to put them on the table. "Did you have fun with Aunty Brynn, Peanut?" he asks Emma.

Aunty Brynn?

It's kind of crazy really, how he treats Emma, but after learning more about him, it's understandable and commendable, and a part of me could fall for a guy like him. I nearly snort out a laugh. A part of me. Jeez, I'm pretty sure all of me could fall for a guy like that, if I haven't already done so, which would be so damn stupid of me.

We dig into the pasta, and Emma gurgles and chews on her teething ring. "Your parents would really love her," he says out of nowhere, a wistful look on his face.

"I think they would too." I shrug. "I just can't say anything, not yet, anyhow." He nods and eats more pasta. "If you want to go practice or hang out somewhere else, Emma and I are fine."

"I have practice tomorrow, then I work for a couple of hours in the afternoon at the coffee shop. I'd kind of just like to take it easy." He loads up his fork and is about to take a bite but stops. A strange expression moves over his face and I can't tell if it's anger, or jealousy. "Unless you want me out of here. Did you want me out of here?"

"No, of course not."

"Good, because a quiet night in sounds nice, really."

We go back to eating our delicious pasta, and while my life is a chaotic mess right now and I have no idea what's going to happen, a new sense of calm comes over me. I feel safe when I'm with Kace.

We finish eating, and he stands and says, "If you want to go find something for us to watch, I'll clean up here."

"Oh, chick flick it is then." I walk my plate to the counter.

He shakes his head and grumbles. "There's probably a game on we can watch."

"Oh, sure," I say, pretending that's something I might enjoy. Honestly, I don't dislike hockey, but I don't love it either. One thing I do enjoy is watching Kace play and maybe it wouldn't hurt to understand the plays.

"Hey, I'm kidding." He turns to me and we both lean against the counter facing each other. His head dips and there's a seriousness about him when he adds, "You don't need to pretend with me, remember."

I relax. "I'm sorry. If you want to watch a game, we can. Maybe you can teach me some things, so I at least know why I'm screaming at the ref or cheering for the team."

"You cheer when we get a goal."

"People cheer for other things too. Plays I don't quite understand."

"Okay, I can teach you some things, but tonight, the movie choice is yours."

"Do you like all sports?" I ask, not quite ready to move away from him. I like the warmth of his body, this easy conversation we're having. "Or just hockey?"

"I like all sports. Why, do you like something better than hockey?" He eyes me like that had better not be true.

"I'm not much into sports, to be honest. I was into gymnastics when I was younger, but it wasn't for me."

He arches a brow. "Gymnastics, huh. You've got twisty moves I don't know about."

That makes me laugh. "Sorry to disappoint. No twisty moves that won't land me in traction." I shrug. "I watch the Olympics. I like the downhill skiing, and I would watch skating, but..." He arches a brow. "I get so stressed out, Kace. I can't even breathe when they start spinning and when the female skater gets tossed in the air, I feel ill."

"I don't love it either. I think it's more dangerous than hockey."

That gives me pause and something inside me tightens. "Have you ever been badly hurt?"

"Concussion once, years ago."

I consider that. "I'd hate for you to get hurt. My God, I can't imagine the stress the girlfriends and wives must feel every time their loved one steps on the ice."

He puts his hands on my arms, a small grin on his face. "Worried about me, Jem?"

"Of course." I lean closer and breathe him in. "I don't want anything to interfere with your career. I know it's important to you." I go up on my toes and kiss him, and teasingly add, "Also, Emma needs a male role model."

He frowns and pulls me against his body, placing a kiss on the top of my head. "She needs a real father in her life."

We stay like that for a while, until Emma starts fussing. "I'd better go check her diaper, and find us something to watch."

He slides his hand down my back and gives my backside a little slap to set me into motion. I yelp. "Are you trying to turn me on?"

He chuckles. "Maybe."

I laugh and gather up Emma and take her upstairs to change her and wash her up for bed. By the time I make it back downstairs, the dishwasher is running and Kace is plunking himself down on the sofa. He holds his arms out and takes Emma from me, passing over the remote.

Since I already know what I want to watch, something I think that will make us both happy, I flick through the apps, and find what I was searching for.

I turn to Kace to see his reaction, but honest to God, when I see his head bent, smiling as he plays with little Emma's fingers, boom...pregnant. I have never in my life seen anything so adorable before. As if sensing me watching his head lifts.

"Find something?"

Since I'm not sure I can talk, I nod toward the TV, and he grins. "Friday night football series from years ago. You like all sports and I like—"

"Let me guess, Taylor Kade."

I chuckle. "Yeah."

He shakes his head and laughs with me. "Figures."

"Come on," I begin, completely animated. "Have you seen him in his football gear?"

"Okay, Jem, I get it."

"If you want to know the truth, you look better in your gear."

"Oh, sure. You're just saying that because I'm helping you out."

"Believe what you want, but it's true." I wiggle against the sofa cushion. "Now shh, Taylor is on."

He rolls his eyes at me, and for the next couple of hours we watch TV, eat some popcorn, and nuzzle a sleeping Emma. It's late by the time we finally make it upstairs, and I suggest he sleep alone, as he has an early morning and Emma is beginning to fuss.

He seemed a little reluctant, and maybe even concerned at first, but then he concedes. Like I said before, I don't want anything coming between him and his career.

I fall into a restless sleep, and wake around midnight to a fussing Emma. "Hey, Peanut," I whisper and take her into my arms. "Are you hungry?"

I quietly walk downstairs, not wanting to wake the guys up. In the kitchen, I turn on the soft light over the stove. I set Emma in her seat and give her a soother while I get her bottle ready. She settles a bit, and I open the fridge. I wince as the bright light hits my eyes, and I'm left blinded when I close the fridge and turn to find a figure behind me.

"Hey," I murmur softly. "Sorry, I didn't mean to wake you. But I did miss your arms around me."

I step into Kace, simply wanting to feel his body next to mine, and when his hands go around me, and I breathe him in, I instantly realize my mistake. The kitchen light flicks on, and I jump back when I find Sebastian grinning down at me, his erection pressing against me as Kace glares at me with hard eyes from the doorway.

21

KACE

The puck lands on the tip of my stick, and with only seconds before the buzzer goes off, I shoot...and score. The crowd goes crazy and the guys all storm me as we win the game. We all cheer and I notice Sebastian hovering around the circle of players.

Jemma explained to me that she thought Sebastian was me in the kitchen, and while I believed her, I think it really pissed Sebastian off, because he's jealous. While he might be into sharing, I'm not, and that's obviously put a strain between us. I need to tread carefully, though. He pays half the rent too, and if he wants Jemma and the baby out, he has every right to demand it.

Maybe if I accepted my father's money, I could move out and get a place of my own. Wow, now there's a thought I never had before. Being with Jemma has softened my hate, and maybe that's not a bad thing. I automatically glance up, searching for her in the stands, but then remember she's at home with Emma. I spot Brynn and she waves wildly. Maybe I should talk to Brynn about my father and half-brothers.

We eventually make our way to the locker room to shower, and after a talk from Coach, we'll head out for nachos and beer. Except I don't want to go. I want to head back and have a quiet night in with Jemma. I note the way Sebastian is watching me as I walk back to the locker room to get dressed. I'm about to ask him if he has a problem, but he heads outside with a few of the other guys.

I eventually follow along and find Brynn and a few of her friends waiting for me. Sierra jumps on my back and we saunter toward the waterfront. I catch Brynn's eye and she gives me a questioning look, obviously picking up on my mood. "Later," I tell her quietly, and she nods.

Inside the pub, the music is playing and the crowd is lively, and I'm pretty sure I've outgrown all this. I grab a beer and reach for my phone to text Jemma. I wait a long time for her to answer. She's probably busy with Emma. I lift my head and glance around as the place fills up. A strange, uneasy sensation grips my gut when I search for Sebastian, and don't see him anywhere. My mind instantly goes to the worst-case scenario: he's with Jemma. Has she suddenly decided to choose him over me. Has she not been genuine with me all along?

I shove a nacho into my face, down my beer and shove that thought to the back of my mind. It's true, my father's betrayal has done a number on me, and maybe the only way I'll ever get past it is to go see him, and find a space in this world where I can breathe again. I just want to reach a point, where my father's actions no longer hurt. In order to have a life or move forward I need to find a way to heal, and really, it's up to me to heal myself, right? My happiness is in my own hands, not in the hands of others. Jesus, am I a hockey player or a damn therapist?

That thought makes me laugh, and I turn to see Brynn muscle her way through the crowd to sit beside me. "Hey, big bro."

"Sis," I respond.

She gives me a shoulder check. "You did good tonight."

"Thanks."

She pulls a cheesy nacho from the pile and holds it in front of her mouth. "So why aren't you celebrating?"

I exhale, and run my hand through my damp hair. "Do you see much of Dad?"

Her body stiffens, and her eyes widen. "Where is this coming from?" she asks, instead of answering my question.

"I guess I was wondering about our brothers." And maybe accepting his funding for the next semester, so I can get a place of my own, and spend more time with Jemma. I keep that part to myself.

"I see him." She pops the nacho into her mouth. "Not a lot, but I do see him."

I nod realizing that, and toy with my glass. "You see your brothers?"

She smiles. "Yes. I see *our* brothers." She pokes me. "But all they want to do is talk about you."

I swallow, and it hurts like a bitch. "They know about me?" Christ, I sound like I'm eating sliced hockey pucks, and not nachos.

"Of course, they do, Kace."

"They play hockey?" I have an odd little jolt of excitement in my chest.

"They do."

"Maybe I haven't been fair," I concede, a bit of the fight draining out of me. "Treating them poorly because of our father's actions. In a way, they were victims too, right?"

She nods in agreement. "They were. Do you want to know their names?"

"I think maybe I do." I never used to. Maybe that made it all too real, even though I knew it was real anyway.

"Luca and Lincoln. There both in high school now."

I shake my head. "Stupid names," I mutter, even though I don't mean it.

She laughs and then we both go silent, exchanging words with a look between us. "He hurt us, Kace. He chose them over us. I get that. Like you and Mom, I'm still struggling with it too. We all deal with things differently." She puts her hand over mine. "I don't think making our father suffer is in any way helping you or me."

"I don't want to be friends with the man."

"Me either."

"But...I don't want to hurt him as much as I use to either." She smiles and nods in understanding. "Are you doing okay?" I ask, and put my arm around her, to pull her in for a hug.

"The thing is, Kace, I had you growing up. You were everything a little girl needed. A brother and father figure, all in one. You didn't have that. I couldn't give you what you gave me." She swallows, and tears pool around the guilt in her eyes.

I hug her tighter. "Hey, I wasn't your responsibility."

"Yeah, but I wasn't yours either." I open my mouth and she puts her hand up to stop me. "Let's agree to disagree." I laugh at that, and my chest loosens. "Emma isn't your responsibility either," she says cautiously.

"I know. I just don't want her to ever feel..."

"I understand. Trust me, I get it. I just...I want you to be caring for her for the right reasons and I don't want you getting hurt, big brother."

"What are the right reasons, Brynn?"

"To lend a hand to someone you care for."

"Jemma is your friend, which makes her—"

"Nope," she blurts out, cutting me off. "I'm not buying that." I grip my glass and finish the last mouthful, not buying into my own bullshit either. But caring for someone and trusting them, well, those are the kinds of things that can rip you apart. With Jemma, the sweet girl who was simply looking for acceptance, maybe it's not so scary with her. "It's nice to see you trusting again," Brynn continues, cutting into my thoughts. "I know that's scary for you, but it's nice to see, Kace."

I go quiet. Does she even know the real Jemma like I do? Would she want the two of us together if she knew Jemma had been deceiving them all? As I debate on asking—I realize Jemma is fearful that they'll all hate her if they find out—my phone pings, and a picture of Jemma and Emma appears. Unable to help myself, I smile like the goddamn village idiot.

Sis nudges me. "Maybe you should get out of here." I nod and she slides from the bench to let me out. She touches my arm and I face her. "Kace."

"Yeah."

"When you want to go see them, I'll go with you, if you want."

I hug her to me and kiss the top of her head. "I'd like that." I spot Sebastian coming through the front door and his gaze lands on mine. He looks away, like he's still pissed, and I let my sister go. "Be good tonight."

"I'm always good," she tells me and makes a fist to nudge my jaw. "And if I get into trouble, I always have my big brother."

"Yeah, you do." With that she goes back to her friends, and I head outside. The night air is cool and I zip up my jacket as I hurry through the streets, anxious to get home to Jemma and Emma. What a cute little family. A chuckle catches in my throat. We're not a family, but right now it feels like we are. I used to worry that I'd turn out like my father. I'm not so sure I'm worried about that anymore. If I had a family at home, someone like the two girls there now, there's no way I'd want anyone or anything else.

My father was a complete asshole to do what he did. I shake my head. To think about what he had, and what he walked away from. It was his loss. I almost feel sorry for him. But I'm done feeling sorry, especially for myself. My father made his choices, and those are not the choices I would have made, so past mistakes are on him, not me, and maybe I am enough for someone. Truthfully why would I even care if I was enough for a man who could do something like that. I'm a good person, and not to sound egotistical, because I'm not, but I am good enough for someone who's kind and considerate. Someone who deserves Brynn and me in their lives.

I pick up the pace and as I approach the house, I spot Jemma pacing back and forth in the living room, bouncing Emma in her arms. My heart does a weird little jump at the sight, and I take the front steps quickly, putting my key into the lock, only to find the door open. Didn't I lock it when I left for the game?

"Hey," I say over a crying Emma, when I enter the living room. Jemma looks relieved to see me. "Were you out?"

"No," she replies quickly. "Why?"

"The door was unlocked. I thought I locked it." Was Sebastian here? An uneasy tightness knots my stomach and I hate it. I refuse to let past hurts resurface, right after I convinced myself I was enough for someone. I kick off my boots and shrug out of my coat.

"Let me help you with her." I take a wiggling, crying Emma from her and let my gaze race over Jemma's face. "You're tired."

"I'm okay," she answers and puts on a smile, but it doesn't reach her eyes.

"Why don't you go get some sleep? I'll feed Emma and get her ready for bed." She looks like she's about to protest, until I say, "Then, after I take care of Emma, I'll take care of you."

She draws her bottom lip between her teeth, a new brightness in her big eyes. "Okay." I give her a little tap on the ass to send her on her way and she hurries up the stairs.

"All right, Peanut. Let's get you settled." I hold Emma tight against my chest, and she snuggles into me, her tears subsiding a little. In the kitchen I fix her a bottle, and head back to the sofa. The shower turns on upstairs, and I flick the lights out and feed Emma in the dark. Once I'm done, I head upstairs to change her and settle her into her bed.

I walk back into my room, and a few minutes later, Jemma walks in, dressed in nothing but a towel. My heart thumps as I step up to her, place my hands on either side of her face and hold her still as I devour her mouth with a hunger I can't seem to sate.

She moans into my mouth and sags against me. I hold her to me and breathe her in as I walk backward, until I hit the bed. I turn her in my arms, and give her a nudge until she's sitting. She stares up at me, and there's something so sweet and needy in her eyes it tugs at the emotions I've always kept buried. Honestly, I'm losing myself in her, and I don't even want to fight it.

"Babe," I say quietly, and reach out to release the knot holding her towel to her gorgeous body.

"Yeah?"

"Tell me what you want."

She reaches for me, and tugs on my shirt. "I want you."

Yeah, okay, I'm falling for her.

"I want you too," I say, the words coming straight from my scarred heart.

While I've been nervous all week, with my upcoming trip to Montreal tomorrow, it's also been an amazing week with Kace. We've fallen into a routine of school, hockey, cooking, cleaning, caring for Emma, and falling into bed together every night. It's been bliss, and while I know it's going to come to an end, there's a part of me that doesn't want it to.

"What do you think of this?" Kace asks, and slides a piece of paper my way.

I stare at the cartoon drawing of a dinosaur and laugh at the accentuated eyes and nose. "Ohmigod, it's perfect." He gives me a big smile, clearly liking the compliment, and I turn my laptop to show him what I've been working on. "So, my main character needs friends, and I was thinking of a kitten, and a puppy, and even a dragon."

"I can try."

"They have to be really cute and shy characters, even the dragon."

He eyes me. "Dragons are not cute or shy."

"I know but my story is about a boy who pretends to be a dinosaur, because he's nervous on his first day of school, and scares all the kids. So, we have to make the friends in school look intimidated."

"Okay, let me try the kitten first."

I go back to my computer and play with the words on the screen. I should be going over the lectures from today, but this project we've been working on has been so much fun for both of us. I'll have to stay up late to work on my lectures, which means tomorrow, when I fly, I'll be tired. But that's okay. I don't want Kace tired, though. He's going to see his half-brothers this weekend. A burst of anxiousness careens through me. I really hope, for his sake, that the meeting turns out well, and brings him a sense of peace with everything that's happened.

As I write, I glance at Kace and take in the deep concentra-tion on his face. Could the man be any cuter?

"Why are you staring at me?" he asks without lifting his head.

"I was just thinking you were cute."

"Cute, huh? Like I'm some innocent character in your book? Some prehistoric creature you can move around and make do whatever you want?"

He's not saying it like it's a bad thing. I laugh at that. "Yeah." I poke his chest. "I'm going to model the dragon after my very own dragon." I lean in and kiss him and when my lips hit his, I realize what I'd just said. I break away and backtrack. "I don't mean you're mine. I just mean...well, we're playing house here."

He nods, and his shoulders tighten. Is he upset that I alluded that what was happening here was real, or is he upset that I clarified it wasn't?

Okay, clearly, I'm in deep here, deeper than I ever should have allowed, and will have to find a way to deal with real life when this is over. Do I go back to being puck bunny Jemma with all the friends, or do I back away and go back to being book nerd Jemma, who spent many hours alone, and only had one true friend?

Damn, I miss Alison.

She doesn't even know what is going on in my life. Just like I don't know what's going on in hers. Maybe I should call her. Would she even talk to me? Or would she turn her back on me, much like the girls in the sorority would if they ever found out I was a fraud.

"You okay?" Kace asks, and I lift my gaze to his.

"I was thinking about my friend Alison. I haven't talked to her in a long time."

"Give her a call."

If it was only that easy. "Yeah, I think I will." Honestly, I'm not sure I will. If I were her, I'd hate me.

Sebastian comes strolling into the warm kitchen—Kace lit the fireplace earlier—annoyance all over his face as Emma's cries comes through the baby monitor.

I jump up. "I'll get her."

"I thought she'd be gone by now," Sebastian mutters with a snarl. I walk toward the door and he stands in my way, blocking me.

"It'll be soon," Kace explains. "Jemma is going to see her sister this weekend, and get things straightened out."

Sebastian arches a hopeful brow. "Yeah?"

"Yes," I answer.

"Then things can get back to normal?" He has a suggestive look on his face that makes my skin crawl.

"I'll be moving back into the sorority, yes." If he thinks I'm going to cozy up to him again, that's not going to happen. Jeez, so much has happened over the last couple of weeks, I'm not even sure I can pull off puck bunny.

"So then, you and me—"

"If you'll excuse me," I say quickly, cutting him off. I don't want Kace thinking Sebastian and I had a past relationship, even though Sebastian seems to think otherwise. Maybe he did put something in my drink that night. Maybe he'd had something all planned out. Thank God Kace rescued me from that situation. Anger mars Sebastian's face and his eyes harden as he moves to the side to let me pass.

I hurry upstairs, and only hear the fridge open and close, no exchange of words between the guys. My stomach cramps. I'm coming between the two of them, and they're players on the same team who need to get along. A sense of panic overtakes me. I have to find answers, and as much as I don't want this living arrangement to end, it has to be over. The sooner the better.

"Hello, Peanut," I say and a smile lights up her sweet little face as I pull her to me. We're bonding, that's for sure, and giving her back won't be easy, for Emma or me. "Are you hungry again?" She gurgles and her fists go wild as I cradle her. "I take that as a yes."

I head back downstairs, hoping Sebastian is gone by the time I reach the kitchen. I enter and find the space empty. Kace isn't even at the table. I prepare Emma's bottle and walk into the living room to feed her. A yawn pulls at me, and that's when I decide I should get a good night's sleep and work on the plane tomorrow.

I close my eyes as Emma eats, and a short time later, the sound of Kace's voice pulls me awake. "Hey, you should get some sleep," he whispers. I open my eyes. "I'll keep Emma in my room, so you can get rest before your trip tomorrow." He walks over and takes her from my arms and I sense a strange shift in him, like he's trying to put a measure of distance between us, physically and emotionally.

"Okay," is all I say, and push to my feet, wiping my brow because the house is so hot. "Good night and thank you." I'm about to walk around him, when he captures my arm, bends and gives me a soft kiss.

"I just want you to get a good night's sleep," he explains, like he's privy to my unease.

"I appreciate that." What I don't tell him is I'd probably get a better night's sleep if he was beside me, and dammit, I've gotten far too used to that.

"I'm sorry I can't drive you tomorrow."

While it would be nice, I'm not upset. "Hockey has to come first."

"I'll be gone before you're even up."

"Are you sure you should keep Emma in your room?"

"Yeah, it's okay. Brynn is coming over early to watch her." He chuckles. "She loves playing Aunty Brynn."

I chuckle but it holds no humor. We've all happily fallen into roles that will soon be ripped out from beneath us, when I get this situation straightened out, and I'm hoping to have it all sorted before Thanksgiving next weekend. Emma going back to Krista is the best thing for everyone—I think.

I head up to the bathroom to wash up and brush my teeth, and when I enter my bedroom, it feels empty. I check my phone for messages and before I can talk myself out of it, I shoot off a message to Alison, to see how she's enjoying her classes. No response comes, and I set my phone down and pull on a thin nighty and nothing else. It's too warm for blankets, so I kick them off and fall into a fitful sleep. At one point, before sunrise, a noise wakes me and I open my eyes. Is Kace in my room? Was my light just on?

"Kace," I ask quietly and reach for my lamp. I flick the light on and wince as I glance around my empty room. Maybe I was dreaming. I go back to sleep, and wake to my alarm. Dread fills my stomach and before I push to my feet and get ready for my day, I send a message off to Kace, wishing him well at his practice.

A noise rings out from downstairs and I laugh. I guess he'd forgotten his phone at home again. I shower, dress quickly and grab my overnight bag. Downstairs, I find Brynn asleep on the sofa, Emma snoozing beside her in her bassinet.

Not wanting to wake them, I grab a muffin and head out the door, thankful that I didn't have to see Sebastian this morning. The air is cool as I toss my bag onto the back seat before I jump behind the wheel and start the car, or at least try to start it. The damn engine won't turn over. I try again and again, with no luck. I check the time. If I call for a ride, will I get to the airport on time?

Seeing as I have no choice, I open the app, and nearly jump from my seat when knuckles rap on my window. I turn to find Sebastian standing there, frowning down at me.

"What's wrong?" he asks, as he opens the door.

"Car won't start. I'm going to call a ride."

"Want me to take a look under the engine?"

I hesitate. I'm not sure Kace would want him messing with his vehicle. "No, that's okay. I'll just grab a ride."

He points to his car on the street. "I can drive you."

"You have practice."

He shrugs. "It's just practice. You're more important than any practice, Jemma," he says, and I can't help but think it's a dig at Kace. They're really not getting along and me being at their place with Emma has everything to do with it. Then again, he's not trying to get into the NHL. He plans to follow in his father's footsteps and go into politics.

"I..."

"Come on." He opens the back door and reaches for my bag. "It's not a problem."

I reluctantly slide from the driver's seat and follow him across the street. He hits the fob and I get into the driver's seat as he puts my bag into the back. I sit quietly as he gets in beside me and pulls onto the road. There's a very uncomfortable silence between us as he drives.

"I appreciate this," I say, wanting to ease the tension.

"Not a problem. Coach will understand." He casts me a fast glance. "You're going to straighten this all out today?"

"That's the plan."

"Good." He snorts. "Then you and I can get back to where we left off."

"I don't think that's a good idea."

"Why not?"

His voice holds an edge of anger, and I get it. He's not used to hearing no. "I just..."

He laughs. "Oh, you think Kace is into you?"

"No, it's not that. I just missed a lot of classes and need to catch up before exams."

He looks at me like he doesn't believe me. "You're different," he points out. "Not much fun anymore."

My chest tightens. "I've had Emma to take care of."

"No, I'm not sure that's what it is." He eyes me, taking in my yoga pants and jacket. "You think this is what Kace wants?"

I try to keep my voice even. "Kace and I are friends."

"Friends who are fucking," he clarifies and he's not wrong.

I swallow and lower my eyes.

"When am I going to get some of that sweet pussy?"

Oh God.

He laughs. "I guess you'll be back in my arms when Kace grows tired of you. It's what he does. I don't mind his leftovers. We're all used to it."

Leftovers? He thinks I'm going to be one of Kace's leftovers.

"Used to it?" I croak out.

"Yeah. You girls all go for his type first. He likes it that way. Don't think he doesn't," he adds, a warning in his voice. He flashes me a smile, but there's anger there. I sense it. "He likes to score fast and first, on and off the ice. I guess when he saw we were together at the party that night, he didn't like it. Wanted you first. He's kind of a bully like that. Probably why he had that pretty titty picture of you."

"Picture of me?" I gulp out. Sebastian knows about that? Embarrassment floods me, and I know I must be fifty different colors of red. Wait, he couldn't know about that unless Kace told him, right? No, they're not even friends. Which makes this more messed up.

"Yeah." He shrugs. "He used it to play the hero and get you to go for him first. Dude is fucked up." He points to his head. "Needs to be number one you know. Lots of daddy issues."

While I agree that Kace has issues, I can't believe that he took the picture and used it. "He said he took it off the wall in the locker room."

He laughs. "Yeah, that sounds about right." He grins at me. "Funny, he kept you around longer than most." He licks his lips. "You must have a real sweet pussy." I stare at him as his vulgar words turn my stomach. That's when it occurs to me that Kace might have been right and if I'm with him, then Sebastian can't sleep his way through the sorority. That's probably pissing him off. I'm pretty sure he's trying to sleep with Brynn too, and I'm pretty sure Kace would lose his mind. Not that I think Brynn would go for Sebastian. Maybe the tension between the two doesn't have to do with Emma and me staying with them. Maybe it has to do with Kace keeping Sebastian from what he wants.

"Then again, you're Brynn's friend and he'd do anything for his sister."

I gulp as the world grows fuzzy around me. I realize Kace has been with other women, and I've heard he doesn't keep anyone around for long. I'd like to believe we're still sleeping together because he likes me, the same way I like him. Not because he's keeping me around to help out his sister.

He pulls onto the highway, easing into traffic. "I think he's starting to get tired of you now, though. I can see the signs."

Signs like him sleeping in his own room last night? Not bothering to take his phone with him to make sure I got to the airport okay?

No, no, no. He's always forgetting his phone. It has nothing to do with tiring of me, right? Or...ugh. Maybe it does. I don't know. God, am I allowing Sebastian to get into my head, or has Kace been toying with me while helping out his sister and is now growing tired of it all?

What do I believe?

I briefly close my eyes and take a deep breath. Kace is a good guy. That's what I believe. Sebastian is just playing some messed-up head games with me. Right?

23

KACE

It's late Sunday night as I stand inside Stansfield International airport and scan the luggage carousel area searching for Jemma. I have to say, I really fucking missed her this weekend. Sure, we texted and talked, and she tried to keep me updated on everything that went down with her sister—although it was hard because she had very little privacy—but it's not the same as having her in my bed.

Okay, yes, it's true. Granted, I was fucking pissed off—at myself—when I found out Sebastian drove her to the airport. If only I had my phone with me, she could have called me and I would have figured something out. I hated that she couldn't count on me, and I was almost certain I'd put my phone in my bag after I handed Emma off to my sister. Although it was a hectic morning, so maybe I didn't. I am known for never knowing where I put it.

There's a part of me though that can't help but think Sebastian set the whole thing up. Then again, it'd be a lot of trouble to take my phone from my bag, and mess with my car after I left for practice. Strangely enough, my car worked perfectly fine when I tried it.

Maybe that scenario is a real stretch, and my brain is coming to its own conclusions because of my past. Sebastian has always been an entitled asshole, and I feel a new kind of hatred coming from him. But I'm not sure he'd go to such measures just to get Jemma alone, even though I'm pretty sure he wants her for himself and he's not too happy that I'm in the picture. Fuck you, Sebastian. Truthfully, Jemma has every right to be with whoever she wants. I just hope it's not with a guy who disrespects women the way Sebastian does.

My heart jumps as I see her coming from the escalator, and warmth goes through me as she searches the crowd, seeking me out. A tentative smile full of uncertainty—one that feels a little distant and cautious—touches her mouth and oddly enough, it feels like a slap. What the hell? What, is she suddenly uncertain about me? My stomach clenches, and my first thought is Sebastian said something to her, even though she assured me he just gave her a ride when I asked during one of our brief weekend conversations when she called to check on Emma.

Maybe she didn't want to get into it over the phone, or maybe I'm reading too much into this, and she's just stressed about her visit with her sister.

Even though there's a security gate to keep those picking up passengers away from the carousel area, I jump it and step up to her. I put my arm around her waist, and pull her to me.

"Hey, everything okay?"

She's tight for a brief moment, and then, as if exhaustion takes over, she sags against me. "It's been a long, stressful weekend."

"I know. Let's get your bag and get you home." At home, I can take care of her, and that's what I want more than anything. I grab her luggage as it circles the carousel and put my arm around her and lead her out to the parking garage.

"You could have just picked me up at the passenger pickup. You didn't need to park."

"I wanted to," I tell her and once again I spot uncertainty in her eyes. Did more go on with her sister than she's telling me? My entire body tightens. We reach the car and I put her bag in the back as she slides into the passenger seat. I climb in next to her and we remain silent as I negotiate the parking garage, pay for parking and hit the highway.

With her head rested against the seat, she turns to me. "I'm so happy you met your brothers. I'm sorry I wasn't there for you."

Tension eases inside of me and I reach out and capture her hand. "It was really nice, Jem."

She smiles. "I love that you offered to show them some pointers on the ice."

"They were so excited. They're kind of cool kids, even though they have stupid names." She laughs at that. "It was nice having Brynn there with Emma. It kept things light, especially between my father and me and Emma gave us all something to talk about."

She squeezes my hand. "I'm glad, but I'm sure it still wasn't easy."

"No, and when he congratulated me on making the NHL, it was nice, but I didn't feel like I wanted to rub it in his face anymore. I haven't forgiven him for what he's done, but I'm just trying to find my place in it all, you know."

"I know." She briefly closes her eyes, and I know the weekend was hard on her.

"Do you think Krista will keep her word and come for Emma next weekend?"

"I don't know, Kace," she says, her voice a bit shaky. "She was so shocked to find me at her door."

"I can imagine." A beat of silence and then. "Do you want to talk about it?"

She swallows. "I talked her into counselling, and even set up an appointment for her." She stares straight ahead. "The thing is, I'm not sure she's able to take care of Emma."

Jesus, this is an awful lot for Jemma.

"Her boyfriend left her after he found out she was pregnant, and she struggled through the pregnancy alone. It breaks my heart that she felt she couldn't reach out to her family."

"Why did she keep it a secret?"

"She was sure she was going to give her up for adoption, but then after she had her, she couldn't bring herself to do it."

I shake my head. "But to drop her off at your door."

"I know, Kace. She was ashamed and wasn't sure where to turn and I guess she knew I'd care for Emma until she was ready, but what she did was wrong, there's no question about that."

"You still don't think she's ready?"

She gives a humorless laugh. "No more ready than I was, but hey..." My heart squeezes. Jemma is such a good, caring person, putting her needs second, even though it could affect her school year, to take care of her niece. "If she doesn't come home, and if I don't think she's ready or capable, I'll have to make some serious decisions."

"Are you thinking child protective services?"

She swallows again, and folds her arms across her body. "I don't know. What will happen to Emma? She could end up in another province. I want to be in her life. I don't want her growing up not knowing her family. Her mother made a mistake. People make mistakes and I think people deserve a second chance, you know."

She's right and I guess I all I have to do is look in my own backyard, to see the mistakes made by my own father. Does he deserve a second chance? I guess the fact that I went to see my brothers means I'm kind of giving him one, and there's no doubt Dad was trying to make amends. He knows what he did was wrong. I swore I'd never take anything from him, but when he really insisted on helping with college and I knew how that could help Jemma and me, I accepted, with the caveat that I'd pay him back when I was in the NHL. It was a truce we were both happy with.

"I'll have to talk to Mom and Dad," she says, her voice weak and exhausted.

"I think that's a good idea. Let's get through the week, and after she shows up, if she shows up, you can be the judge of whether you think she's capable or not."

She exhales, and sinks into the seat. "That's all I can do. The problem is, I'm not a doctor, and hey, she fooled us when Mom, Dad and I video chatted. What if she comes here, appearing to have herself together, and I can't see the truth right in front of my face?"

I nod, not really knowing what to say, but it's definitely a legitimate concern. "Your sister must be a great actress."

She snorts. "Yeah, who knew."

She turns to me, catching my eye and I wonder if she's thinking the same thing I am. That Jemma was acting when she came here too and the only one who could see through it was me. That's only because I grew up with a man who lied to me constantly, which means maybe Jemma is a good actress too.

"If I kept her..." she begins and lets her words trail off. She groans and shakes her head. "What am I saying? That's impossible. I'd never be allowed back in the sorority house." She goes quiet, like she's considering that, and I'm a little shocked, to be honest. Does she want to go back to the sorority, and become the girl she was when she first arrived? "I guess I just mean, I'd have no place to go. I don't have the funds to find my own place."

I open my mouth, about to tell her I've been thinking about my own place, but shut it again. Am I moving too fast? Thinking there's more here than there really is? Hell, we're not even a real couple, and she likes to point out that we're just playing house. How many times has she reminded me?

I flick on my signal and pass a car on the highway as she turns back to look straight out the window, her body tight again. Twenty minutes later, I pull into my driveway and I'm happy that Sebastian's car is nowhere to be found. I really need to get out of the house, sooner rather than later. I guess I can't really put any offer on the table until I at least have my own space.

"Come on, let's go see Emma."

Her face lights up, and my heart tumbles. My God, I am fucking crazy about this woman. She hurries from the car and practically runs to the door as I grab her bag. I love her enthusiasm and yeah, I get it. She's bonded with Emma. Heck, we all have. If her sister doesn't want her, no way can Jemma just let her go into the system, and I need to do everything I can to make sure that doesn't happen.

She's inside by the time I reach the front porch and the sounds of her cooing with Emma fills my heart with so many emotions I could damn near sob. Fuck, it's been one hell of an emotional roller coaster ride this weekend for both of us, really.

"Thanks, sis," I say when Brynn looks at me, searching my face for answers. "I'll fill you in later."

"You know I'd do anything for you, big brother."

"I'd do anything for you to, sis."

Brynn steps up to me and I note the way Jemma watches us with warmth—and wait, is that uncertainty again—in her eyes as my sister throws her arms around me and gives me a hug. I kiss the top of her head before she pulls away.

"Emma has been fed, changed and bathed, and Jem, I'll take our notes tomorrow."

Jemma pats Emma on the back and starts rocking her. She was so uncomfortable with Emma at first, but look at her now, she's got it mastered. "Thanks again, Brynn. I really appreciate all you're doing for me."

"Hey, you're a sorority sister, and us sisters have to stick together."

Jemma briefly casts a glance my way. To gauge my reaction to that maybe? Because I know she's faking it to fit in? My vibrant, outgoing sister, though. I don't think for one second she'd cast Jemma away because she wanted to be a part of something, using any means possible. But it's not my place to out Jemma to my sister.

Jemma stifles a yawn as Brynn heads out the door. "Are you hungry?" I ask, taking in the dark circles under her eyes.

"I don't have much of an appetite, to be honest?"

"How about a sandwich?"

"Actually, that sounds kind of good. I need a shower after traveling."

"Why don't you go get Emma settled in and grab a shower. Crawl into bed if you want and I'll bring it to you in bed."

She smiles. "That's a service a girl could get used to."

"Good, get used to it," I tell her and she frowns. "What?"

She looks down. "Nothing. Thanks."

A moment later, she heads upstairs with Emma, and I pull my phone from my pocket when it pings. I'm trying to get better at carrying it around. Jesus, I'm still mad at myself that I left Jemma in a bind. It's a message from Conner, wanting to know if I'm hitting up the gym tomorrow. After I hear the shower turn on, I walk to the kitchen and answer him. We exchange a few more messages and when I'm done, I go to the fridge and pull out some fresh chicken I cooked earlier for Brynn and me. I make a sandwich, grab a bottle of water, and start upstairs.

I find Jemma pulling on a pair of pajama pants and a T-shirt. She turns and smiles when she sees me at the door. I walk into the room, set her sandwich and water on the nightstand, and strip down to my boxer shorts.

I don't miss the way she's watching me as I pull the covers back. I'm about to climb in but stop when she asks. "Are you sure, Kace?"

"Sure, about what?"

"You must be exhausted and in need of a good night's sleep. It's been a long and hard weekend for the both of us," she continues as she glances down. "You and Brynn, you've both done so much for me, and well, you've..." Her gaze slowly lifts, and once again I spot uncertainty. "...gone above and beyond for your sister's sorority friend."

I exhale. What the hell has gotten into her head? Or better question is, who's gotten into her head? "Yeah, well, maybe I'm not just doing this for my sister, anymore..."

24

JEMMA

I pace around the living room, anxious and exhausted as I wait for my sister to show. Last night I was so stressed, I never slept at all. I texted her Kace's address earlier in the week, and again last night before I crawled into bed, and the fact that I haven't heard back has crumpled my expectations and left a knot in my stomach. If that isn't making me anxious enough, I lied to my parents this week as well. Telling them I had a huge assignment and wasn't sure if I could make the family turkey dinner tomorrow. I told them I'd let them know by the end of the day today and how fair is that when they have to shop and prep?

I'm a little, or maybe even a lot angry at Krista, that it's come to this. My plan for today was to assess my sister, and if I thought she was okay, we'd travel to Shelburne together tomorrow, along with Emma—Kace said I could have his car if I needed it. I'd support her while she told Mom and Dad the news. If she doesn't show, or if I was worried about her mental health, well...I don't really know, but Kace said one day at a time, and we'd sit and figure it out if we had to cross that bridge.

Speaking of Kace. My God, I can't believe he told me he wasn't helping me because of his sister. I can only hope that meant he's doing it because he cares about me. I never got the chance to ask, as we ended up making love well into the wee hours of the morning. That brings a smile to my face, and momentarily pushes back the panic coursing through my veins. Then again, he could have meant he was doing it for Emma. From his past, it's clear he can't stand the idea of any child feeling abandoned the way he had. I have to say, though, I'm seeing a change in him, a mellowing of sorts, since he started visiting and texting his brothers.

He'd left earlier after he got a text. He seemed a bit cagey about it, but I am not going to question him or let anyone get in my head again. He told me he was going to pick up his sister and get a turkey for tomorrow. His mother is cooking, and I'm invited to dinner if things go south with my sister. While dinner with his family sounds nice, I need for my sister to show.

A noise sounds on the front steps and I stop packing and suck in a fast breath. She's here. *Breathe, Jemma breathe.* I hurry to the front door, but the second I pull it open and find Sebastian standing there, key in hand, I step back.

"Oh, it's you."

"Nice to see you too," he grunts with a scowl.

"No, no. I didn't mean that." I sort of did mean that, but I'm not about to tell him that and upset him. I might have to stay here longer. "I thought you were my sister."

"She's coming to get the kid?" he asks as he glances at Emma with disinterest, and maybe even annoyance.

"Yes, hopefully."

"Hopefully?" He shoves his key into his pocket. "Either she is or she isn't."

I step away and walk back into the living room to check my phone, not wanting to have this conversation. We've barely spoken since he drove me to the airport, and I like it that way.

"She might be running late," I hedge.

"I guess you'll be moving out after she picks her up."

"Um...that's the plan." That is the plan, right? I can't stay here. Kace never put that offer on the table, and that would be crazy anyway.

He snorts. "I'm sure Kace is happy about that."

I stiffen. "What's that supposed to mean?"

"Come on, Jemma." He throws himself into a chair and puts his feet on the coffee table, looking like he's not going anywhere in a hurry, and I don't want him here if—when—my sister shows up. "I told you. He's tired of you. How is he supposed to bring a chick home with you and the baby here?"

Don't listen to him Jemma.

"Yeah, you're right," I agree, hoping that will put an end to this. I glance at my phone and fight the urge to call Kace.

"He's with Sierra now."

My heart stalls, and I spin to face him, and catch the smirk on his face. My heart jumps into my throat. Why do I get the sense that he's telling the truth?

"Okay," I respond for lack of anything else. I swallow, and after my weeks of training as a puck bunny, work to pretend it doesn't bother me. Kace might be with Sierra but that doesn't mean anything is going on, right?

He bangs his fists together. "She's a good fuck."

"Oh, you had her before Kace, did you?" Why the hell did I say that? Oh, maybe to piss him off. Probably not my smartest move, but I'm a hot freaking mess inside right now.

His face goes red. "What the fuck?"

"Nothing," I reply quickly and walk to the window to look out. I honestly don't care if he was with Sierra. I only care if Kace is with her, and God, Sebastian is getting in my head again.

He pushes to his feet. "Listen," he says his voice softening. "Let's get back to where we were before that kid showed up."

Standing behind me, he puts his hands on my shoulders and gives a squeeze, but his touch turns my stomach. I shrug him off and walk away, and can almost feel the rage coming off him.

"I'm just...things have changed."

He gives a derisive snort. "If you're really holding out for Kace, baby, you need to stop. I wasn't lying about him."

Don't ask, Jemma. Don't freaking ask. He's baiting you.

"About what?" I ask, hating myself that I'm walking right into his trap.

He frowns and glances down and for a minute I think I see real sympathy on his face, and the fact that he's feeling sorry for me turns my stomach even more. Something bad is going down. I feel it in every bone in my body. Does everyone know I'm a fake, a liar? I hug myself, an uncontrollable quiver going through me.

"What is it?" I ask working to sound casual, like whatever he has to say won't bother me.

He sighs and his shoulders sag. "I didn't want it to come to this, but I think it's for you own good."

"Tell me."

His hand slips behind his back and he pulls his phone from his back pocket. He runs his finger across the screen, and I stare, my entire body on edge as I wait for some bubble to burst and the sky to crash around me.

"Here," he says and holds his phone out.

I step closer, and my heart sinks into the pit of my stomach, when I see a picture of me, sprawled out on the bed, my nighty scrunched around my waist, exposing the naked lower half of my body. Tears prick my eyes, and I take the phone from him, trying to figure out when and how this was taken.

"What...where." I stare at the phone and that's when I realize it was taken upstairs, in the bedroom. I grip the phone tighter and back up. I blink the tears from my eyes as my breath comes so fast I'm sure I'm going to pass out. "Wait, did you do this?"

"No, baby," he says, his voice soft and sympathetic. "I told you. Kace likes to do shitty things."

"How do I know you didn't do this?"

He nods his head toward the phone. "Look who sent it?"

I glance at the phone to see that it came from Kace's number. I stumble backward and before I fall, Sebastian puts his arms around me and pulls me to him. "I...don't believe you. Kace would never do this."

"It's right there, baby. He sent it around. Ask anyone. He's pretty messed up."

"None of this makes sense." I wrack my brain. "You said he did it before to play hero, so I'd go for him instead of you."

"I don't know why he's doing it now. Maybe to push you away, or maybe to fuck around with you, get a good laugh. Did you forget that I told you he was a bully?"

The world closes in on me as Sebastian watches me, waiting for me to react. I stare at him, flabbergasted. Is this some sort of punishment for pretending to be something I wasn't? Is Kace that messed up? Has he just been messing with me all along, waiting for the right time to strike, and make me pay for my lies? I pinch my eyes shut, and work to dispel those negative thoughts. Kace is not like that. I don't care what Sebastian says. It's just my old insecurities coming back to haunt me.

"Ask around, Jemma." He sticks his bottom lip out in a pout, like he's feeling especially sorry for me, but a part of me can't help but think he's enjoying my misery. "You'll see the picture has been sent out. Lots of guys on the team have a copy."

Mortified, I gulp and grab my phone. I take deep breaths as I pull up my contacts and call Brynn—instead of texting. I need to hear her voice and if anyone knows anything about this it will be her. She answers on the second ring.

"Hey Jemma, what's up?" she asks sounding normal and cheerful. She certainly wouldn't be acting casual if she knew what was going on right? "Is Emma okay? Did Krista show?"

I relax a bit and lift my face to meet Sebastian's eyes. I watch him as I say, "Yeah, I was just wondering what you were up to."

"I'm just getting to my dorm room now." The sound of our dorm room hinges creak, and I know she's arrived. "Hey, are you okay?" She must hear the trauma in my voice but before I can answer, I hear, "Oh, hey Kace. What are you doing here?"

What is he doing there? In her dorm room? He told me he was picking Brynn up to go turkey shopping. Did she not know he was coming, or was Sebastian right? A laugh rings out in the distance. A female laugh.

"Brynn," I murmur my fingers tightening on my phone. "What's going on?"

"I don't know." She sounds as confused as I feel. "Kace and Sierra are here." Her voice is muffled, like she's covering the phone as she talks to Kace and Sierra. I try to hear but can't. I also get the feeling Brynn doesn't really want me to. She comes back on and says, "Um, can I call you back?"

"Okay." My heart is beating so fast, it nearly jumps from my chest as the call ends and I stare at the picture of Emma and Kace—my screensaver. I continue to stare, as Sebastian hovers over me and my thoughts are so confused and chaotic, I don't know which way is up or down anymore. All I know is I need to sit before I fall.

I stumble again, and Sebastian catches me. "I...I need to sit," I tell him my voice as shaky as my hands.

Just then my phone pings, and I reach for it, hoping it's Kace telling me none of this is what I think it is. I see my sister's name through blurry eyes and when I read her message that she's not coming, my legs go out from underneath me. A strangled cry catches in my throat.

"Let me take you to your room," Sebastian says, and I glance at Emma. He puts his arm around me to support me and picks up the bassinet. Why is he being so nice to me? "Come on," he says, giving me a nudge to set me into motion. As my throat clogs, I don't answer, I just nod in agreement, and blindly let him lead me to the stairs.

I walk, unable to believe this is all happening. There has to be some mistake. Kace is not like my sister's bully. Luring her in and then making fun of her. No, he's a good man. The best man I know and in my heart, I am sure there's a good explanation to all of this. My brain is just too fried at the moment to figure it out, and I have Emma to worry about, not to mention my sister.

What am I going to do?

25

—

KACE

I stand inside my sister's dorm room—Jemma's dorm room—with Sierra giving me an *I told you so* look as Brynn's confused gaze goes back and forth between the two of us.

"What is going on?" Brynn asks, as I stand over the box tucked in the corner. The box Jemma hadn't unpacked and appeared agitated when I jokingly asked if she had a dead body in it. It's not a dead body, but the contents are damn near killing me. This just can't be right.

"I told you it was her baby," Sierra says again, a smugness about her as she folds her arms and glares at me.

Brynn stiffens and cranes her head to see the contents of the box. "No way is it her baby."

"How do you explain this then?" Sierra reaches inside the box, moves a few books around and pulls out baby clothes. "She was hiding these in here, Brynn."

Brynn's brows pull together as she drops down onto Jemma's bed. "Maybe she put them in there after Emma arrived?" She frowns, and I get the sense that she doesn't even believe that.

"She came with these. It's obvious the baby is hers, and she came up with some elaborate scene to hide it, and maybe even to snag herself a hot hockey player."

"Sierra, that's insane," Brynn blurts out.

"Is it? I mean come on. Everyone knows and sees how good Kace is to you. Under all the gruff, he's nurturing and sweet. You can't deny that."

"I was the one who asked Kace if she could stay with him." She shakes her head. "I was trying to set the two of them up because she's—"

"She's not who you think she is, Brynn," I finally explain, cutting them off. "She was pretending to be a puck bunny, a girl who liked hockey and went to games and was up for anything. She's not that girl."

Brynn goes still, her gaze meeting mine. "I know that."

I swallow, hard. "You do?"

"Yeah, I do. She's sweet and quiet and a total book worm, which is why I thought you and her would make a great couple."

"But the way she acted at the parties. The drinking...taking her top off, hanging out with Sebastian." I note the way Sierra's body goes tight at the mention of Sebastian. I turn to her. "What?"

"Nothing," she answers quickly, and backs up a bit. "I think you're both wrong. I think that's who she actually is, and was playing you both, so you'd think she was some sweet, innocent girl." She snorts. "I think she got to you both, because she needed a rich baby daddy." I eye her. "You're going play in the NHL, Kace. You're going to be rich," she says with an eye roll. "When it came to fucking, Sebastian would do, but when it came to the future, she wanted to snag you."

No. No. No. This is all coming at me so fast, I can no longer think straight. I back up and sag against the wall, my gaze going back to the contents in the box. The problem I'm having is she's barely left my place. When would she have had the time to go buy clothes and put them in here? The second-hand things we purchased for Emma came from the online marketplace and I picked them up. None of these clothes were in that pile.

I bend forward and put my hands on my knees, my brain racing. Krista didn't seem distraught when Jemma video chatted with her. Jemma explained that to me, but still, it never sat well in my gut. Then she went to Montreal to visit her sister, and didn't want Brynn or me to go with her. Granted, I had a game and Brynn took care of Emma. Krista is supposed to come today, to get Emma, and I sensed Jemma didn't want me there when they arrived. Oh, and I can't forget about the time I found her in Sebastian's arms in the kitchen. She had an explanation for that too. I scoff. She seems to have an explanation for everything.

"She's still fucking Sebastian," Sierra states. "You should know that."

A headache begins in the back of my skull as the sudden need to see Jemma and get to the bottom of all this has me pushing myself off the wall and stalking to the door.

"Where are you going?" Brynn asks, her voice shaky and worried.

I tug the door open and turn back to see Sierra's fingers racing over her phone.

"I need to talk to Jemma and find out what's going on."

Brynn jumps up. "Want me to go with you?"

"It's up to you." I stare at Sierra as she continues to text. "Sierra," I snap harshly and her head lifts. "Don't be spreading any shit around until we know the truth."

She blinks at me, feigning innocence, but I know who she is and what she's all about. Then again, do I? Maybe I really still am a bad judge of character. Has my past with my father taught me nothing?

"I'm not spreading shit," she says and gives me a pout. "I'm just answering a text. I'm as upset by all this too, Kace. I can't believe she'd do something like this to you. I would never treat you like that." She comes closer. "Why don't I come too? You might need me."

I'm about to tell her it's not necessary when Brynn's phone pings. She slides her finger across the screen, and her eyes go wide as the color drains from her face. My heart jumps.

"What?" I ask, everything in my gut telling me something else is going down and it's going to be bad.

"I..." Brynn stares at her phone and a horrible knot tightens in my gut.

"Brynn, what is it?"

She holds her phone out and that's when I see a picture of Jemma, dressed in nothing but a thin nighty, which is bunched around her waist, as she lays spread eagle on her bed —or rather, the spare bed at my place.

Rage and worry go through me as I see red. Who did this to her, and why? Then as my mind goes back to the night she took off her bathing suit top, another thought hits. Was she aware? Did she want this?

"Who sent you that?" I ask.

She gulps and hands me her phone. "This came from Olivia. Ally got it too. They said it came from your phone earlier."

"What the fuck?" I snatch it from her and stare, sure this is some kind of mistake. "I didn't send this to anyone. I've never even seen this before." I search my pocket and tug my phone out. I used to leave it laying around the house a lot, but I've been getting better and better at taking it with me when I leave in case Jemma needs me.

"I got it too," Sierra says. "I think it's been sent out to a lot of people."

I check my phone to see that over half the hockey team received it. Jesus Christ.

"She's up to something," Sierra tells us with a little bob of her head. "She probably did this for sympathy or something."

Still not wanting to believe that, I storm out of the room and tromp down the stairs, Brynn tight on my heels. Outside, I zip up my coat against the cool wind and hurry to my car. Brynn slides in beside me.

She casts me a fearful look. "Sierra can't be right. I know my roommate."

"Yeah, we thought we knew our father too, didn't we?" I blurt out much too harshly and she flinches. "I'm sorry," I say quickly and give her hand a squeeze.

"You and Dad. I thought you had come to a better place."

"We have," I tell her. Thanks to Jemma. She was the one who thought the path to healing was dealing, and not hating.

"What if we were wrong?" she whispers so quietly, I struggle to hear.

"We're not. We can't be. Someone has to be behind this. You know I didn't send that picture around of Jemma."

"Yeah, but it was taken from your phone, Kace. You could be in a whole lot of trouble for this."

My hand stills on the shifter. Fuck, I hadn't thought of that. "Jesus."

"The NHL," she says with a wince. "Nonconsensual distribution. Kace, this isn't good."

She's right. It isn't good. I pound the steering wheel, but I'm not just worried about me. I'm worried about Jemma and how this would hurt her—especially if she had no idea about it.

Of course, she had no idea, Kace.

That's when my brain reminds me she didn't seem too fazed by the half-naked photo I tore off the locker room wall before anyone saw it. I pinch my eyes shut. That's because she was pretending to be something she wasn't—someone she thought she needed to be in order to fit in and be liked.

But was she pretending? Could this sweet vulnerable version that I've been getting to know not be the real Jemma.

"Fuck me."

I start the car and head toward my place, trying not to speed. A lot of people are out enjoying family time on this Thanksgiving weekend. I work to keep my shit together as I approach the house and spot Sebastian's car parked on the road. I thought he was going back to Lunenburg, to be with his family this weekend. Why the fuck is he still here? The knot in my stomach tightens and when I cast a glance Brynn's way, I find her watching me.

I pull into the driveway and kill the ignition. "Do you want me to come in?" she asks.

"Why don't you wait here," I suggest. It's clear from the look on her face, she feels responsible for all of this—whatever this is. But she's not. I didn't have to agree to letting Jemma and the baby stay with me.

I walk up to the front door and find it locked. I tug my key from my pocket and let myself in. Silence fills the air. I walk quietly, and peer into the living room half expecting Jemma to be sitting with her sister—or maybe it's just what I'm hoping for—but I find it empty. I stalk through the place, stopping to glance at the pictures I'd drawn of dinosaurs. I pick one up, and despite the storm going on inside me, a smile tugs at my face as I remember how we worked together on Jemma's story. I set the drawing down, and take one last look around. Once I've concluded that the main level is empty, I walk back down the hall and glance up the steps.

I'm about to call out, but stop myself. If Emma is asleep, I don't want to wake her. Maybe Jemma is asleep too, exhausted and distraught after meeting with her sister. Or maybe no one is here, because they've gone out with her Krista, to the park for ice cream or something. I start up slowly and listen for sound.

I pass my room and Sebastian's, and they're empty. Unease spreads inside me as I reach Jemma's closed bedroom door. I lift my hand, and debate on knocking, but again stop myself in case they're asleep. I put my hand around the knob, twist slowly and cringe as the hinges creak.

The second I take in the vision before me, I can no longer stay silent. "What the fuck?" I ask, as my gaze meets Sebastian, who is laying on the bed, his arm around Jemma. Jemma's lids fly open and she stares at me. She blinks like she has no idea what's going on. But then the shock on her face turns to anger and then sadness.

"Kace," she says and tries to move, but Sebastian, who is completely fucking naked is holding her down. She glances over her shoulder, and a little gasp catches in her throat. What, is she pretending she didn't know Sebastian was in her bed? She shoves his arm and jumps from the bed, glancing down at herself, and looking almost relieved to see she's dressed.

As Sebastian rolls to the other side of the bed and pulls on his jeans she asks me, "What are you doing here?"

I snort. "I came to get answers, but I guess I now have them."

"No," she answers quickly. "Nothing was going on here." She pinches her eyes shut. "You...wait...Kace, were you with Sierra?"

I straighten. "Yes."

A strangled cry catches in her throat. "I thought..."

Wait, does she think I was sleeping with Sierra? Does she think I'd do that to her? "It's not like that," I say but she just shakes her head.

"You. Me." Tears fill her eyes. "I don't know what I thought."

"I thought things too, Jemma. I thought you were helping your sister out." I throw my arms out and make a show of glancing around. "Let me guess. She didn't show?"

Her brow bunches together, as she places a hand on her stomach. "No, she didn't. She's unwell. I don't know what I'm going to do now."

"Maybe you should take care of your baby," I shoot out.

Her head jerks back. "What?" She stares at me for a long time, and I hold my ground as her lips begin to quiver and the color drains from her face as she sinks back onto the mattress, like she just had a lightbulb moment. "Really, Kace. You believe the rumors?"

"How could I not? I found the baby clothes in the box in your room. You obviously brought them with you."

"What were you doing in my dorm room?"

I shove my hands into my pockets before I punch the door. "Does it really matter?"

"Why were you going through my stuff?" She crosses her arms. "Stupid question. You don't trust me, obviously."

"Trust," I say and wave a shaky hand toward Sebastian. "Come on, Jemma. This is who you were all along wasn't it? You fucking fooled me and my sister. You were looking for a baby daddy."

Despite the tears pooling in her eyes, her face hardens, and the look she aims my way hits like the butt end of a stick. "If we want to talk about trust, maybe you might want to explain this." She glances at Sebastian and with a nod, gestures toward his phone on her nightstand.

He reaches for it, and opens it to show me the half-naked picture of Jemma, sent to him by my phone. Enraged and ready to kick the shit out of him, I stare at Sebastian. I have no idea how or why he did it, I only know he's somehow behind that picture, and likely the last one. Fucking bastard, and now Jemma is in his arms. How the fuck has this become my life?

"Maybe you're the one who's not who you say you are," she says.

"You think I did that?" I ask as I slowly turn back to Jemma.

Instead of answering, she says, "Maybe you should be careful who you trust."

Jesus, is she admitting all this? Admitting that she wasn't genuine with me after she moved in? That maybe I saw things in her what I wanted to see but that wasn't really who she was at all?

I back up an inch; the sight before me has my stomach churning. I turn, and that's when I set eyes on Brynn in the hall. I asked her to stay in the car, but I guess at least now I won't have to rehash what just went down here. With my back to Jemma, I clench down on my teeth and say, "I want you gone before the day is over."

26

JEMMA

"**I**'m sorry I've been such a horrible friend," I say to Alison as she drops down next to me on the sofa and hands me a tub of ice cream and a big spoon. I've been at her place for three days, but up until tonight I haven't felt like talking. Tonight, however, I kept nothing back.

"You haven't been a horrible friend, Jemma." She waves her hand around the apartment she shares with three other girls. "This is college. It's where we find ourselves."

Well, I wish I would have moved in with her here to find myself, instead of into a dorm with a bunch of girls who turned on me. Although I'm not entirely sure that's true, and Brynn certainly hasn't. For the last three days, since Kace kicked me out, she's been texting to check up on me and Emma, but I'm too embarrassed to message her back. That's pretty shitty of me, actually. She was so good to Emma and to have her taken out of her life isn't fair. God, I'm just making mistake after mistake, aren't I?

Now, I'll likely fail my first year at the academy, too. I haven't been able to go to class or even watch the lectures online. I'm just grateful it was the long weekend, and I didn't miss too much, but I also haven't completed any catch up either. I've been so exhausted taking care of Emma, and trying to figure out how to deal with this crazy turn of events. I'm going to need help, whether that's from child protective services, who I don't want to call, or from my parents. In the back of my mind though, I'm holding out hope that Krista calls and we can work things out. One thing is for certain, she needs help, and if she'd just talk to me, I could try to arrange that for her.

A sleeping Emma gurgles in the bassinet beside me, and my heart aches for the abandoned child. None of this is fair to her, and right now I can't be wallowing in myself pity. I need to be thinking of her.

"Do you think you should talk to him?" Alison asks quietly.

"Kace," I blurt out. "No way will he want to talk to me. He thinks I've been sleeping with Sebastian, and don't forget he was with Sierra."

She frowns, uses her spoon to dip into the ice-cream and licks it from the tip. "Was he with her, though? You know, like actually having sex with her?"

"That's what Sebastian led me to believe."

She snorts out a laugh. "Yeah, but from everything you told me, Sebastian is an asshole. Why would he be naked in your bed, Jemma? He was obviously up to something."

"Yeah, true," I say. I hadn't had time to really dig into that, with everything else going on. But Alison is right.

"Do you think he knew Kace would show up?"

"I don't, actually. Kace said he was going to get a turkey for Thanksgiving." I hate that I didn't even go home to be with Mom and Dad. They love it when we're all together, and I let them down. I've been letting everyone down.

"Maybe he was getting a turkey. Why would he lie about that? You did say he invited you to his mother's, right?"

My heart pinches tight. I really wanted to go to his family home with him and Brynn. "Brynn seemed surprised to find Kace in her room, though. I could hear it in her voice."

She shrugs and glances at Emma as she makes a sound in her sleep. "Maybe they were meeting somewhere else."

I take a big spoonful of Chunky Monkey and let it melt on my tongue as I try to slow my tired brain down and really think about this. "I guess that's a possibility."

"Okay, so let's go with that. He was meeting Brynn elsewhere. Then why would he be in your room? Do you guys keep your doors locked?"

"No, not usually. I...I guess Sierra took him there, to show him the baby clothes in my box." I give a big eye roll because that's all crazy. "There were no baby clothes in the box. It was all my books. I just...I like to keep them close. They give me comfort, it's weird, I know."

She gives my arm a supportive squeeze and tears form in my eyes. I am so lucky to have a true friend like her. "It's not weird, it's who you are, and I love that."

"You're the only one who loves a book nerd. Look at us in high school. We were never invited to anything, and I didn't want anyone here to see that side of me." I glance at the big bay window as the moon rises higher in the sky. I should be asleep right now, I'm exhausted, but Emma was up fussing and Alison joined us on the sofa. "I didn't want Kace to know."

"That didn't turn out so well."

I shake my head and give a humorless laugh. "Tell me what you really think?"

"That you got yourself into something that could only end in failure." I eye her and she holds her hands up. "Hey, you know I love you. We've been friends since we were kids and nothing is going to change that. I just don't like seeing you unhappy, and you had to go find yourself. What you don't realize is..." She stops to poke my shoulder. "This girl here, the one who likes quiet time in the lighthouse to read and is working on a children's book. She's actually pretty cool. Maybe you should have given her a chance, and high school is high school, Jemma. It sucks for everyone."

I nod, remembering when Kace said the same thing. I dig my spoon back in the ice cream. "That's the girl Kace liked," I whisper. "He liked it when I wasn't pretending to be something I wasn't."

"See, told you."

"Yeah, but he doesn't believe I'm that girl now. He actually thinks Emma is mine and that I was trying to trick him." A big hiccupping sob catches in my throat. "My God, Alison. Someone spread pictures of me half naked in my bed." I groan and bury my hands in my face. "It's humiliating, and how will I ever show myself on campus again?"

"That person needs to be up on charges."

My mind goes back to my last conversation with Kace. I guess I sort of led him to believe he couldn't trust me. When I first told him to be careful who he trusted, I was talking about Sierra, knowing she had to be lying to him, but when I saw the hurt in his eyes, I knew he thought I was talking about myself, and I was so angry and hurt, I wanted him to hurt too. Wow, I'm a horrible person.

"You're right," I say with a heavy sigh as a fresh wave of tears threaten. How could this have happened? I guess Kace easily could have come into my room that night the house was over-heated. I vaguely remember hearing someone and calling out to him, but nothing about that sits right. Kace is kind and sweet and so damn nurturing. It's not like he does things to purposely hurt people. Could Sebastian have done it? I hold my stomach. Then again, the picture came from Kace's phone.

"Are you going to pursue it?" Alison asks, pulling my thoughts back.

I groan as her eyes narrow in on me. "I kind of just want it to all go away."

"If Kace did this, he should be held accountable."

My gaze flies to hers and I get the sense she's testing me somehow. "I don't think..."

She cocks her head, a challenge in her eyes. "You don't think he did it, huh?"

"No," I blurt out with absolute confidence.

"All roads point to it, Jemma. Even the picture he 'supposed-ly'..." she pauses to do air quotes around that one word. "... found in the locker room. He could easily have been behind that."

"He's always losing his phone," I point out coming to his defense.

She shrugs like that's nothing. "What was it you told me Sebastian said, Kace wanted to play the hero, because he likes to score first and fast."

"He's not like that."

"Daddy issues?" she challenges, and again, I get the sense that she's going somewhere with this and trying to pull something from me.

"Yeah, but he's working on that." My heart does a little happy dance to know he's been seeing his brothers and is working on his issues with his father. Love and hate, there's a fine line, and life isn't fun walking around feeling indifferent. I'm glad he's not doing that anymore. Jesus, I still care for him, love him. But hate, I'm sure that's what he must be feeling for me now.

"Crazy rumors spread over in the sorority, huh?"

"Yeah, totally."

"Rumors like Kace was sleeping with Sierra and you were hiding clothes in the box." She examines her spoon. "How do you think the clothes got there?"

"Anyone could have put them there, I suppose. But I'm guessing it was Sierra, not that I can ever prove anything."

"Why would she do that, though? How would it benefit her?"

"I...to push me out so she could be with Kace."

"Do you think she did that all on her own?"

I sniff and shrug. "I don't know."

"If she wanted Kace, and Sebastian wanted you..."

My stomach tightens as I remember all the things I've heard about Sebastian. How he was sleeping his way through the sorority. He obviously had his own agenda. What other reason would there be for crawling into bed with me naked? And how did he know Kace would show up when he did? Did Sierra tip him off? I thought she was my friend. God, why did I ever believe a word Sierra or Sebastian said to me? I sink into the cushions, a new kind of ache in my stomach and my heart. "I guess Kace isn't the only one who had to be careful who he trusted. I am such an idiot."

"No, you're human and you made a mistake. Looks like lots of people involved made mistakes." She shifts closer, crossing her legs, her gaze meeting mine. "Who do you trust?"

Deep in my heart, I know Kace wasn't responsible for the pictures. I lashed out to hurt him, thinking he was with Sierra —based on my own insecurities—and then to accuse me of trying to find a baby daddy. What a freaking mess we've made, all because we listened to other people.

I sink into the cushions, a new kind of ache traveling from my stomach and my heart. "I trust you." I smile at my best friend, thanking her for opening her door to Emma and me, and still being there for us when I needed her most.

"Let me rephrase that question. Do you trust Kace?"

Tears fall hard and Alison takes the ice cream from me and sets it on the coffee table. I try not to ugly cry. I don't want to wake up Emma. She's been kicked around enough as it is. Alison pulls me to her, and I weep as she holds me.

"You love him, don't you?"

I don't speak. I'm not sure I can, so I just nod and get her shirt soaked as I cry. I just hope when she grows up she never has to experience this kind of pain.

Alison rubs her hand over my hair to smooth it out. "I think you need to talk to him, Jemma," she tells me in a low, comforting voice.

"After the things I've said, and accused him of doing? No way will he talk to me, and I don't blame him."

"He did the same to you, don't forget."

My heart breaks a little more at the reminder. "I didn't forget," I manage to get out. "I don't want to talk to him after he accused me of something like that anyway."

"But you do. You both need to talk. You both said hurtful things because they were coming from a vulnerable place. Love is hard, my friend."

We both go quiet and I push upright. Alison hands me a box of tissues and I wipe the tears from my eyes. Wanting to stop feeling sorry for myself, I glance at a sleeping Emma. "I need to do one right thing this week and call my parents."

"I think that's exactly what you need to do. They deserve to know and they'll know how to get Krista help."

I crush the tissue between my hands, determined to move on and never think about Kace again. What's the point? While Alison could be right, and we could use a conversation, he's never going to talk to me again. I sniff as Emma gurgles. "She's sweet, isn't she?"

"She is," Alison answers quietly.

"Kace really loved her."

God, I need to stop thinking about him. But I'm sure losing her from his life is hard after the two of them had bonded. What will become of us all now?

On that thought, I push to my feet, so tired that standing is difficult. "Tomorrow is a new day," I say and try to inject enthusiasm into my voice. "Things can only look up." Lord knows they can't look down, considering I'm at my very lowest.

"Sleep is a good idea." She stands and picks up Emma. "I'll take her up and get her changed. You look like you could use a minute to yourself."

She turns to leave, but knuckles rap loudly on the door and we both stop. My gaze flies to Alison. Who could be here this late?

27

KACE

My chest aches and it's almost impossible to breathe as I storm out of the house, hop into my car and slam the door harder than necessary. Brynn slides in beside me. Her movements are stiff, and she's quiet as I start the car. I'm about to back out of the driveway when I glance at her and take in the worried look on her face.

"What?" I ask.

"Something...I don't know, Kace." Her eyes dart from me to the front door, back to me again. "Something isn't right. I feel it in my bones."

"You were in the same room as I was," I harshly point out, even though I shouldn't be taking my anger out on her. "You saw what I saw, right?" I add, softening my tone.

"What exactly did we see?" she asks, her voice shaky and hesitant, just as upset as I am.

I back out of the driveway and start toward her sorority, not wanting to remember what I saw—ever.

"I mean it, Kace. What exactly did we see?" she insists.

Does she really need me to spell this out for her? I take in her scrunched-up face and shake my head. "First, we saw baby clothes in the box, and them we saw Jemma in bed with Sebastian."

"Jemma was fully dressed," she reminds me.

"And Sebastian was completely naked."

"Exactly."

What is she getting at? I cast a fast glance her way, my brain on overload, unable to put two and two together. Which makes me think of the time Jemma said one plus one equals one. I groan. "She's not who we thought she was," I remind Brynn as old insecurities grip my throat. I forcefully try to swallow against the pain.

"You didn't send that picture around," she states quietly and I appreciate her trust in me.

I pound on the steering wheel. "You're right. I didn't."

"I'm sorry Jemma accused you of that, but I think she was reacting...just like you're reacting." I cut her a glance and she holds her hands up, letting me know she's on my side, as she hurries on with, "Who had access to your phone? Which, by the way, you're always misplacing or forgetting." She's not wrong. Her voice trembles when she adds, "If Jemma presses charges..."

The road before me wobbles as the world closes in on me. Fire ravages every nerve in my body. "Sebastian is behind the picture. He had access to my phone. It has to be him. But why, and how the hell am I going to prove it?"

"I don't know."

We both go quiet as I stop at the red light. I tap the steering wheel, the anger coursing through my body making me restless and anxious. I glance to my left and see a For Rent sign on a cute little house that I had already been looking into renting—for Jemma and me, and Emma if need be. I'm not sure what's going to happen now, but no way can I stay at my house and see Jemma and Sebastian together. I told her I wanted her gone, but do I really have the power to demand that? Half the place is Sebastian's and if he wants her there, she has every right to be there. Didn't I ask the same of him?

The light turns green and I step on the gas. Once I drop Brynn off at her sorority house, where am I going to go? Jesus, I have no idea. Maybe I'll have to stay with her in the dorm until I get my shit together. I suppose I could go stay with Mom, or Dad even, but I'm a grown-ass man, and don't want to go back home with my tail between my legs.

Fuck me.

I reach the sorority house and ease into a parking spot. I kill the ignition and just sit there, frozen in place. Brynn doesn't look like she's in any hurry to move either. I glance up and spot Sierra, a duffle bag in her hand as she exits the house and glances around. Why the hell does she look like she's sneaking around?

"She called me," I explain as I turn to Brynn. "Told me there was something I needed to see in your room."

Brynn's hand flips over on her lap. "Why would she even be going through Jemma's things?"

I wrack my rattled brain. "Isn't that a good question."

"I honestly don't think the baby is Jemma's." She shifts in her seat. "I know they have the same eyes. Even Sierra pointed that out, but—"

"Jemma and her sister could pass as twins," I tell her, cutting her off. "I saw pictures of them."

"If Sebastian was behind the nude picture...maybe..."

As she lets her words trail off, the unease in my stomach intensifies, not because Jemma deceived me, but maybe because...she didn't. Fuck. Something is wrong here. I take a deep breath, willing my brain to settle. As I become less reactive, a measure of logic settles in, helping me think with a bit more clarity. I work to puzzle things out. "Jemma knew I was with Sierra. It was one of the first things she mentioned. How would she have known that?"

Brynn grips her seat belt, and tugs it off. "Another good question." She frowns and stares at Sierra until she walks around the building and is out of sight. "Jemma was with Sebastian. Maybe he told her." She eyes me. "Maybe there's a common denominator here."

"But the clothes. He wasn't behind that." I run my hands through my hair. "How would he even know I was with Sierra?"

"I don't know. Sierra was texting someone from my room. Maybe she was texting Sebastian. Maybe this was all a set up. Maybe there's more than one common denominator and maybe the baby clothes are in the duffle bag and she's giving them back to whoever they belonged too."

Jesus, if only I was better at math. "Why?" I unbuckle and push back in my seat. "I get that he wants Jemma. He's always wanted her, but he's always wanted every woman in the sorority."

"Sierra has always wanted you, Kace." My heart jumps into my throat. She's flirted with me yes, and not to sound egotistical, but a lot of girls flirt with me. "My guess is she wanted to break you two up. Why fill the box with baby clothes if it wasn't to come between you and Jemma?"

My breath comes faster even though I can't' seem to fill my lungs. "You think she did that?"

"I don't think Jemma had baby clothes hidden in that box. Do you?"

I swallow hard. "No, I just...reacted." Brynn gives me a sympathetic smile and nods. "Why go after Jemma so hard, and I'm not even sure Sebastian is smart enough to put some ludicrous plan together to get her."

"He wants what he can't have." She glances at the spot where Sierra disappeared. "And maybe he's not the brains behind it all."

If Sierra wanted me, and Sebastian wanted Jemma, if they were willing to do anything to get what they wanted...My heart sinks into my stomach. "Two birds, one stone," I say, the math becoming clear. Fuck, what have I done? I glance at my sister as bile punches into my throat. "I reacted...I fucked everything up."

"I think you reacted because maybe you expected the worst from Jemma. Maybe it was easier to react and run away, then stay and fight because there's a part of you that's still afraid and unable to trust."

I drop my head onto the steering wheel. "Oh, fuck, sis."

"I know, but right now, we need to figure out the truth before Jemma gets hurt and you..."

She doesn't need to finish the sentence because I know how bad this is for me. I also know how bad it is for Jemma. Panic erupts inside me, and I need to move, to do something, anything to make this right. "How?"

"I'm not sure." She opens her door. "Come on, you're staying with me tonight."

I follow her inside, and once we reach her room, I throw myself onto Jemma's bed, remembering the first time I 'slept' with her. Then my mind goes to the time I really slept with her, back at my place. Something niggles in the back of my mind. "Sis?"

"Yeah?"

"Sebastian always led me to believe he slept with Jemma and she never corrected him."

"That's because she was trying to be something she wasn't."

"I think...I think I was her first." My heart thunders in my chest, to know she trusted me enough to be her first. I grab the sides of my head, as a tortured sound crawls out of my throat. After the way I reacted, I didn't deserve to be her first. What if I can't make this right? "She tugged the bed sheets off when I went to the bathroom."

"Yeah, big brother. I think you were her first too."

I close my eyes and lay there as Brynn climbs into her bed and reaches for her phone. Voices sound in the hall as the time ticks by and just when I think there's no way to make this right, my sister jumps to her feet.

"What?" I ask.

"I was texting with Sierra. I told her how happy we were that she showed us the baby clothes." I frown, unable to follow. "She's coming over to console you. I told her you wanted to see her."

I jackknife upright. "What the fuck, sis?"

"It's time for you to get to the bottom of things, Kace." I eye her. "Play along." I push to my feet my brain racing. "You've got this."

I don't 'got this' but I have to figure something out and fast if I want to bring the truth to Jemma. Someone knocks on the door, and Brynn hurries to it. She pulls it open and Sierra stands there, her gaze finding mine.

"I'll leave you two alone," Brynn says and steps into the hall.

"You wanted to see me?" Sierra asks, tentatively stepping toward me.

Before I can think better of it, because I'm not great at thinking on my feet, I blurt out, "Sebastian told me you two worked together to break Jemma and me up." Fuck, am I that much of an idiot? She goes completely still, her eyes wide. "I'm glad you did." She relaxes a bit.

"Really?"

"She was all wrong for me. Those two belong together, just like you and I belong together." As much as I don't want to, I hold my arms out to her, and she steps into my arms.

"You're not mad?" she asks as she wiggles against me and it's all I can do not to cringe in disgust.

"I understand why you did what you did. Drastic times call for drastic measures, right?"

"Right." She angles her head and searches my face, worry in her eyes. "You're really not mad?"

"Mad, why would I be mad?"

I cup her face and lean into her, like I'm going to kiss her and she softens, "Sebastian said if you ever found out, you'd kill him."

"Nah, it's all good. Were the baby clothes his idea or yours?"

"Mine. I had to give them back to an old friend, though."

I smooth my hand over her hair. "Of course, you're smart like that."

She smiles, loving the compliment. "Getting in bed naked with Jemma was his idea, though. I told him you'd be mad and want to talk to Jemma after I showed you the clothes."

I laugh, like I mean it. "You texted him to give him the heads up?" She nods. "So smart, Sierra...and so fucking busted." Her smile fades. "What the fuck, Sierra? Do you have any idea how fucked up this is?"

She blinks rapidly. "But I thought..."

I step back, needing distance between us as the dorm room's door creaks open. "Get out of my room and never step foot in it again," Brynn says, her arms folded as she glares at Sierra. Sierra opens her mouth. "Forget it, Sierra."

I stand there staring at Sierra as she whimpers and scampers out the door, and that's when a plan forms in my mind. The first thing I do is pick up my phone and check my text messages, noting everyone who received the picture of Jemma. I nod to Brynn, walk down the hall, and knock on Olivia and Ally's door. It opens and Olivia stares at me, the surprise on her face turning to anger.

"It wasn't me," I explain. "I'm here to make sure you both delete that picture from your phone."

"We already have," she answers.

"Thanks." I walk away, and find Brynn standing there. "Let's go." We step into the night. As the cool air falls over us, we jump in my car and I head to Storm House and knock on every door. Once all the guys delete the picture—most of them had already—I get back in my car. I explain to Brynn what's happening and drive to my place to confront Sebastian —and to talk to Jemma, although I'm not at all certain she'll even listen to me.

With determination driving my actions, I park in my drive-way, nod to Brynn and get out of the car. I head to the front door, and instead of letting myself in, I knock. A few minutes later, Sebastian pulls the door open and his head rears back when he finds me standing there.

I don't say anything. Instead, I pull his phone out of his hand.

Anger flashes across his face as he lunges for the phone. "What the fuck, dude? Give me that."

I put my hand on his chest and push him back. "You're the one who sent the picture of Jemma around."

He snorts and gives a shit-eating smirk. "Nope, the picture came from your phone."

"Yeah, I know, but you sent them from my phone."

"Yeah, so," he says smugly. "How are you going to prove that?"

"I don't need to. You just did. You're going down, Sebastian, and your father won't be able to help you this time." I delete the picture, and toss the phone back as Brynn comes from around the towering maple tree. "Got it?" I ask.

She nods, holds her phone up to show me the video.

I step closer to Sebastian. "I need to talk to Jemma."

"She's not here," he blurts out blocking me. "She left when you told her to leave."

"Where did she go?"

He puffs his chest out. "Like I'd fucking tell you anything."

I pull my arm back, about to punch him in the mouth, but Brynn grabs my hand to stop me. "Let's go," she says and Sebastian stands there cursing at us, accusing me of taking what's his, and wanting all the girls first. While I'd like to knock his teeth out, I walk back to the car with Brynn, and while I'm happy that Sebastian is going to go down for all this shit, I need to find Jemma, and fast. Did she go back to Shelburne? Do I call? If I do and she's not there, I don't want to alarm her parents.

I numbly drive back to the sorority, and while I have no idea if Jemma is going to forgive me, or where to find her, I need to keep moving forward with my plan. Over the next few days, I go through the motions of school and hockey, and go to the police with information on Sebastian—who has mysteriously disappeared from campus and the team. Late one night after practice, just when I'm at a loss, not knowing what to do next, I walk into my sister's dorm and find her with a big smile on her face.

"I found her," she blurts out.

My heart jumps. "Where is she?"

"At her friend Alison's."

I don't know how she found her, I'm just grateful that she did and I'm also cursing myself for not thinking to check with her friend. I hurry out the door. "Send me the address." Ten minutes later, I'm sitting in my car outside a house in the north end of the city. I spot movement behind the sheer curtains and jump from my car. I hurry to the front door, and while I know it's late, and they're probably getting ready for bed, I knock.

I stand there, shifting from one foot to the other, my stomach is a hot mess as the door creaks open and I come face to face with the woman I love.

"Kace," she murmurs, her eyes big. "How did you..."

I glance past her shoulder and spot Alison with Emma. At least I assume it's Alison. A cold breeze washes over me. "Can we talk?"

She stands there for another second, and my hope begins to fade as my bones chill. "I'll take Emma upstairs," her friend says.

Jemma nods, and a second later, she backs up, letting me in. "Thanks."

"What are you doing here?" she asks.

Where do I begin.

With the truth, dude. Always begin with the truth.

"I love you, Jemma."

She stands there staring at me like I'm speaking a foreign language. "I'm so fucking sorry. I never should have accused you of trying to trick me, for not being genuine, or for sleeping with Sebastian the other day. I understand if you never want to talk to me again. I really hope that's not going to happen, because I love you and I'm an idiot and I said stupid things because...because...I'm an idiot. Wait, I already said that, didn't I?"

Is she smiling? Wait, no she can't be. It's dark in here and I'm imagining things.

"I am so sorry about the picture being spread around. I promise it wasn't me, I know you don't believe that, but believe this. I went to every person who received a copy and personally watched them delete it. You'll be happy to know most of them had already deleted it anyway. Sebastian will pay for what he's done. I know you're embarrassed, but no one is going to shame you, Jemma. If they do, I'll be talking to them, with my fist."

This time, I'm sure she's smiling, but I have to be wrong.

"I spent the last three days trying to find you. It was my sister who figured it out." Wait, did her smile just get bigger when I said sis? "I rented a bungalow. I'm moving out of my house. I can't be around Sebastian, not that I think he's going to be on campus long, but I take possession in a week, and there's room for you, and Emma." She doesn't say anything, so like an idiot I add, "If you need a place to stay." She arches a brow and I shake my head. "I don't mean it like that. I mean, I want you to live with me. I want to be with you, and help you take care of your sister's baby. I'll be away in Edmonton next year, but this is my home base. We can make a life here, or you can move to Edmonton when you finish college. Whatever you want."

I stop long enough to take a breath, and just when I'm about to say a million more things, she puts her fingers to my lips to stop me. A tortured groan crawls out of my throat as she shuts me down.

She doesn't want to hear any more, dude.

No, no, no. I can't leave things like this. "Please," I begin and she shakes her head no. Tears prick my eyes. I can't lose her. She stares at me for so long, my body begins to shake harder. Is she waiting for me to leave? I open my mouth and she cocks her head, a gesture to stop me.

I nod in understanding. I love her and don't want to lose her, but I have to respect her wishes. "I'm sorry," I push out. I'm about to take a step back when her hand lands on my arm.

"I'm sorry too, Kace."

My heart is pounding so hard, I'm not sure I'm hearing her correctly. "Jem?"

"I'm sorry for pretending to be something I wasn't, for accusing you of being with Sierra, for not trusting you, and for letting you ever believe I slept with Sebastian. That never happened. Ever."

"I was your first," I murmur quietly as my heart fills with all the love and emotions I have for this kind, incredible, caring woman standing before me.

"You were."

I glance at the floor. "I didn't deserve that."

She touches my face and I lift my head. "Yes, you did. You're the best guy I know, Kace." I stare at her through blurry eyes. "We both made mistakes and said things that came from a dark place. I know you didn't send that picture, and I know that you didn't sleep with Sierra."

I nod, not knowing what to say, but that's okay because she says it for me. "I also know that I love you, and these last three days without you have been miserable. I want to be with you. I want to move in with you. I still don't know what will happen with Emma, but as long as you're by my side, I know things will be okay."

A cry catches in my throat as I wrap my arms around her and lift her clear off her feet. "I promise not to be an idiot ever again."

"I'm sure you will be," she says with a laugh. "I will be too. Just like Jack, sometimes we act the way we do, and say the things we say, out of fear."

"Jack?" I ask, a bolt of jealousy zipping through me.

She cups my face and laughs. "Our dinosaur," she explains and when I cock my head, she adds, "In our book."

Our book. I love that. "I'm as barbaric as Jack, aren't I?"

"We both are, but you know what? Jack gets a happy ever after in his book, so why don't we go upstairs and start working on our own."

My heart soars, and I let loose a growl, much like Jack does in the book and Jemma winks at me. "Come to think of it, sometimes barbaric isn't such a bad thing. Or maybe we can work on getting the dragon to breathe fire."

I grin as she teases me about my nickname, and give her ass a playful slap, the way she likes. She yelps and hurries up the stairs. As she goes, taking my heart with her, I know that with Jemma in my life I've scored—not fast—but definitely, big time.

"Who wants watermelon?" I ask as I step into the back yard, the screen door to the cute little bungalow I rented last year slamming shut behind me. Our little home is nice, in a great location too, close to campus and to Emma's daycare. Plus, the yard is big enough to have my family and Jemma's over for a Canada Day celebration. Mom even came, and I was worried at first. But maybe she too has found peace with everything that happened to us, and right now she's having a lovely chat with Jemma's mom.

"Me," Emma calls and holds her hands out, waving her fingers toward herself. My heart grows a little more as she smiles and showcases her two front teeth. She is so damn adorable and I'm lucky to have her in my life. In fact, I'm lucky to have all these people in my life. While I've spent time in Edmonton this summer, and I'm going to be happy playing in the NHL this fall, I also love coming back to my family.

"Need any help, son?" my father asks, as he shades the after-noon sun from his eyes. At least he didn't bring his wife to the party, that would have been a lot for all of us.

I shake my head, my heart no longer full of anger. "Got this, Dad." We might not be buddies, or even best friends, but over the last year we've come to a comfortable place, all thanks to Jemma. He and my brothers have even flown out to see a few of my practices, and that makes me happy. He's proud of my successes and I no longer want to hurt him with it. Right now, Luca and Lincoln are out front, playing a game of street hockey with some neighboring kids. I kind of like their names.

Krista smiles as she stands, takes a piece of watermelon from the tray, and hands a piece to Emma. "Come and sit on my lap, Emma. I don't want you running around and choking on this." She scoops a very busy Emma up and carries her to the table where the others are gathered.

Last year, after Jemma and I made up, the first thing we did was visit her parents, with Emma in tow. It was a shock to them, for sure, but we all put together a plan to get Krista the help she so clearly needed. She's currently living with us, and getting counselling on a regular basis and I see a huge differ-ence in the state of her mental health.

I catch Jemma's eye and she gives me a warm smile. I love having everyone here, but I can't wait until later, to have my fiancée all to myself. She steps up to me, puts her arms around me and gives me a loving kiss that curls around my heart.

"Get a room," Brynn calls out and I turn to her, noting the way she's going from one foot to the other. Her wave of anxiety falls over me, but I don't sense she's upset about something. In fact, she seems very happy.

"What's up, sis?" I ask. Her gaze flies to Jemma's and they exchange a look that says they're up to something. I don't like it. Not one little bit. Okay, that's not true. I love how close my fiancée and my sister are.

Brynn stayed at the sorority house her first year, but one year was enough for her. She wanted to experience the sorority life, and she did, but now she's in one of our spare rooms, and she also helps out with Emma. I understand how tiring dorm life can be. That's why I moved out my last year with Sebastian, who, last that I heard, had moved back home and had been charged with nonconsensual distribution of intimate images. But I don't want to think about him, not when my heart is full of happiness.

"What's up?" I ask again, and glance at my beautiful fiancée.

"Well..." Jemma begins, and I eye her. "I sort of did a thing, and wanted to surprise you."

"What did you do?" Brynn darts into the house, and comes out with something behind her back. "Not another baby on the doorstep, is it?" I whisper to Jemma and she laughs.

"Not quite." She squeezes my hand as everyone at the table looks on. "Remember I've been asking you to draw those dragon pictures for me?"

"Of course, I remember. While all the guys were out partying after practice this summer, I was in my room drawing pictures." I would draw and redraw from her descriptions until I had it exactly how she wanted it. Who knew she'd be so particular? Not that I minded.

"Aww, I'm sorry." She pouts. "I didn't mean to keep you from partying."

I shrug and admit, "I didn't want to party, babe. I like drawing. It made me feel closer to you." It's true, I was homesick.

"Well," she begins. "I finally got a hold of Brandon Cannon like you suggested a long time ago." My brow crinkles and I take in the twinkle in her eyes. She hugs her hands to her chest, and gushes, "He helped me so much."

"Helped you with a book?"

Brynn squeals and Jemma nods, and that's when Brynn pulls a book out from behind her back. I stare at the gorgeous cover and recognize the dragon on the front. My heart thumps. "You did it, babe. You published a book."

She pokes me. "We published a book."

"I can't believe it." I take it and flip through the pages. "It's gorgeous."

"I'm going to be doing a big signing at Dartmouth Book Exchange in a couple of weeks." She crinkles her nose. "Do you think you'd want to do it with me? I bet everyone would love to meet the artist."

That makes me laugh. I never considered myself an artist before. "Yeah." I give her a kiss, so proud of her accomplishment, and so happy she wanted me to be a part of this book. "If you want me there, you know I'll be there."

"I guess you should probably read it first, though. To know what it's all about."

"Of course." I close the book. "I'll read it later."

She crinkles her nose. "I'd actually rather you read it now. In fact, everyone should read it when you're done."

I glance around at our guests. "I'm not sure now is the right time."

"It is. I'll refill everyone's drinks and Brynn and I can get the barbecue going while you read."

"Okay," I agree. If it's that important to her, I'd better read it. At the head of the table, I drop down into a chair and conversation resumes around me. I read through the book, and it's a fast, easy read because it's for six- to eight-year-old children. I grin as I read, realizing I'm reading a book about a dragon who wants nothing more than a family but can't get close to anyone because he can't control his fire. He burns everyone he touches, and is very sad until he meets a girl dragon who helps him tame his flame. I continue to read, seeing so many elements of Jemma and me in the book.

I glance up at her as I flip to the last page, and she has an anxious smile on her face as she watches. So much for getting drinks and the barbecue going. I look back down and grin when I see Papa Dragon and Mama Dragon with the Baby Dragon. I close the book and feel the warmth and love between the pages.

"I love it, Jemma."

She stares at me long and hard, and since I'm not sure what she's waiting for, I put my hand behind her head and bring her lips to mine.

"You're the papa dragon," she whispers, for my ears only.

"I kind of figured." She inches back and I lower my voice to match hers, "And you're the mama dragon." She nods, and I ask, "Is Emma—"

She shakes her head no, and I stare at her. Who was her inspiration for baby dragon? The second her hand goes to her stomach, I jump from my chair so fast, it falls backward. Brynn squeals, and I put my hands on Jemma's shoulders.

"Are you saying..."

She nods, leans in and whispers in my ear, "We're going to have our very own baby dragon."

I pick her up and spin her around, while everyone at the table looks on in confusion. I turn to them, and toss the book to my mother, who is sitting closest to us.

"Read," I say. "We'll be back in about thirty minutes."

Jemma squeals as I scoop her up and carry her across the yard. "Are you happy, Kace?"

I step into our house. "Happiest man in the world, babe, which is why I'm going to take you upstairs and show you."

"What about our families?" Her eyes are wide, like she might actually care about that.

"They can take care of themselves for thirty minutes," I tell her. "This dragon is burning up for the most amazing woman in the world."

"We can't have that. It could be dangerous," she teases as I hurry up the stairs and kick open our bedroom door.

"Very dangerous."

I set her down and give her backside a little slap. She yelps and backs up, dropping onto the bed and crooking her finger. "Then get over here, dragon, and let me see what I can do to extinguish that flame." She winks and adds, "Wait, do I call you Daddy now?"

***

Thank you so much for reading Jemma and Kace's story. I hope you loved it as much as I do. Be sure to check out the other books in the series. Up next is Opposing Teams.

ALSO BY CATHRYN FOX

Scotia Storms

Away Game (Rebels)

Warm Up (Rebels)

Crash Course (Rebels)

Home Advantage (Rebels)

Shut Out (Rebels)

Moving Target (Rivals)

Face Off (Rivals)

Scoring Fast (Rivals)

Opposing Teams (Rivals)

Deal Breaker (Rebels)

Hard Burn (Rivals)

Fake Out (Rivals)

End Zone

Fair Play

Enemy Down

Keeping Score

Trading Up

All In

Blue Bay Crew

Demolished

Leveled

Hammered

Single Dad
Single Dad Next Door
Single Dad on Tap
Single Dad Burning Up

Players on Ice
The Playmaker
The Stick Handler
The Body Checker
The Hard Hitter
The Risk Taker
The Wing Man
The Puck Charmer
The Troublemaker
The Rule Breaker
The Rookie
The Sweet Talker
The Heart Breaker

In the Line of Duty
His Obsession Next Door
His Strings to Pull
His Trouble in Talulah
His Taste of Temptation
His Moment to Steal
His Best Friend's Girl
His Reason to Stay

Confessions

Confessions of a Bad Boy Professor

Confessions of a Bad Boy Officer

Confessions of a Bad Boy Fighter

Confessions of a Bad Boy Doctor

Confessions of a Bad Boy Gamer

Confessions of a Bad Boy Millionaire

Confessions of a Bad Boy Santa

Confessions of a Bad Boy CEO

Hands On

Hands On

Body Contact

Full Exposure

Dossier

Private Reserve

House Rules

Under Pressure

Big Catch

Brazilian Fantasy

Improper Proposal

Boys of Beachville

Good at Being Bad

Igniting the Bad Boy

Bad Girl Therapy

Stone Cliff Series:

Crashing Down

Wasted Summer

Love Lessons

Wrapped Up

Eternal Pleasure Series

Instinctive

Impulsive

Indulgent

Sun Stroked Series

Seaside Seduction

Deep Desire

Private Pleasure

Captured and Claimed Series:

Yours to Take

Yours to Teach

Yours to Keep

Firefighter Heat Series

Fever

Siren

Flash Fire

Playing For Keeps Series

Slow Ride

Wild Ride

Sweet Ride

Breaking the Rules:

Hold Me Down Hard

Pin Me Up Proper

Tie Me Down Tight

Stand Alone Title:

Hands on with the CEO

Torn Between Two Brothers

Holiday Spirit

Unleashed

Knocking on Demon's Door

Web of Desire

ABOUT CATHRYN

New York Times and *USA today* Bestselling author, Cathryn is a wife, mom, sister, daughter, and friend. She loves dogs, sunny weather, anything chocolate (she never says no to a brownie) pizza and red wine. She has two teenagers who keep her busy with their never ending activities, and a husband who is convinced he can turn her into a mixed martial arts fan. Cathryn can never find balance in her life, is always trying to find time to go to the gym, can never keep up with emails, Facebook or Twitter and tries to write page-turning books that her readers will love.

Connect with Cathryn:
Newsletter https://app.mailerlite.com/webforms/landing/c1f8n1
Twitter: https://twitter.com/writercatfox
Facebook: https://www.facebook.com/AuthorCathrynFox?ref=hl
Blog: http://cathrynfox.com/blog/
Goodreads: https://www.goodreads.com/author/show/91799.Cathryn_Fox

Pinterest http://www.pinterest.com/catkalen/

9 781998 943241